If Thy Right Hand

Robin Lamont

© 2011 Robin Lamont
All Rights Reserved.

No part of this publication may be reproduced, stored in a retrieval system, or transmitted, in any form or by any means, electronic, mechanical, photocopying, recording, or otherwise, without the written permission of the author.

First published by Dog Ear Publishing
4010 W. 86th Street, Ste H
Indianapolis, IN 46268
www.dogearpublishing.net

ISBN: 978-145750-026-8
Library of Congress Control Number: 2011924732

This book is printed on acid-free paper.

This book is a work of fiction. Places, events, and situations in this book are purely fictional and any resemblance to actual persons, living or dead, is coincidental.

Printed in the United States of America

R0426101797

To Kenny, always.

CHAPTER ONE

H E CARRIED ONLY the tools he needed, in one hand a liter bottle of rum and Coke, and in the other a heavy rope. Just past the pool house, he stopped and squinted up at a sixty-foot pine. This was the spot. He threw the rope over a low, sturdy branch, then tested his weight to see if it would hold. Next he made a loop and attempted to tie it off, but his gloved hands had trouble with the knot and, already drunk, he couldn't remember whether the end went underneath or over the first twist in the loop. Throwing off his gloves, he worked the knot until his fingers ached from the cold.

When he thought he'd gotten it right, Chris Owen took another slug from the bottle. Sweet courage. It wasn't that he was reconsidering. There were just things he didn't want to think about, like his parents' faces when they got the news. At least they'd get their deposit back from the university. Shit, all he did was cost them money and heartache.

Mostly, Chris didn't want to think about Heather. But that was impossible, she was always on his mind. He shoved his hands in his pockets and scanned the park. This was where he had first seen her, with her long legs and sparkly, sapphire eyes. She had her head cocked to one side as she wrung out her wet hair by the pool and caught him staring. She stuck out her tongue like a six-year-old, and they both laughed. Heather was his best friend; with her he felt worth something. Flushing hot in the cold night, Chris remembered the satiny feel of her breasts and how perfectly they fit in his hands.

All that ended with the trial. For five days, he sat at the burnished wood table with his attorney, the smell of furniture polish fusing with the sting of the accusing eyes that filled the courtroom. The sound of the kids at school whispering behind his back became the soundtrack to his life. Through it all, he clung to the belief that his friendship with Heather would survive, even if he had to go to jail. But when he learned that he had lost her forever, the guilt and isolation brought him to his knees.

Chris took a final hit on the rum and Coke and steeled himself. With the rope in one hand, he climbed up using the knurls in the trunk as footholds. The night sky was awash with stars. He remembered that even though they looked real, in fact they had all burned out millions of years ago. Excruciating loneliness surged through him and brought with it the adrenaline he needed. He fitted the noose around his neck and with a promise to himself that this would be the last pain, he pushed off from the tree.

His body jerked heavily against the rope, and right away the knot began to slip. But not before panic took over. His legs kicked wildly, his hands clawed at the thing around his neck. And then the rope snapped free and he thudded to the ground. His body convulsed as he gasped for air, fighting for each breath.

After a few moments Chris realized where he was and what had happened. An irrepressible urge to laugh caught in his damaged windpipe. *I fucked it up! Just like I fucked up everything else in my life!* He rolled onto his back and lay still. Soon, his fists unclenched and his arms spread to welcome the sweet air pouring into his aching lungs. Maybe it wasn't supposed to be. Maybe he was meant to grow up, grow old, be someone, or possibly ... someday ... be happy. The all too familiar pain of losing Heather slammed into his chest again. Still, he didn't want to die. Not now.

Chris slowly pushed himself to a sitting position and felt in his jacket for his cell phone. Dr. P did say he could call him any time. Chris scrolled down his meager list of contacts and when he got to the therapist's home number he hit send, only to realize there were no bars. No cell service out here.

Just then, a pair of headlights appeared. A car heading slowly toward him, tires crunching on the snow-crusted road. Chris rose unsteadily to his feet and put his hand over his eyes to block the blinding beams. For one crazy second, he thought it might be Dr. Paradiz and hope lit up his face. But then he realized that was impossible – no one knew he was here. The driver rolled down the window.

"Chris?"

The voice sounded familiar. He tried to speak, but could barely croak out a sound. He stumbled forward a few steps until he saw who it was. His eyes flickered with recognition, then surprise.

But before he could respond, an explosion knocked him backward. From such close range, the bullet blew a ragged hole through his sternum, taking with it half his heart.

CHAPTER TWO

ILENE HELD HER breath as the judge polled the jury. She didn't believe any of them would have a sudden change of heart, but she'd been a prosecutor long enough to have encountered the occasional rogue juror. When the last "guilty" was voiced, it seemed the entire courtroom exhaled with her, including the defense attorney Avery Flint, who looked utterly deflated. Nonetheless, he gathered himself and clamped a reassuring hand on his young client's shoulder. The judge remanded the defendant, set a sentence date, and the drama over, the spectators quickly dispersed. A short, thickset man with a dark five-o'clock shadow walked up to Ilene as she stood organizing files and stuffing her briefcase at the State's table.

"Thirty-eight minutes," he said.

"That's all? It felt like hours."

"It always does. I heard Judge Brower nearly fell over when he heard they had a decision. He thought we were going to be here all night. *Thirty-eight minutes* on three counts! Might be a record on a rape case," he said appreciatively. "You be hittin' any more home runs they gonna check you for steroids."

Ilene could barely muster a weary smile for the bureau's investigator Hector Moran. Trial prep was a grueling affair, long days re-writing her opening and closing arguments, and sleepless nights worrying about whether they had gotten a decent jury or if witnesses would show. For the first time in weeks she was looking forward to a relaxing evening at home.

With Sam, of course, home was never completely stress-free, but she would take trial-free any day. There was only one more thing to do and it seemed to be getting more difficult with every case.

The Chief of Special Prosecutions gathered her things and headed out of the courtroom with Hector. As the heavy doors closed behind them, Marielle, the sixteen-year-old victim in the case, broke away from her parents and rushed to embrace Ilene who returned the hug and whispered, "It's over now. I'm proud of you."

Folding Marielle into a farewell embrace, her own emotions threatened to break the surface though she fought to keep them submerged. She had grown attached to this brave, wounded teenager who reminded her so much of herself at that age. But her work was over; it was time for Marielle to move on with her life. Time to say goodbye.

"Hey you," Ilene held her at arm's length and gazed affectionately into the girl's teary brown eyes, "I expect to hear you've made honor roll again next term. I'll be waiting for that call."

Taking a deep breath, Ilene gave Marielle a last squeeze, picked up her trial bag and headed to her office. The heavy briefcase hardly slowed her and Hector had to hurry to keep up. They were just about to enter the crowded elevator going down when Anita Flores, the Special Prosecutions' secretary popped out.

"Glad I caught you," she said to Ilene. "Mr. Malone wants to see you as soon as you're done."

Ilene's heart sank. "Do you know what about?"

"Sorry, he didn't say."

"All right, I'll be up in a minute."

She was about to get in the elevator going up to the fifth floor when she was stopped again, this time by Avery Flint, who was running down the hall calling out her name.

"Can I have a word?" he asked breathlessly.

"Gotta be quick."

Hector excused himself while she and Flint walked over to an alcove that was often used as a conference area for last minute plea deals or cautionary advice to a prospective witness. Ilene set her trial bag on a marble window sill and refastened the oversized barrette that held the mass of wild, chestnut curls away from her face; she had long since given up trying to style her hair, settling for merely containing it.

She didn't look down at the street, but if she had, she would've seen a small group of picketers on the sidewalk in front of the court house with placard signs reading "Close down the Westerly" and "Keep sex offenders in jail." She might even have heard their distant, angry chanting. Instead, she studied the defense attorney, who ran a hand across his haggard face.

"What's up, Avery?" she asked.

"I really thought they would have some problems with the force issue," he said. "The only evidence was her testimony that at some point before penetration he held her shoulders down. That was *it*. No other physical force and no threat of physical injury. I mean, he's not that big a guy. I felt certain the jury would have at least considered his explanation."

Ilene stayed busily silent.

"Well, I guess that's water under the bridge now, hunh?" Flint looked exhausted.

"Yeah."

"Yeah. I was just wondering if you would think about the sentence we discussed during negotiations. If you're not ... comfortable with that, maybe you boost the lower end and call it 'two to four' with sex offender treatment?"

"Avery," Ilene scolded, "that was the *plea* deal. Your client chose not to take it and forced a sixteen-year-old kid to relive the event on the stand with her entire family watching, not to mention putting the State through the time and expense of a trial. Why would I even consider such a lenient sentence?"

"He supports his aunt. She's been diagnosed with cancer and he's her only means of support. Nobody knows where the father is, and if the kid goes in for a long time..."

"Get the aunt to write a letter. Anyway, Judge Brower's not going to max him out, you know that. He's not a repeat offender."

"I know, but Brower is always swayed by your department's input. Especially you."

Ilene forced a tight smile. "I'll think about it."

Flint had dealt with Ilene before. "Please," he implored. "He's only twenty-one and doing any kind of time is going to be hard enough."

"Quite honestly," she replied, "it's really not my problem." She reached for her bag, but Avery stopped her.

"You did a fantastic job with Marielle," he said.

Ilene straightened. "What's that supposed to mean?"

"Well, her performance on the—"

"Her *performance?*"

"The way you were able to draw her out."

"I prepped her, Avery. Prepped, not coached." Ilene's hazel eyes threw off sparks. "And I'll have you know that she was very restrained on the stand. Let me remind you of what I *couldn't* ask her and thus what the jury *didn't* hear: Marielle Arroyo was a virgin. She hadn't even gotten into kissing because her braces just came off. She plays flute in the school orchestra and listens to Ravel and Debussy on her iPod pretending it's rap music so she'll look cool to her friends. She trusted him – and he raped her. Your client held her down and raped her. And this sweet kid still feels like it was *her* fault."

Ilene snatched her bag off the sill and stalked off.

"I didn't mean…" Avery trailed off, knowing he'd blown it. More than his disappointment with the verdict, he felt personally insulted that the jurors had come back so quickly. And in his urge to take it out on someone, he violated a rule well-known in the defense bar: do not question the veracity of Ilene Hart's victims – she'd react like a cornered wolf protecting her cubs, and her bite was just as bad as her growl.

* * *

She was still smoldering when she found Hector.

"Everything okay?" he asked.

"Yes, yes," she responded brusquely. "Walk me up to Malone's office, so we can go over a couple of things before you leave. I don't know what he wants, but as soon as he has his say, I'm going home. I'm done for today. D...U...N... done."

Kept waiting by the female centurion who guarded passage to her boss, Ilene and Hector compared notes about the next day's work until Gerald Malone filled the doorway to his office. Literally. The Westover County District Attorney was a burly six-foot-four and even in a custom-made suit he looked like he'd be more comfortable sacking a quarterback, which he had done plenty of in college.

"Come on in, both of you," he said jovially.

He waved them over to the chairs facing his desk.

"I thought you were on vacation," he said to Hector.

"Leaving day after tomorrow."

"Excellent. You deserve it."

"Thank you."

"You going with the family?"

"Yes, sir. Looking forward to it."

"How many kids you got now, Hector?"

The stocky Moran didn't hesitate. "Twenty-four," he answered without a smile. "And that's just with my wife."

"Heh, heh," Malone chuckled, "I didn't mean any offense. But I understand you have quite a brood."

Ilene rolled her eyes in spite of herself. Hector was more than a co-worker, he had become a friend. He'd been in the bureau for years and was an indispensable part of the team, communicating well with Social Services, school officials, police and distraught relatives, both in Spanish and English. Most important, the children liked and trusted him. He said it was because he was short like them, but Ilene knew it was his kind, open face and his ability to listen without judging.

Malone plucked the crease in his trousers as he eased into the enormous leather chair behind his desk and crossed his legs. Ilene balanced on the edge of her seat.

"How can we help you, Gerry?" she asked.

"Congratulations on the verdict," he answered. "Nice work, both of you."

"Shucks, boss. Just doin' my job."

"Everything going well over there?" asked Malone.

"I'm sure you'd know if it weren't," she smiled.

In the pause that followed, Ilene shared a brief look with Hector, both knowing that the District Attorney did not request one-on-one's to applaud a trial win, not with more than a hundred Assistant DA's in the county trying cases every day. She waited for him to get to the point.

"Mind if I smoke?" he asked innocently, reaching into an inside pocket.

Ilene did; it had been years since she gave up smoking and she wasn't tempted to take it up again.

"If you must," she said.

Malone lit right up. "You've seen what's been going on out there today?" he asked.

"Going on where? I've been on trial all day," Ilene replied.

"Take a look outside, see if they're still there."

Ilene went over to his window and saw a few women circling on the sidewalk. "Who are they?" she asked.

"It's a group of angry citizens voicing their concerns about the Westerly rehabilitation facility in Branford."

Branford? Oh, boy. Ilene took another look. It didn't look like a demonstration, more like an orderly parade of Ugg-booted suburban moms, but she could smell trouble brewing. "I was wondering when the drums would begin to sound," she said.

"What do you know about it?"

"The Westerly? It's a rehab program for juvenile sex offenders, therapy and general monitoring services. It's only been open a few months. They took over part of the Westover General Hospital."

"It's all convicted sex offenders?" the DA queried.

"All 'juvies,' sir," Hector broke in, "or young adult. And all low-risk as I understand it."

"Any problems up there that you know about?"

Ilene shook her head. "I haven't heard anything."

Malone mulled it over, then asked, "Does it really work? Between you and me."

"Does *what* work?"

"Sex offender rehabilitation."

Hector answered. "Jury's still out, but so far the research seems to indicate that it does to some degree. It's pretty complex; you have to look at the length and type of treatment, what kind of sex offense, what kind of environment they're going back into, etcetera."

"What do *you* think?" the DA asked Ilene.

"I don't think about it, Gerry," she responded flatly, returning to her seat. "Frankly, I have my hands full getting convictions in the first place."

"Right," Malone brushed a piece of lint from his suit. "Like I said, this Westerly business is making the natives restless about sex offenders. There are a bunch of parents who are using the Branford Elementary School for a meeting tonight. I got a call from the principal who's asked that we send someone from your bureau to be on hand."

She knew where he was going and gamely offered to send her deputy chief.

"He specifically asked for you."

"Listen, Gerry, my son Frankie goes to Branford and I know many of the parents. I really try to avoid mixing home and work. Besides, I'm not the one to answer questions about The Westerly."

"The clinic's director Dr. Paradiz will be there to do most of the talking. And I think your … friend will be on hand as well."

Ilene colored, feeling exposed. Most of her co-workers knew that Ilene, a widower, and the Chief of the Branford Police Department, Matt Bingham, had been an item for years. But more than many of her colleagues, Ilene worked at keeping her personal affairs private. Likewise, she had rigid rules to help manage her home life. Mostly because of Sam.

"Are you sure Bess can't cover for me?" Ilene pressed. "I told my boys I'd be home tonight. I can't just leave at the drop of a hat."

"You'll have plenty of time to get home. The meeting doesn't start 'til eight." He had it all figured out for her. "And you don't have to speak, you're only there for reinforcement and reassurance," he insisted, turning on the charm. "Bottom line – I need you. I think this has the potential for getting out of hand and I want the best I've got to keep things under control."

Before Ilene could protest further Malone put the closer on his request. "Please," he added nicely.

CHAPTER THREE

I LENE'S CLIPPED FOOTSTEPS echoed in the dank, underground parking lot. It was well past six and the lot was
nearly empty – county government didn't pay overtime. She
reached into her purse for keys and hit the remote button to
unlock her Toyota Highlander. The taillights blinked in recognition. Striding toward the car, irritation mounted with every
step. The evening was shot and she couldn't think of a way to
break the bad news to Sam.

That damn Branford meeting! All week long he had been
looking forward to trying out the new computer keyboard he
had designed, and now she'd have to tell him he couldn't go to
practice tonight. Any nineteen-year-old would be unhappy
about a last-minute plan to stay home and babysit a younger
brother, but Sam wasn't just any teenager. They were in for a
stormy evening.

Out of the corner of her eye, Ilene saw a shadow in the next
row moving in tandem with her and she quickened her step.
She had almost reached her car when the shadow became flesh
and blood as the figure vaulted over the concrete divide. One
of his feet caught and he fell heavily into her path. Ilene leapt
back, prepared to run. But the man splayed on the concrete
floor didn't move; she thought he might be unconscious. Stepping closer, she eyed him warily.

As she leaned in, she saw who it was. "Simon? Is that you?
Are you hurt?"

Simon McColl moaned and slowly pushed himself to his knees. His coat was torn and missing a button, and his hair lay plastered with sweat against his face.

"Sorry. Wanted to catch you before you left," he mumbled, staggering to his feet. He swayed until he got his balance. "Thought I could make it over that thing. Stupid."

"Are you okay?"

McColl locked his rheumy eyes on to hers and broke into a sick grin. "Counselor, how the hell are you? We haven't heard from you in quite a while."

Ilene was taken aback. "I've been so busy, really," she said defensively. "How is Rebecca?"

"Peachy. Thanks."

"I've been meaning to call."

"She joined a grief counseling group."

"Oh, that's good."

McColl thrust his face aggressively toward Ilene, exhaling a gaseous form of scotch. "Useless waste of time!" he hissed, and a drop of spit landed on Ilene's arm. "All they do is eat and talk about 'sharing.'"

Ilene recoiled. "What are you doing here, Simon?"

"Thought we could go have ourselves a little drink. To celebrate."

"Celebrate?"

"Yeah!" he shouted, throwing his arms in the air. "Owen got out. Son-of-a-bitch does one year in that cushy Westerly hotel and he's free an' clear."

McColl, of course, was talking about Chris Owen. The year before, Ilene had successfully prosecuted him for the statutory rape of Simon McColl's daughter. The judge had showed leniency, and with Chris adjudicated a youthful offender had sentenced him to probation and rehabilitation treatment at the Westerly Center. She wondered if McColl was one of the protesters at the court house. A rush of guilt overcame her seeing Simon in such obvious pain. She knew what he and his wife had been through during and after the trial and had stayed in contact, at least for a while.

"Yessir," McColl went on, "he goes free as a bird. And my baby's dead." His puffy eyes filled with tears.

"Simon, go home and get some sleep," Ilene cautioned, resting her hand on his shoulder.

McColl threw off her hand with a wild gesture that nearly toppled him again. "No!" he shouted. "I'm gonna have my say!" Ilene took a step back. "That place is a fuckin' joke! They can't re'bilitate 'em. Once a rapist, always a rapist. Everybody knows that."

Two security guards who had heard the commotion trotted down the garage ramp and appeared around the corner behind McColl. Ilene looked up and tried to hold them off with a small head shake, but the two officers crept closer. Unaware, Simon continued his slurred verbal assault. "'Nother reason to celebrate. Guess what today is? Heather's birthday. You know how old she was gonna be? Do ya?"

Ilene knew but couldn't bring herself to say.

"Fifteen. Fif-teeeeen!" screamed McColl holding his head as though it would split apart. "He raped my little girl. He killed my baby! We *killed* her!"

One of the guards stepped up behind McColl and asked Ilene, "Do you know this man, Miz Hart?"

"Yes, Charlie. Yes, I do."

"Okay," he conceded, but he wasn't about to let Simon continue. "Sir," he said firmly, "we're going to get you home now."

Simon McColl spun around ready to fight off his attacker, but when he saw the large security guard and his partner, he went limp. Palms pressed against the hood of Ilene's car, he hung his head and sobbed openly. The guard waited a few seconds and then took McColl's arm and led him up the ramp. McColl went along meekly, whimpering his way out.

CHAPTER FOUR

"PASS THE KETCHUP."

"No more ketchup, Frankie. It's too salty."

"I have to cover up the taste of this meatloaf. It sucks."

Ilene rapped her knuckles gently on her eleven-year-old's head. "If that's an adjective, choose another one, Mister."

"Revolting, disgusting, puke-ridden..."

"How about inedible?" his brother suggested.

"What does that mean?" asked Frankie. "Gross?"

"Never mind," said Ilene. She handed Frankie the ketchup. "How was school today?"

"Okay."

"What'd you do?"

"Nothing."

"Didn't you have a math test today?"

"Good." Frankie wasn't listening. Busy pounding the end of the Heinz bottle, he had gone into his increasingly frequent robo-response to her questions about school and friends. Ilene gazed wistfully at her younger son. Only six months of fifth grade had transformed him from her sweet, affectionate boy into a five-foot-three, incongruously pale and freckled "gangsta." He now swaggered into the gym at Branford Elementary with his best friend Kevin to challenge all comers to a game of HORSE, dribbling a basketball with one hand and tugging at baggy pants with the other. Words like "yo!" and "dominate" sprinkled his vocabulary. There were still moments when her child re-emerged, the tip of his tongue resting against his upper lip as he concentrated on his homework or when he broke out into the unguarded, angelic smile that she loved so much. But the moments were becoming fewer.

Ilene sighed inwardly and turned to Sam who was slowly chewing a bite of potato and looking suspiciously at five string beans carefully segregated on one side of his plate.

"Sam."

He lifted his head and kept chewing, but didn't look at her.

"How did the computer lab go today?" she asked brightly.

Sam had reluctantly agreed to try a part-time job at Branford Elementary working on their computer system while he attended classes at a nearby community college. His mother hoped the experience would give him a sense of independence while keeping him close to home where she could monitor the situation. But his true passion was doing statistical analysis for the basketball team at a state university about twenty miles away. And although Ilene thought the commute might dampen his interest, so far it hadn't.

When he finished his mouthful, Sam put his fork down and said in his low, gravelly voice, "I don't like it when they push the chairs around. It hurts my ears."

"Sure."

"And when they scream in the hall, I have to put my hands over my ears."

"I'm sure a lot of teachers feel the same way," his mother commiserated.

Ilene's oldest son had been diagnosed at the start of kindergarten with Asperger Syndrome, a high-functioning form of autism. Looking back, she had known early that something was wrong: he didn't play like other toddlers, he seemed to move awkwardly, bumping into tables and chairs at home and preschool, and he shunned certain types of physical contact. But she had been so overwhelmed as a single parent in college and then with her all-consuming push to get through law school, Ilene had convinced herself Sam was merely experiencing some delays that would sort themselves out.

Choosing to keep the baby and refusing to divulge the name of the father had been the ultimate act of rebellion. Her father, William Caldwell, nearly wept in anger and frustration. "My God, Ilene, you're so young. You don't know what you're doing!" But the more he insisted that she was dashing her chances at Yale Law School and, *a fortiori*, ruining her life, the more Ilene was determined to prove she was salvageable without following in his oversized footsteps.

"Please, honey. Your mother would be so unhappy," he pleaded.

His twenty-one-year-old daughter glared at him. "Maybe we should have thought of that while she was still alive."

"What ... what are you talking about?"

"Think about it, Dad," she shot back and marched out the door for good.

They never discussed the pregnancy again. And five years later, Ilene handed in her final law school exam, knowing she had a chance at magna cum laude, even if it wasn't at Yale or Harvard. She sold her books, paid the month's rent, and used what was left to buy Sam a graduation present. But when she got to the pre-school to pick him up, one of the teachers took her aside. Sam should be tested by a neuropsychologist – he needed more than they could provide at KinderCare.

Stunned and disbelieving, Ilene carted him around to a series of specialists until she finally acknowledged they were all saying the same thing. At the last appointment with the doctor who had been the kindest to Sam, she wept in his office as he patiently explained Sam's form of autism and described the patience and extensive services he would require. Then she dried her eyes, applied to the District Attorney's office for the regular hours and health care benefits, and began her own crash course on Asperger parenting.

Ilene learned that Sam was extraordinarily bright with an uncanny gift for math and problems in logic. But he had significant social deficits. Unlike most other children, Sam's interaction with people proceeded by way of his intellect, not intuition. He wasn't good at figuring out what people were thinking, couldn't read their behavior or body language. His slow social processing alienated his peers and made interruptions in his routine problematic. In addition, Sam had unusual sensitivities to isolated, sharp noises and to certain physical sensations. At nineteen, he had finally learned to tolerate an affectionate squeeze to his shoulder and more formal hand-shaking, but generally didn't like to be touched, particularly anywhere on his head.

"How about the computer work itself, Sam?" Ilene asked. "How is that going?"

He thought about it for a few seconds. "I got the WSAS up and running."

"What is that?"

"The Westover School Alert System. It's an automated program that can send simultaneous email messages and trigger phone calls to tell parents about school delays or closings, that kind of thing."

That got Frankie's interest. "Can *you* send the message?"

"Only the District Superintendent can authorize it, but I could override his password, I suppose."

"Sick!" his brother exclaimed happily. "You could like, cancel school any time you wanted."

Ilene made a face at him and went back to questioning Sam about his work in the computer lab. "And how about the day-to-day stuff? Is it interesting?"

"Indeed. Who would not get a thrill out of downloading the newest version of 'Froggy Phonics' and cleaning peanut butter off mouse pads?" He folded his paper napkin and laid it over the string beans so he wouldn't have to look at them. "But occasionally the opportunity arises that I can work on some calculations."

As soon as he heard that, Frankie jumped into the exchange again, this time in an attempt to de-rail Sam from picking up steam on the subject of his "calculations" – his all-consuming passion. He gulped down his milk and blurted out, "Yo, I have a good one. Knock, knock."

Ilene glanced at Sam to see if he remembered what he was supposed to say. He apparently didn't, so Ilene responded.

"Who's there?"

"Interrupting Cow."

"Interrup–"

"Moo!" Frankie yelled, nearly jumping out of his seat.

Ilene giggled while Frankie laughed delightedly. Sam sat impassive.

"Get it?" Frankie asked him.

"The cow interrupted," Sam offered solemnly.

"Right."

"But a cow can't speak, so it couldn't say 'knock, knock.' Nor could it have the intellectual capacity to identify itself as an 'interrupting cow'. So in that sense, the joke is internally inconsistent. And anyway, it's rude to interrupt."

"That's what makes it *funny*," Frankie pointed out enthusiastically.

Sam glanced at his mother to question which one of them was correct. But a bona fide knock at the front door spared her.

Frankie clutched his head in mock horror. "Oh, my God, Sam! It's the Interrupting Cow!"

Ilene got up to see who it was while Frankie attempted to explain the joke to his brother one more time.

* * *

Matt Bingham had already let himself into the foyer. He was wearing black jeans and a Branford Police Department parka. His square face was clean shaven and dominated by gold-flecked brown eyes topped by heavy eyebrows. At six-foot-three and a fit two hundred fifteen pounds, he moved comfortably and confidently, and although he didn't smile frequently, when he did, his grin was infectious.

As soon as she saw him Ilene clapped her hand over her mouth. "Oh, shit," she exclaimed.

"Uh … hello to you, too," said Matt looking slightly befuddled.

"Sorry, you reminded me about the meeting at school tonight. I completely forgot."

Matt ran a hand through his thick brown hair, now graying at the temples. "That's not like you. I left a message with Frankie."

He took off his coat and hung it on a hook near the door, then sat down on the bench in the front hall to unlace his boots, first shifting his ankle holster and Glock 9-millimeter to a more comfortable position. "I tried to get you at the office, but you'd already left. They told me you'd been tagged to attend the love-fest tonight. Thought I'd swing by beforehand, grab a cup of coffee. We can go over together."

"I'm going to wring Frankie's neck. I've told him a hundred times to write messages down. How am I going to tell Sam *now* that he can't go to Hudson?"

"He has practice tonight?"

"It was going to be his big night to try out the keyboard."

"It'll be okay."

"No, it won't," Ilene insisted. She was furious with herself; between Simon McColl and the immediate clamor for dinner as soon as she came through the front door, the school meeting had slipped her mind entirely.

"Why don't you skip the meeting then?" Matt asked.

"Can't, Malone asked me personally."

"It'll work out," Matt reassured her again. He stood up and gently pulled her close, his eyes twinkling. "Can we have a do-over on the greeting?" he asked.

Ilene looked up at him, the light catching on her high, angled cheekbones and the edge of her strong chin. The distinctive planes of her face, however, yielded to the softness of her full lips. It was here that Matt placed a lingering kiss, and he held her until she relaxed into his embrace.

"Hi," he said.

"Hi."

"You look great," Matt said brushing back her hair.

"Are you kidding? I'm exhausted."

"Me, too. I was up at four-thirty."

"How come?"

"Homicide," he said, his eyes taking on a far away look. "Gunshot victim in the town park. He was just a kid."

"Oh my God, that's horrible. Was he from around here?"

Matt's eyes suddenly showed his fatigue. "Yeah," he nodded. "You knew him, in fact. Christopher Owen, your guy on that rape case last year."

Ilene drew a quick breath. Chris Owen?! She tried to picture him, but found it was Heather's face etched in her memory. Chris was more elusive; he had a smoky look about him, indefinable, a hazy kind of smile – although when she saw him he wasn't smiling much.

"What happened?" she asked.

"We're trying to find out. It looks as though he was killed sometime last night. Brad Collins found him on a routine swing-by at the park. At the scene, Feinstein's people thought he'd been dead about five, six hours. We'll have more information tomorrow."

"Someone shot him? My God!" Ilene exclaimed, "I saw Simon McColl today."

"Heather's father?"

"I don't think he knew about Chris. I'm sure not or he would have said something."

"When was this?"

"After work. He came to see me, but he was very drunk."

"What did he want?"

"To be honest, I'm not sure he knew why he sought me out. He was a mess. Today is the anniversary of Heather's birthday."

Matt gave Ilene a searching look. "If anyone had reason to be angry at Chris, it would be Simon McColl," he offered grimly.

"Angry enough to *kill* him?" Ilene asked in surprise. "I can't believe that. And anyway, if he had wanted to go after Chris, he would have done it a long time ago. Why wait until now?"

"For one reason, Owen had just finished his relapse prevention program. That pretty much finishes his sentence, right?"

Ilene looked away. "He did mention something about that."

"As I remember, McColl wasn't too happy about Chris's sentence. Maybe he thought it was time for some home-grown retribution," suggested Matt.

Ilene felt suddenly uneasy. McColl didn't just *know* Chris had completed his probationary sentence at the Westerly, he was *enraged* about it. And that Chris's release coincided with Heather's birthday – the circumstances were ripe to make Simon a time bomb.

Raised voices from the kitchen distracted Ilene and reminded her again that she had more immediate concerns.

"I'd better deal with Sam," she said, returning to the kitchen.

Matt followed her and found the boys deep into their favorite subject – basketball.

"Yo," Frankie said, his smile peeking out from his practiced slouch.

"Ola, Big Guy," Matt returned. "Your mom tells me you're taking Spanish this semester. I'm impressed."

"Don't be," Frankie moaned. "A second language is one too many for this brain."

"Stick with it, kid," Matt ruffled Frankie's hair. He sat down in Ilene's chair. "Hey, Stats," he said, using the nickname he'd given Sam, "How's it going?"

"It's going very well. I'm trying out the keyboard tonight at practice," he said, making a gallant effort at eye contact. "Coach Boone and I are working on individual offensive ratings, so even though they're just scrimmaging, I'll have a chance to–"

Ilene interrupted, "I'm sorry, Sam." She crossed her arms anxiously. "You can't tonight. Something came up, and I have to go to a meeting at school. I'm really sorry," she added gently. "I should have told you earlier, but I forgot."

"No, I have to go to the game," he replied, shaking his head back and forth. "Coach is expecting me."

"I need you to stay with Frankie," Ilene said firmly, trying to head off what she knew was coming. "You can call the coach, he'll understand."

"He doesn't have to stay," Frankie piped up. "I don't need a babysitter. I'm almost twelve."

"I have to go to the game," Sam repeated more insistently.

"No." Ilene's tone made clear she was digging in. "I may not be home until late."

"But, Mom!" Frankie protested.

"He'll be all right, Ilene," Matt chimed in. "We're not going far. Bring your cell phone."

Ilene's back stiffened imperceptibly.

"Frankie," Matt cautioned with mock officiousness, "you going to have any girls over while we're gone?" The boy made a face and put a thumbs down on that. "Any drug dealers? Vicious criminals? Angry rappers?"

"Not *tonight*," Frankie grinned.

"He says no, Ilene," rephrased the Chief.

After a moment's hesitation she said, "I don't know."

"She's caving!" Frankie pronounced.

Matt held a cautioning finger to his lips.

"Just this one time," Ilene relented unhappily. The pressure from the three of them and the prospect of a meltdown by Sam was too daunting. "But keep the front door locked and call me if you hear anything unusual or get worried for any reason at all."

A delighted Frankie hopped up to clear his plate and promising he had completed his homework, retired to the family room to do video games. Ilene began the kitchen clean-up while Matt helped himself to a large portion of meatloaf.

"How's the team looking this year?" he asked, taking in a mouthful.

"Not bad."

"And what are you working on?"

Sam's eyes lit up. "I'm designing a program that utilizes a simplified keyboard to record offensive score sheets. Then I take that information and use certain equations for determining, amongst other things, a given player's floor percentage and his offensive rating."

"I see. This is new for Hudson State?"

"Very new. They've been using only the most rudimentary statistics."

"Like rebounds, assists, that kind of thing?"

"Precisely. Very limited. Rather like describing my mother as a woman with red hair. It may be accurate, but insufficient if one wanted to know what she is capable of."

"So true," said Matt with a playful glance at Ilene.

"To date, I've had to do all the offensive score sheets by hand. The keyboard will allow me to work more efficiently."

"What do you record?"

"Everything. I'll show you." Sam withdrew a crumpled piece of paper from the pocket of his worn corduroy pants and spread it out on the kitchen table. On it were handwritten notations, the first line read:

46 HS   42d 6 42d/ 10 6d 10 6-*C* 11r 32++*A*

Matt peered at the paper uncertainly. "What kind of equation is that?"

"It's not math, it's code," Sam corrected. "This is a single possession by Hudson State at the end of the second quarter of Sunday's game. They've scored forty-six points as you can see from the first number and the team designation. The other numbers relate to the players on the floor." Sam began to speak more rapidly as he pointed out the progression, "Here we have Jones dribbling up the court to start the possession, small 'd' for dribble. He passes off to Marshon, number six, who passes it back to Jones, who again dribbles, and this time passes at mid-court to Odell. Odell gets it back to Marshon who shoots from the top of the key and misses. Then JT gets the offensive rebound, throws it back out to Vojacek, who's set up on the left side and hits the jumper. JT gets the assist."

"All *that* in just one line?" asked Matt incredulously.

Sam hesitated only to assure him he was correct and then continued. "Okay, so now it's 48-39, and LI Tech has the ball–"

"Whoa, Sam," Ilene interrupted. She had to repeat herself twice before he registered her. "If you're going to make the practice, you'd better be on your way. It's after seven."

He checked his watch. "Four-and-a-half minutes after seven, to be precise." Animated and beaming, he stood and shoved the score sheet back in his pocket. At six foot, he had a good five inches on Ilene and looked even taller because of his broad shoulders and mop of frizzy hair, sand-colored wiry corkscrews that stuck out in all directions and bounced whenever he moved his head. For years, Sam's hair had drawn stares from children, and from adults remarks about the sixties being over, but he had learned to shake them off; it was the price he paid for refusing to go to a barber. Because of his sensitivity only Ilene could embark on the occasional hair trim. Now he merely brushed back a wayward curl with his long fingers and disappeared to pack his keyboard. He re-emerged briefly to announce his departure.

"Come home right after the game," Ilene cautioned sternly.

When he had gone, Matt pulled out a chair and she forced herself to sit for a moment while they sipped their coffee.

"It's remarkable what he does," said Matt. "And his passion for it is wonderful. Is the university still considering hiring him?"

"I think so," Ilene said, rubbing her temples.

"You don't like the idea?"

"I want him to be happy, Chief. But he has to finish the year out at Community College and stick with his computer job at the elementary school. Then we'll see what opportunities are available."

"But if the opportunity exists *now* to do something he really loves, why not? I'll bet he could transfer his credits to Hudson State and graduate from there."

"He can't live on his own yet."

"College is not really being on your own. He'd be in a dormitory. Heck, he's already driving back and forth."

"Hudson State is not in a good neighborhood. There's a lot of crime and as it is, he's hanging out at the school with the hip-hop guys on the team who are in a completely different place, socially and psychologically."

"Do they treat him badly?"

"No, it's not that...." Ilene put her head in her hands. She felt too wrung out to have an argument with Matt. "Please don't push me."

"I'm only trying to get you to lighten up on him a little."

"You don't understand."

"I think I do. I'm aware of Sam's limitations, but he's almost a man."

"Do you want to take over as parent?" she challenged, feeling close to tears.

"Ilene," he answered slowly. "You should know by now that I think you're doing a fantastic job with the boys. They're great kids. And to answer your question – I would love to co-parent with you." Ilene stared down at the table.

"Sometimes I wonder what we're doing," he continued. "I'm nuts about you. I care for the boys more than you can imagine. I'd like nothing better than to be part of their lives in a more … meaningful way. I want to marry you. It's been six years since Daniel died."

"It's not about Daniel," Ilene said sadly.

"Then what *is* it?"

"I love you," she said lifting her head. "I do. I'm just not ready."

Matt heaved a frustrated sigh, he was always so careful with her. Screw it. "Is it about Sam and Frankie? Are you waiting for them to grow up before you can resume a life?"

"And are you anxious to push them out the door so you won't have to share me with them?" Ilene retorted, her face flushing with hurt.

"Oh, I see. You're bent out of shape because I suggested Sam might do all right on his own and that Frankie is old enough to stay home by himself for a few hours."

Ilene stood up quickly from the table. "Can we fight about this another time?" she asked, resuming her post at the sink and keeping her back to the kitchen table.

They were both tired. Matt decided not to pursue it and was at once saddened to find himself making that all too familiar choice.

CHAPTER FIVE

T HE SMALL TABLES in Mrs. Reynolds' room were color-coded, as were the cubbies stuffed with the inexhaustible supply of black-and-white marble notebooks awaiting the next morning's science or social studies assignment. The shelves were labeled: "Pencils, Pens, Rulers," "Markers, Crayons," as were the book sections, "Adventure," "Animals," "Sports," "Just-Right Books." Under a flickering fluorescent bulb in the corner, something was being cultivated in two large fish tanks, although it wasn't readily apparent what. The smell of glue sticks and graham crackers lingered.

With a few minutes to spare before the meeting, Ilene headed straight to Frankie's classroom. Her work schedule didn't allow her to participate in class projects the way most of the stay-at-home moms in Branford did. To combat her envy and keep involved in Frankie's school life, she visited his homeroom whenever possible, seeking clues to the parts of his life he was guarding ever more vigilantly. After switching on the overhead lights, she wandered down a row of brightly decorated posters. The project was called "What Our Elders Can Teach Us." She quickly zeroed in on Frankie's "My Grandparents, by Franklin Hart," and suppressed a grin. His handwriting was terrible, but his spelling wasn't bad and his text captured their voices perfectly: *My dad's parents, Evelyn and George Hart, live in California in a condominium. I don't see them much because Evelyn refuses to fly. Not after 9/11. End of story. And she thinks trains are disgusting. Grandpa plays golf every day and once shot two over par* on the Rio del Mare course next door. They took me to Disneyland when I was eight, but it wasn't half as good as the one in Florida. What I can learn from my grandparents is that "life goes on."

Ilene's smile faded. Life hadn't gone on for Daniel Hart, George and Evelyn's son and Frankie's dad, who had an unforeseen, fatal heart attack during one of his early morning runs.

A hand rested on Ilene's shoulder and she jumped.

"Oh, hi," Ilene recovered and gave her friend Roz Wohlman a quick hug.

"I feel as though I haven't seen you in ages," said Roz, returning the squeeze. "How's Frankie?"

"Doing great. At least, I think so. He doesn't share much with me anymore."

"It's the age," Roz laughed. "Kevin only speaks to me when he wants food, otherwise he just grunts." Kevin and Frankie had been best friends since pre-school.

"Did you go through this with the girls?" Ilene asked, referring to Roz's twin daughters who were seniors in high school.

"Not really. Girls are different, and Lizzie and Kate are so accustomed to talking incessantly to each other, if one is out of the house I'm the stand-in." She gave Ilene a sympathetic smile. "Are you having separation issues?"

"Probably. This is the last year of elementary school and I get sad knowing I have to say goodbye to all this…" Ilene opened her arm to include the classroom, "this … innocence."

Roz nodded. She hooked her elbow through Ilene's and read Frankie's poster. "Wow, Evelyn and George sound like a pair," she commented.

"You can say that again. Although I'm sorry they're not a bigger part of Frankie's life – as grandparents."

"What about your dad?" Roz inquired.

Ilene stepped away and wandered down the row. "We don't talk much," she said casually over her shoulder.

"Terry showed me a picture of your father in the *Times* the other day, at some big fundraiser for the New York Ballet."

Ilene examined another poster.

"He looked very distinguished in his tuxedo," Roz went on, "and his wife is lovely."

Ilene mumbled in response.

Sensing she was treading on sensitive territory, Roz brought the subject back to Evelyn and George. "Are Daniel's parents not particularly grandchild-friendly?" she asked.

"They prefer being long distance grandparents. Frankie's energy has always been exhausting for them, and Sam – well, that's another story."

Roz looked sympathetically at her friend. "From the little you've told me, I gather they weren't too supportive of Sam," she said.

Ilene's mind drifted back to her early years with Daniel and the tension that his parents injected into their lives as newly-weds. She had hoped they would embrace Sam, but it had been difficult. Along with a daughter-in-law they got an illegitimate six-year-old with autism who could be a royal pain in the ass. He had a gagging reflex in response to Evelyn's perfume, and even if she hadn't doused herself with it in the morning, the smell was all over her clothes. He threw up on her a couple of times, he couldn't help it. That may have been what finally drove them out west Ilene thought wryly.

She gave her friend a wan smile. "I think they viewed Sam as a kind of stain on the Hart lineage – like George's career in the pharmaceutical industry and Evelyn's year-round tan qual-ifies them as titled aristocracy. Do you know they actually tried to talk Daniel out of the formal adoption proceedings?"

"Ouch," said Roz.

Yes. That had hurt.

"But Daniel and Sam got along pretty well, didn't they," Roz asked optimistically.

Ilene struggled – she longed to open herself completely, but when it came to Sam, she had carried her deepest feelings in isolation so long they felt like a part of her body, solid and unyielding.

"Actually, Daniel was never really a father to Sam, more like an uncle or something," said Ilene. Truth? Even parenting his own son had been a burden. He tried on occasion, but the effort always showed. There was simply no joy in it. "When I got pregnant with Frankie," Ilene continued, "he was happy about the *idea* of having his own flesh and blood child. But the reality of diapers and oatmeal flung to the far corners of the kitchen – that was a different story. Daniel would have been a good husband if we didn't have kids."

"Yeah, it's the little things that get in the way," Roz said with feigned irritation.

Ilene smiled. "Really. He was a good, smart man, just not wired for parenting. Heck, he worked endless hours downtown, and the nights he came home before the boys were asleep he'd manage to play dinosaurs with Frankie for a few minutes. But then after dinner and a drink, he'd crash. He had nothing left for Sam."

"Who took a lot of energy."

"Still does, but not in the same way."

"It must've been overwhelming. How did *you* manage?"

Ilene squeezed her friend's arm. "Life goes on."

They laughed.

"Say, did you hear about that boy killed in the park?" Roz suddenly remembered.

The door inviting Roz deeper into her life clicked shut. Ilene made it a point not to discuss her cases outside of work, and she was still trying to make sense of her encounter with Simon McColl right on the heels of Chris's murder. With a noncommittal nod, she went back to studying the Elders project.

"The girls knew him," said Roz, "but not well. He was a year ahead of them until that whole thing last year. He missed a lot of school and was held back because of it. They told me he was real loner and used to get into trouble for bringing alcohol to school. It's horrible that he should be killed, but no one's that surprised."

"No?" asked Ilene nonplussed. "That a boy should be shot to death in the town park?"

"That it happened here, sure," Roz corrected, "but let's face it, he was not a good kid. He could have been mixed up in drugs and was shot as part of a gang thing. Then there's the fact that he was a sex offender which makes everyone think, 'what was he doing in the park in the first place?' I mean, as far as that goes, it makes me nervous to know they can be set free to wander into the town park where our kids play. Which is exactly why this meeting tonight is so important! We really have to do something about this supposed rehab place. You'd know more than me, of course, but...."

"You're worried about the Westerly Center?"

"You better believe it," said Roz with such conviction that it gave Ilene pause. There hadn't been many protesters, but if solid, unflappable Roz was worked up, the trouble she had sensed earlier had the potential for whipping up a real storm.

She found out soon enough.

* * *

As they neared the doors, the two women were greeted by the din in the gymnasium. Over a hundred parents were talking over the clatter of metal folding chairs the custodian was setting up to accommodate the crowd. On an elevated stage at one end of the room, Matt was talking to the school principal who glumly surveyed the growing audience. People began to take their seats. Roz went off to find her husband, and Ilene scanned the room for familiar faces.

She spotted a woman from Child Protective Services. Lynette Kulik sat by herself in one of the chairs near the front. They had worked together on a few cases, and Ilene was about to go over when she was stopped by a handsome couple.

"You're from the DA's Office?" asked the husband. He was sharply dressed in a business suit, his black hair heavily gelled and his cologne in assault mode.

Without waiting for a reply, he thrust out his hand, "Jason Schatz. I'm an attorney – Case, Barney."

Ilene knew the firm, an elite crew that handled mergers and tax dodges for big corporations. Everyone there was an "Attorney," all others, including lowly prosecutors were "lawyers."

Schatz inclined his head to a slim, blond woman at his side. "This is my wife, Mary Beth."

She gave Ilene another firm shake and asked, "You're from the Sex Abuse Bureau?"

"Special Prosecutions, yes."

"Thank you for coming tonight," said Jason heartily.

"We have two little girls," Mary Beth stated.

When Ilene didn't immediately respond, she continued, "You know, we moved up here from the city. So, for us to learn about a refuge for sex offenders right here in Branford is very disturbing." She looked as though she were about to cry.

Ilene heard her name called from the stage. Matt was motioning for her to come up and she turned to make her excuses to the couple.

But Jason clasped her forearm. "Just to say we're really glad that there's someone else around here who's got the you-know-what to go after molesters." He wagged a finger in her face for emphasis. "Not here. Not in our community."

Unnerved, Ilene drew away quickly and rubbed his trespass from her arm as she joined Matt on the stage. If Roz and the Schatzes were any indication, parents were more than "voicing their concerns" as Malone had promised, they sounded aggressive and scared. She also wondered if Schatz's comment about someone else going after molesters was a reference to Chris's murderer. What had happened to make the Westerly Center so threatening all of a sudden? She asked Matt.

"I don't think many people knew about it," he replied. "The clinic didn't exactly advertise when it opened. But there was a piece in the Sunday paper a couple of weeks ago and I guess word gets around."

He turned to a man standing near them, "I think you know Dr. Jeffrey Paradiz, the head of the Westerly Center."

"Of course," said Ilene as she shook hands with the trim psychologist. He was in his early fifties and comfortably dressed in slacks and a V-neck sweater. Thinning hair accentuated his high brow and aquiline nose, but most noticeable were his clear eyes that focused intently on whomever he was listening to. Tonight, however, he looked distraught and Ilene guessed why.

"Chris Owen was a patient of yours?" she asked.

"Yes," replied the doctor.

Ilene was searching for the right words to express her sympathy when Harvey Carle, the principal, began to tap on the microphone and ask everyone to sit down so the meeting could start. With an apologetic nod to Paradiz, she took a seat behind the podium hoping to keep a low profile. The auditorium had quieted somewhat, and Carle addressed the crowd, acknowledging their apprehension about the clinic but emphasizing that everyone on the staff was committed to keeping their children safe. He introduced Dr. Paradiz. As one body, the crowd leaned forward.

"Good evening," said Paradiz, his voice squealing and crackling through the speakers. He cleared his throat and fussed with the microphone, finally reconciling himself to standing back a few feet.

"I'm glad to have the opportunity to speak here tonight," he started. "Let me begin by telling you about the Westerly Center and what it is we do. The Westerly provides group and family therapy for juveniles who have been convicted of various sexual offenses. The Center is located in the annex of Westover General Hospital which provides additional staff for other therapeutic services."

Paradiz was not a good public speaker. His presentation was stiff and his obvious lack of comfort made him appear defensive. Furthermore, it was evident that his audience wasn't interested in the elements of group therapy as part of the "complex process for therapeutic change" or his young patients' needs "to overcome impaired social and intimacy skills." The harder he tried to provide some insight into why they acted out as they did, the more restless his listeners became. A few began to interject questions.

"Do the juveniles live at the clinic?" asked one.

"No. We work on an out-patient basis."

"What kind of security do you have?"

Dr. Paradiz was confused by the question, but responded gamely. "Out-patient means they don't reside at the clinic. But general security is provided by the hospital."

"That's not what I meant," the questioner said irritably. "How do you monitor your patients' whereabouts?"

"Most of the young men and women live at home. But naturally, we take a great interest in, and do our best to supervise, our attendees' outside activities."

"Why don't you call them what they really are? Sex offenders!"

And another. "What evidence do you have that therapy works?"

Paradiz jumped on that one. "That's a good question. Although only recently researched, a major report came out a few years ago following up on almost thirty thousand sex offenders."

Several gasps escaped from the audience and Ilene winced inwardly. She knew the doctor was merely trying to demonstrate the impressive scale of the study, but thirty thousand sex offenders was too big a number for this crowd.

"In that study," Paradiz went on, "it was found that only thirteen-point-four percent of sex offenders committed another sexual offense—"

"That's comforting," someone threw out.

"...which contradicts the prevailing and uninformed view that almost all sexual offenders re-offend—"

"I don't care about numbers, I want to keep my child safe!"

"...and that those who were motivated to seek therapy were at lower risk to re-offend – only about eight percent."

He was losing them rapidly.

"They belong in *prison*, not group therapy!"

"Don't we have rights here? What does the law say?"

"Let's hear from the DA's office!"

After these last two remarks, Paradiz seemed to recognize that his time had expired and looked back at Ilene with a silent plea. Seeing no means of escape, she stepped up to the lectern and took the mike.

"Hello. I'm Ilene Hart from the District Attorney's Office," she said. This time, there was a genuine round of applause. She took a deep breath and launched into an attempt to allay the crowd's anxiety. She started well, at any rate.

"First, I join with Principal Carle and want you to know that all of us here tonight are dedicated to ensuring the safety of your children. In that light, the most important thing to know about the Westerly is that it's a treatment center primarily for juvenile offenders who are not at high risk to re-offend. Let me explain. When an offender is sentenced after conviction, he or she is given a risk assessment factoring in the type of sexual crime, any prior convictions, level of force used, alcohol and drug abuse, among other things. Obviously, any priors, a very young victim, deviant fixations, and certainly violence, would result in a higher risk. The offenders who are attending the Westerly are all considered low risk."

Ilene acknowledged Jason Schatz in the second row with his hand up.

"How can you be sure they're low risk?" he asked intently.

"Well, we can't be a hundred percent sure of anything, but the assessment is made by professionals in law enforcement, including Probation and Social Services."

"But you have to admit that there *is* a risk," he persisted.

"Of course."

A woman at the back of the room stood up.

"Why can't they do their therapy in prison, and if it's successful, then they can be released?" she asked apprehensively.

"In short, because our Penal Law has designated certain offenses as not worthy of incarceration. That includes, by the way, other crimes that cause damage to persons and property, not just sex crimes."

"Child molesters are different!" rang out an angry voice.

"They are," Ilene agreed. "But as I said, the age of the victim is taken into consideration in the type of crime and risk assessment."

The audience was not as receptive to Ilene as their initial applause had indicated. More people began to speak up and there were choruses of, "Let 'em do their group therapy, just not around our kids," and "*Any* risk is too great. I say, lock them up!" One person loudly advocated for castration.

It had been a long, stressful day, and Ilene had reined in her patience long enough. Unwilling to put up with the same disrespect given Dr. Paradiz, she put out her hands to quiet the group.

"Okay, I hear that many of you are uncomfortable about the center. I understand your feelings, I'm a parent myself. But if you want to talk about *risk*, let's set the record straight. Your child is far more likely to be sexually abused by someone in your own community than by a stranger. Significantly more so." She let her words sink in and continued, urgency creeping into her voice, "Your fear of the Westerly Center is misplaced, and if you imagine there are predators haunting the streets just waiting for a chance to snatch your child from the yard, you're watching too much TV. Does it happen? Yes, in rare instances. But if you really want to protect your child, *educate* yourselves. Learn to recognize the social and psychological qualities in a child that make her – or him – vulnerable: a sense of insecurity or isolation. These are the feelings that pedophiles exploit by trying to make the child feel accepted, special. It's called 'grooming' the victim, and they'll take as long as they need to win over the child's trust. Read up on these grooming techniques and understand that they are also used on parents and guardians to instill a similar trust. So, don't be taken in, telling yourself, 'Oh, but he's so nice,' if the person fitting that profile is your kid's teacher – coach – troop leader – your priest – or Uncle Charlie who seems overly-interested in taking little Suzie for ice cream every Sunday."

The sound of stunned outrage from the audience was pure silence.

Ilene glanced at the front row where Lynette Kulik was seated. The CPS worker gave Ilene a small encouraging smile.

After a moment, a lone, male voice from the back protested loudly, "Whose side are you on?"

"I'm on the *victim's* side, sir," Ilene said hotly. "And I'll prosecute anyone – and I mean *anyone* who uses a child to gratify himself sexually. "

The man angrily pushed over his metal folding chair with a crash and strode out the door. He looked familiar, but Ilene couldn't place him. A few others followed more quietly, at which point she handed off the microphone to Matt. As she did, she made a silent, but firm resolution to refuse further community engagements even if Gerry Malone got down on his knees.

The outburst had the effect of mollifying the group and those with more questions raised their hands to be called on like good students. But the meeting never got back on firm footing. Most concerns were directed to Matt regarding security around the school, particularly at arrival and departure times. Some lobbed a few questions at Dr. Paradiz. No one asked to hear from Ilene again, and the assembly began to dissolve. Matt noted the time and suggested that they wrap things up for the evening.

* * *

As the last of the chairs were folded and stacked, Ilene slumped against a piece of scenery tucked in the back of the stage, trying to avoid any lingering parents while she waited for Matt. Roz, lacking her usual sunny smile, found her.

"You didn't exactly make a lot of friends tonight," she said hesitantly.

Ilene frowned. "I couldn't join the posse and try to run the Westerly Center out of town."

"But do you think you might have gone a bit heavy on the, 'it could be your *coach*, your *teacher*,' that kind of thing?"

"It's the unfortunate truth, Roz. If people are so concerned about their kids, they should be knowledgeable about the abuse that really takes place, rather than getting hysterical about a non-existent boogeyman."

"It might not have been the ideal time or place to enlighten them, especially with a lot of teachers, troop leaders and Uncle Charlies in the audience."

"If not here, where? And when is the *right* time?"

Roz was becoming exasperated with her friend. "I see your point, but everyone is pretty worried about the Westerly Center."

"I wasn't trying to fire anyone up. I was trying to educate them about where child abuse really occurs," Ilene was adamant. "And a number of people out there did not *want* to calm down. Believe it or not, sex with children is a subject that gets some people very excited."

Roz's jaw dropped. "Are you suggesting…"

"Let's go, Roz!" her husband Terry called out from the back of the gymnasium, motioning irritably for her to get a move on. He didn't acknowledge Ilene.

Roz sighed and touched Ilene gently on the arm. "Get some sleep. I'll call you in the morning."

"All right," Ilene forced a smile. "But I won't sugar-coat this for anybody," she added as her friend walked away.

CHAPTER SIX

T HE NEON SIGN out front emitted a non-stop, pulsing hum that left him with an ugly headache. It wasn't nearly as bad during the day when customers and street sounds distracted him, but in the evening the throbbing electronic current really got under his skin. Especially because it was easy enough to fix. The bulb on the "u" and part of the "e" was out, making the store "Q'enie's" to anyone who walked by. He had the tools at home, but the owner didn't want to spend the money for new bulbs.

Pulling out the center drawer of the sales desk, Travis Buel hunted for the bottle of Advil he kept tucked behind the three-part delivery forms. He popped two in his mouth, swallowed them dry, and on second thought, took two more. His stomach would probably punish him in about an hour, but it was either a migraine or heartburn, and he'd take his chances on the latter. The clock ticking away over the Simmons and TempurPedics assured him that he could lock up and go home in twenty minutes, but the thought gave him little comfort.

Home. What was that?

Two days ago his landlady had given him notice that he had to be out by the end of the month because of the new Rockville ordinance that prohibited registered sex offenders from living within one thousand feet of any school, park, or recreational center where children "frequented." That pretty much wiped out any place in the city. And without public transportation, how would he get to work?

Buel took off his thick glasses and returned to the classifieds where he had circled a couple of rentals to check out. But it was a crap shoot, there was no way to know. None of the ads spelled out whether the location was within a thousand feet of a school or bus stop or YMCA. Was he supposed to take a measuring tape around the neighborhood? Was he required to tell the landlord up front about his conviction? Hell, it wouldn't make any difference, he had to inform the cops if he moved and they'd go right to the landlord to make sure.

What in God's name had happened to his life? He was fifty-two years old, had a college degree, and for small change and a shit-commission he was a freakin' mattress salesman – excuse me, mattress *consultant*! There was a time when he could get sixty-five bucks an hour as an electrician, but now he didn't have enough start-up money to go it alone and no one would hire him anyway, not if they got wind that he was a registered sex offender.

It wasn't fair. He loved that girl, he loved her *so* much. Buel felt the threat of memories sharpen his headache.

Jessica. My Jessie. He would never have hurt her in a million years. The prosecutors and child welfare workers could say what they want, but he never hurt her. He was always gentle, caring. And didn't he plead guilty so she wouldn't have to testify? Sent himself off to state prison where – hoohah! – you want talk about sex abuse? You want to know what they *do* to pedophiles?!

A familiar surge of toxic and confusing bitterness flooded Buel's body. He couldn't control what turned him on. He'd tried, but he couldn't. It's the way he was wired, like homosexuals are wired to their own sex, or women who were only attracted to tall guys, or guys who only liked blondes. He was captivated by young girls; he loved their sweetness, their purity, their little painted toes in flip-flops – and that made him some kind of monster.

Swiping away a few beads of sweat from his upper lip, Buel took the store keys out of the drawer and got up. Sudden fatigue nearly pushed him back down into the chair, but at that moment, the front door opened and a solitary figure entered, silhouetted by the street lights outside.

He quickly pocketed the keys and straightened his shoulders. He dug deep to produce a big, welcoming smile.

"You're just in time," he said. "I was about to close up."

"Can I just look for a second?" asked the customer.

"Sure thing. You in the market for something on the firm side?" Buel walked over to the most expensive merchandise on the floor. "If so, this is the one for you. It comes with a five-year warranty and there's—"

He didn't get anything else out because a bullet ripped through the back of his skull, pitching him forward. Face down, his body went into spasm and before it had stopped, the killer rolled him over, put the gun in his mouth and fired again.

A minute later, with the store dark and the front door closed, Travis Buel's twisted body lay still, his blood pooling on a king size Posturepedic TrueForm with Memory Foam.

CHAPTER SEVEN

ILENE STEPPED INTO her office and hung up her coat.
"Make yourself at home," she said to Hector. He sat day-dreaming in her swivel chair, feet up on the desk, lost in visions of his upcoming vacation.

Hector abruptly swung his feet to the floor and with his jacketed elbow swiped the area where his shoes had been.

"I brought you the paper and a café latte," he offered smoothly.

"Starbucks?"

"Of course."

"Very well then, you may sit in my seat, but keep your feet down."

Ilene pulled up a chair to the other side of the desk, took the plastic lid off the coffee, and peered into the bag next to it.

"What kind of danish is this?"

"Cheese."

"God, Hector, you are so transparent. You know damn well I don't like the cheese."

"Who said that was for you?" he asked, plucking the bag from her hand. He pulled out the pastry and bit down hungrily. "Have fun last night?" he asked through the mouthful.

"A blast."

"Looks like the party kept on going after the school cleared out."

"How so?"

Hector took another bite, holding his hand underneath to catch the crumbs and pointed with his elbow to the newspaper on her desk. Ilene picked up the news section, and when she got to the middle of the page let out an audible breath.

The article was about the discovery early that morning of graffiti spray-painted across the front doors of the Westerly Center. Someone had written "Perverts!" and "Sex Offenders R Sick + Evil!" There was a statement by Dr. Paradiz to the effect that the vandalism was upsetting to all on the staff but their work would go forward as planned. Then she read: *More graffiti was found on the side of the building: a scrawled message that read, '1 down, 29,999 to go.' None of the personnel interviewed could explain the message's meaning, but one nurse at the affiliated Westover General Hospital called the vandalism 'shameful and ignorant.'*

Hector saw her face. "What is it?"

"Somebody wrote on the building 'one down, twenty-nine thousand, nine hundred ninety-nine to go.'"

"I saw that. What's it mean?"

Ilene looked up. "You heard about Chris Owen, right?"

"I did," he winced. "Why? You think the graffiti has something to do with him?"

Pressing her knuckles against her mouth, Ilene stared back at the newspaper on the desk, disquiet etched in the furrow between her brows. "Do you remember the Canadian study done a while ago on recidivism in sex offenders?" she finally asked.

"The Hanson/Bussiere?"

"Yes. Last night, Dr. Paradiz cited the study, noting that it followed 'thirty thousand offenders.' You do the math."

Hector raised his eyebrows. "You think the artist up at the Westerly knew about the study?"

"No, because the Hanson study was actually about twenty-eight thousand, which means whoever did the graffiti was relying on Paradiz's rounded figure, and that means they were there at the school meeting. But more importantly, the reference to 'one down' points to the fact that the graffiti artist knew Chris Owen was dead."

"It was in the papers," Hector balked. "Two media sources stated that he had been convicted of a sex offense."

"But I'll bet they didn't know that Chris had just gotten out of the rehab program up there."

"He did?"

"See?" Ilene retorted. "Even you didn't know."

"I thought he was in the juvenile program down-county."

"They transferred him to the Westerly when it opened up here."

Hector mulled it over and said, "Okay. So this tells us three things," he ticked them off on his fingers. "One, our graffiti artist was at the school meeting; two, he was aware that Chris Owen was dead; and three, and this we have to surmise – he also knew Chris was a patient at the Westerly. Otherwise, why target the place?"

"Exactly."

"It doesn't, however, mean that whoever did the graffiti killed Chris." Hector got up from behind the desk, balled up the paper bag and swiped the crumbs to the floor. "Besides, I heard a couple things."

"Like what?"

"Like the ME found abrasions on his neck, and at the scene there was a rope hanging off a tree right next to his body."

The newspaper slid off Ilene's lap, but she made no move to recover it. "What does that mean?" she questioned.

Hector shook his head. "Beats me. Maybe whoever shot Chris tried to hang him afterwards, but couldn't pull it off or got scared and ran."

"Why in the world…"

"That's all I know."

He ambled to the door and stopped, changing the subject. "Check out the sports section," he said brightly. "There's a nice piece about the Hudson State basketball team. They're having a real good season."

"I suppose," responded Ilene weakly.

"Isn't Sam working with the team?" Hector asked.

"He's talking to them about it."

"Great! I'll bet he's thrilled."

44

"He likes it. But I think that going from home and Community College to a city university might be too big a leap for him, don't you?"

"Aaah, give him a chance," Hector rebuffed. "Kids make mistakes, but that's how they learn."

Anita Flores breezed in and out, depositing Ilene's mail on her desk. Hector left with a friendly wave that Ilene halfheartedly returned. She took back her chair feeling grumpy. First Matt, now Hector, each so ready to exercise his manly prerogative and send Sam out into what would be an inflexible, unforgiving world for any kid barely out of his teens. Ilene stared at the pile of mail. So easy to let Sam "make mistakes." When was the last time one of them sat up half the night with a disconsolate seventeen-year-old after his first date because the girl had suddenly bolted from the pizza place when he wouldn't shut up about statistics? The girl said she'd be right back, so Sam had waited for two hours before calling Ilene to see what he should do. And what about the time he naively accepted a ride from a fifteen-year-old classmate who said he could drive? They were lucky to have ended up in a ditch rather than wrapped around a tree. Oh sure. Let him make some mistakes....

Just then, the phone rang. It was the District Attorney's secretary who barked a terse request for an immediate audience with Him regarding the "Westerly situation." Malone had obviously heard about the graffiti, and Ilene had an uncomfortable feeling that he was going to ask her to do some damage control. As her feet searched for her heels underneath the desk, she imagined what Dorothy felt when the Great Oz ordered her to bring back the broomstick of the Wicked Witch of the West.

* * *

" 'A rational man is guided by his thinking – by a process of Reason – not by his feelings and desires.' You know who said that?" Gerry Malone was perched on the sill next to an open window in his sixth story office. He took a deep drag on his menthol cigarette, exhaled the smoke into the chilly gray morning and then turned back to Ilene.

She took a guess. "Aristotle?"

"Ayn Rand – my spiritual guru."

"Isn't Rand as a spiritual *anything* a contradiction?" offered Ilene.

"Only if my admiration is blind or unsupported by reality and the conclusions of reason."

"Mmmn," Ilene mused. "And all this time I thought you were just a big ole' linebacker."

Malone extinguished his cigarette on the outside brick of the building and flicked the butt out the window before closing it. As he returned to his desk, Ilene quickly added, "A linebacker with a cum laude law degree, of course."

"My point is," Malone continued, "I'm getting a lot of pressure from the community about the Westerly, and when I speak of 'the community' I refer to the absolute bunch of *nuts* out there."

"When it comes to sex offenders, Gerry, hysteria trumps rationality. Especially when it comes to kids. I'm afraid that's just the way it is."

"Not good enough. What can we do about it?"

"To be honest, I think anything we try to *do* will just bring more attention to the clinic and add fuel to the fire. Things will die down eventually."

"Eventually takes too long. The way I see it, when the irrational group gets to looking over its shoulder for the proverbial monster, it also begins to feel that the police and the DA's office are not doing their jobs. I can't afford to look passive on this one. The whole Westerly business has the potential for getting out of control. The graffiti, the murder of that kid...."

Ilene sat unmoving, waiting for the DA to demand not only the broomstick but the witch herself, along with a solid conviction.

"So, I need you to come up with some ideas on how to nip this thing in the bud," he confirmed. *It's already in full flower, Boss, nothing I can do.* "Work with Chief Bingham, the Branford Town Supervisor, anyone you can think of to tamp down the agitation." *Valium in the drinking water?* "I'd start by talking to the good doctor at the center. I'm sure this isn't the first time he's seen a negative reaction to his clinic." *For goodness sake, just leave it alone, Gerry.* "And keep me posted."

Ilene smiled thinly. "Of course."

Malone rose to signal the end of the meeting. As Ilene headed to the doorway he added, "By the way, I heard about your little speech at the school last night, and I guarantee you that lecturing worried parents and teachers about the 'real' predator in their own community is not productive."

Ilene's fists clenched, but she mustered her cool and said blithely, "Any other approach is unsupported by reality and the conclusions of reason."

"Whatever," Malone sniffed. He looked down and patted his jacket pockets for his cigarette pack.

* * *

Ilene returned to her office even grumpier. She knew the furor would die down of its own accord. But Malone was publicity-obsessed, and when anything threatened to cross his re-election path, he became unglued, couldn't think rationally. Ayn Rand be damned. Ilene began to sort the mail on her desk, throwing interoffice memos in one pile and motion papers in another. She picked up a white envelope addressed to her, but with no postmark or return address. Odd. She opened it and found a folded piece of paper with a short typewritten paragraph that immediately extinguished all thoughts of Malone and the Westerly. When she'd finished reading it, she dropped the paper as though it had burned her fingers.

You are a Prophet, a beacon of light in an ugly world. You are the one who can save me. What I'm doing is wrong, I know that. But I am powerless to stop, I have no choice. You can save the child, too. I have her hidden where no one will find her. Sometimes she cries out and I see the fear in her eyes, the bruises on her soft, pale skin. And I cannot control the urges – they are too strong. Please help me.

Thirty minutes later, Ilene and Hector sat across from Lester Dawkins, who headed the District Attorney's investigative staff. Ilene tapped her fingers nervously on her knee while Dawkins studied the letter.

"What do you think?" she asked.

"Weird," said Dawkins.

"I was hoping for a more professional assessment," Ilene said without much amusement.

Dawkins held the letter, which he had encased in a plastic sheet protector, up to the light. "Looks like ordinary printer paper. And it appears to have been typed on an old manual typewriter. Look at the malfunctioning 's' on the typeset," he pointed out. "We'll run it for prints and try to get some DNA from the envelope where he might have licked it. But I have a feeling we're not going to get anything."

"Why not?"

"Because if this clown really wanted you to find him, he would've given you a few more hints."

Hector chimed in, "The lack of postmark does tell us that it was dropped off by hand."

The thought that the letter writer had been that close sent shivers up Ilene's back.

"True. How'd this get to you?"

"Anita said that it was in with the morning mail which gets sent over from the mail room."

"Roddie Polenko still there?" asked Dawkins.

"Yeah, I showed it to him," said Hector, "but he couldn't tell anything; he comes and goes. Someone could've walked in and dropped the letter in the interoffice pile and he wouldn't have seen."

Dawkins peered over his wire-rimmed glasses and read the letter again. Then he lifted his large black frame from the chair and paced the room.

"Why Ilene?"

"Because I'm the head of Special Prosecutions?" she ventured. "There's clearly a sexual threat in here. He's talking about a child, a little girl that he's holding someplace and trying to fight off his *urges*."

"Maybe. But I think it's more personally directed. After all, you are a 'beacon of light in an ugly world.' A *prophet*, no less."

"Someone who reads the future?" Hector asked.

"That's one meaning." Dawkins removed his glasses and cleaned them on his shirt. "But a prophet is also someone who speaks for a movement or cause, like Martin Luther King, or someone who is considered to speak by divine inspiration."

"Hey, you're a leader of sorts in combating child abuse," Hector said to Ilene, "and it does seem like he's asking for help."

"A prophet can also be an orator," Dawkins added. "Do you do many speaking engagements?"

"No, I try to avoid … although…" Ilene caught herself, "I did say a few words at a community meeting last night."

Hector raised his eyebrows, "About child abuse, yes?"

Dawkins stopped pacing and peered over his glasses, waiting for further explanation.

"The folks in Branford just found out about the Westerly Center," said Hector.

"The rehab place?"

"Yeah. They're unhappy about it."

"What did you speak about?" Dawkins asked Ilene.

She began to rub the tension from her forehead, but her icy hands only made it worse. "It wasn't a *speech*, really. Some of the parents are worried about the center's risk, and I thought I'd set them straight about where, statistically, the risk to children really lies."

"Sounds like you made quite an impression on someone."

"You think the letter was sent by somebody at the Branford meeting?" Ilene asked incredulously.

"It's come right on the heels," said Dawkins. "Be good if we could get a list of all the people who were there."

"I don't see how," said Ilene. "There were over a hundred and fifty, and no one was taking names."

"Too bad. Okay, we'll start with the lab analysis on the letter itself, go statewide to put out feelers for any missing children, contact CPS and have them review on-going cases of suspected child abuse, maybe do a round of unscheduled visits – just in case this is for real."

"What do you mean, 'in case it's for real?'"

Hector shifted in his chair. "I think what Les might be suggesting is the letter could just be an attention-getter. He gets his jollies off while we're running around, bringing in a lot of manpower and draining resources. We've seen this kind of thing before, especially from anti-government, anti-police crazies."

"You can't assume there's no danger here, guys," Ilene's voice rose in alarm. "Whoever wrote this letter is really sick! He says he's holding a child captive!"

"Of course we're taking this seriously, Ilene," Dawkins put in quickly.

"Of course," Hector reiterated. "Just thinking out loud."

Pushing her hair off her face, Ilene buried her head in her hands. Just a half hour ago she had told Malone that the reaction to the Westerly would die down. But if this was connected, there was something seriously wrong in Branford, someone quite unhinged.

"In the meantime, is there anything I should, or should not be doing?"

"I don't see a viable threat to you," said Dawkins. Over Ilene's head, he and Hector shared a brief look. "But keep your eyes open. I'll let you know as soon as we have something."

CHAPTER EIGHT

THE SCRITCHING OF all the pens and pencils was getting under Sam's skin. He didn't understand why his classmates had to write down every word the professor said. For himself, he didn't take notes in class, only jotted down an idea or two. After all, it was just physics – okay, advanced physics, but not that difficult. While the professor droned on and the scribbling continued, Sam stared at an ink stain on his desk and let his mind wander.

He liked to fantasize about his ideal life. There were really just two fantasies, but it was satisfying to refine them, add color and detail. In the first he's on the bench at a Division I school, maybe Duke or UCLA; they're way ahead in their division – because of him. He's wearing a dark blue suit just like the coach, he looks good and no one makes fun of his hair. In fact, as he surveys the modern stadium, he sees that afros have come back in style and he fits in with all the black players.

Now the scene shifts and it's a beautiful Saturday afternoon and he is home. He is working on skill curves for each of the players, charting their shooting efficiency against possession percentages. Here comes his wife who is quiet and lets him work in peace. She appreciates basketball stats herself and they can talk about it in detail. Around the house, she is precise in her communication and therefore easy to understand and get along with. She doesn't just say, "Honey, could you help me in the kitchen?" Rather, she asks him if he will dry the dishes in the drainer and put them away in the cabinet. Everyone agrees that his wife is a "knockout." Indeed, she looks quite a bit like the dark-haired girl in the front row.

He's wanted to ask her on a date, but doesn't know if she has a boyfriend. He sought advice from his friend Toolkit on how one would know if a girl does, or does not, have a boyfriend. Toolkit said that he should just ask her. Toolkit could fix almost anything that was broken, but was clueless about romance. Sam had wondered if Frankie knew, not from personal experience of course, but stuff he might have heard at school. Sadly, his brother's only suggestion was to spy on her and see if some guy ever put his arm around her, but Sam didn't like the idea of spying on his possible future wife. He thought about asking his mother, but rejected the idea out of hand. There were many parts of his life she didn't need to know anything about. Like sex.

Sam could say that he was not a virgin, but his one and only experience had been somewhat stressful. The sex itself felt good. Very good, actually. The girl had seemed as anxious as he to get it on, and he knew all about condoms, had read about foreplay and what women tended to like. Even kissing had been surprisingly pleasurable given his reservations about being touched. This was different. It all worked out quite well indeed. Until afterwards – then he was stumped. The girl wanted him to spend the rest of the night in bed with her. He couldn't fathom the purpose of that and was so flummoxed by her request that he got dressed and left without a word. He needed far more information about the after-sex part before trying *that* again.

Sam rewound his mental tape to fantasy number one and was lost in the ink stain when the professor interrupted his train of thought.

"Mr. Hart, are you with us?" he asked pointedly.

Sam snapped his head up and saw everyone in the class looking at him. "Yes, I'm here," he replied.

"You seemed to be in another world," said the professor.

"I don't know what other world you're referring to," Sam said honestly.

A couple of people in the class chortled, and the professor gave a short, exasperated sigh.

"We're talking about fermions, Mr. Hart."

"Yes, particles with antisymmetric wave functions," said Sam.

The professor paused. "Correct."

"Fermions possess an intrinsic angular momentum whose value is Planck's constant divided by 2 times pi times a half-integer, whether or not it's...."

"Thank you, Mr. Hart," the professor interrupted. "You've gotten ahead of us here, but I would ask that you stay focused on the task at hand, all right?"

Sam nodded and when he looked around, he saw that the pretty dark-haired girl in the front was smiling at him.

CHAPTER NINE

I LENE STEPPED BRISKLY down the brightly-lit hospital hallway toward Dr. Paradiz's office. The receptionist, a pleasant woman in her sixties, said she thought he was in with someone, but Ilene was welcome to wait outside his office. On the way, she passed a makeshift lounge with a TV and a vending machine where a small group of teenagers idled. Two unsmiling boys were playing chess at a card table while a few others, the hipper ones dressed in baggy pants and sideways baseball caps, sprawled on a sofa halfheartedly watching ESPN sports news. There was one girl in the group, about fifty pounds overweight, wearing thick stripes of violet eyeliner and large hoop earrings. She tried to look disinterested but couldn't disguise her keen eye for the boys piled on the sofa. A real mix, Ilene thought, but they all had one thing in common – they were all juvenile sex offenders.

She knew their pathology: adolescents who exhibited anti-social, attention-seeking behavior, with low self-esteem and sexual identity issues, amongst other problems. Probably many of them had been sexually abused themselves as youngsters. But for Assistant DA Ilene Hart their histories were relegated to clinical symptoms and profiling tools. What she knew far more intimately were their victims, most often younger kids, a few much younger: a five-year-old who cringed in fear when any male adult approached; a seven-year-old girl who insisted on wearing sweatpants and long-sleeved shirts in the summer, who couldn't make eye contact, even with Hector. The older victims, kids in middle school, also suffered. Girls like Heather McColl.

Ilene shook off the parade of small faces for whom she'd spent nearly sixteen years fighting in the criminal justice system and tried to focus her attention on the task at hand – devising strategies to take the Westerly out of the spotlight. She still thought that proactive measures were likely to draw more attention to the center, but she had to appease Gerry. She also thought Dr. Paradiz might be able to shed some light on the graffiti which, like the letter, seemed to be connected to the Branford school meeting.

At the end of the hall, Ilene walked through an archway with a small sign marked "Administration" and into a worn waiting area with paint-chipped walls. The one bright spot was a large window that looked out over the hospital's rear parking lot. Outside, light snow drifted lazily from the overcast sky.

A state trooper sat low in a green plastic armchair, legs spread, reading a magazine. When Ilene entered, he straightened and nodded in greeting. Ilene smiled back. The door to Dr. Paradiz's office was closed.

The trooper gave her another look. "Aren't you in the sex crimes unit?" he asked.

"Special Prosecutions."

"Right. M'name's Harris Dodd. I think we worked a case together a few years back. The gay kid who was assaulted at the school in Riverton."

"Sure. Tim Hobner."

"That's right," Dodd slapped his knee appreciatively. "I *couldn't* remember his name."

Ilene studied him. "You took Tim to the hospital."

"Yeah."

Ilene reached out her hand. "I remember you. Tim told me you were very kind to him."

Dodd blushed and lumbered to his feet to shake her hand. Then he sat back down and shifted awkwardly in his seat, at a loss for further conversation. With an embarrassed smile he picked up his magazine again. Ilene concluded that he was here about one of the juveniles and settled in a chair across the room, noting with some annoyance that now she would have to wait for whomever was in with Doctor Paradiz and then Officer Dodd. She reached for an old newspaper.

As she flipped through the pages, Ilene became aware of muted voices coming from the inner office. She couldn't hear what they were saying, not over the low hum of the white noise machine in the waiting area, but it sounded as though there were a few people in there. Understanding the inviolate need for confidentiality between patient and psychologist, Ilene tried to tune out the voices by focusing on stories of local interest.

One was about an apparent botched burglary at a Queenie's Mattress outlet in the neighboring county. Travis Buel, the sole employee in the store at the time, had been killed. It was unknown whether or not he resisted a demand for money, but he had been shot execution-style: one to the back of the head and another into his mouth. Police had found the contents of his desk scattered about and were asking potential witnesses to come forward. At the end of the article, Ilene's eye caught the following: *Travis Buel, 52 years old, was unmarried and lived alone. Court records confirm that Mr. Buel was a convicted sex offender who had been released from Upton Correctional after serving five years in prison. He moved to Rockville and had registered his work and home addresses with the state and local police.*

Suddenly, a woman's high-pitched scream sounded from within Dr. Paradiz's office. Ilene jumped to her feet and steeled herself to crash through the door to see if anyone was hurt. But Officer Dodd, although he looked up from his magazine, didn't budge, and Ilene realized that the scream was not a call for assistance, but a cry of devastation. The sound cut to the bone.

The woman cried out again. "Noooo! Oh God! My baby! Why would he do that?" she lamented in heart-wrenching sobs.

And then, joining her in an anguished duet of misery broke the deep, guttural sobs of a man. He could barely get his words out, but finally cried, "Chris, I'm so sorry, forgive me."

Ilene's heart sank as she put the pieces together. The doctor was not with another juvenile offender, but with Chris Owen's parents. She looked questioningly at the trooper.

"It's about that kid in the park. We informed the parents of the death yesterday," he whispered apologetically. "But the Branford cops are pretty sure he tried to kill himself first. *Hang* himself. He obviously didn't succeed – the ME says he was very much alive when he got shot. But they found a note in his locker, and he tried to call his shrink right before." He nodded in Paradiz's direction. "I guess the story's gonna break tomorrow and Chief Bingham thought'd be best if we brought the parents here to learn about it from the doctor."

"I don't understand," said Ilene, fearing that she did. "Are you saying he failed in his suicide attempt and someone came along at that moment and shot him?" Ilene asked incredulously.

"That's what I'm told."

Ilene stood rooted. Chris's parents had attended most of the court proceedings on the McColl case and she remembered them clearly. The mother had displayed what Ilene thought was immature and erratic nurturing; she either sat too close to her son and babied him, or she nagged him about trivial things, his posture, his choice of sport coat. The father had seemed distant towards his wife and son. Both parents had minimized their son's crime.

There was no minimizing this.

Feeling like a voyeur, Ilene turned to leave, but caught Dodd studying her. He cocked his head toward Paradiz's office and gave her a knowing, hopeless shrug. Ilene didn't know what to do. She felt trapped. She wanted to escape the sounds coming from the office, but Dodd was watching to see what she would do – the Chief of Special Prosecutions – the ice maiden of sex crimes. What would he think if she ran out now?

Ilene resumed her seat and pretended to read. She couldn't erase the scene that the trooper had just described. Chris Owen, desperate to end his life, but somehow failing or aborting the attempt just in time to get a bullet through the chest. Did the killer know this? See it unfold? Who would be ruthless enough to do that? As Ilene listened to the keening of Chris's grief-stricken parents, she knew they must be facing the same unfathomable questions.

Assuming a casualness she didn't feel, she put down the paper and walked over to the window where she tried to focus on the snow dusting the grass and parked cars. A multitude of excuses for walking out right now came to mind: the messy roads, the meeting tonight with the Renegades' coach.... But her feet stayed planted while she rode the waves of her own conflicted emotions, ebbing and flowing with the sounds next door. Finally, the weeping diminished and without warning, the door opened.

Ilene turned and saw the Owens coming out. First Tom Owen, a heavyset, balding man with glasses. His face was red and patchy from crying, and he seemed lost as he came into the waiting area looking around for the way out. Maggie Owen followed, her arms crossed tightly over her chest as though try-ing to physically hold herself together. With her hair pulled back into a ragged ponytail and a frayed cardigan over old sweatpants, it was clear that she didn't care how she looked. Indeed, it was evident that Chris's mother didn't care about anything anymore. As she took in the figure standing by the window, her eyes, devoid of all light and life, looked straight through the woman who had prosecuted her son.

Dr. Paradiz stayed in the doorway until they left. A profes-sional who listened to the grief and loss of his patients every day, he tried to present a neutral expression, but compassion and perhaps his own sense of failure acted as gravitational pulls to his features, making him look older than Ilene remembered. She turned away, fixing her gaze on the parking lot to avoid looking at Dr. Paradiz or watching the Owens and the trooper walk down the hallway. And then, even though it seemed that no time had gone by, she saw the couple exit the building and shuffle slowly to their car, their feet leaving smudges on the slushy asphalt. Tom Owen opened the passenger door for his wife and helped her in. He shut it after her and was rounding the back of the car when his knees buckled and he sagged against the hatchback, his shoulders heaving. Ilene pulled her-self away and was almost startled to see Dr. Paradiz.

"I'm sorry to keep you waiting," he said gently. "Won't you come in?"

Ilene risked one more glance out the window before following Dr. Paradiz into his office. She moved to a chair on the other side of his desk while she tried to forget her last view of the parking lot.

"Thanks for taking the time, Doctor," she said.

"Please, I wish you'd call me Jeffrey," Paradiz said. "I think I'm done being a doctor for today."

"I'm very sorry about Chris. I ... just learned about his suicide attempt."

"Thank you." The doctor paused. "I liked Chris."

Caught off guard by her empathy for the Owens and the hurt echoed in Paradiz's face, she tried to change the subject. "When did he finish his treatment here?"

"He completed the probationary requirements about three weeks ago, but I encouraged him to keep seeing me privately. He was depressed, but I didn't see this coming."

"He showed up for his appointments?"

"Yes."

"I recall he had a drinking problem. That might have contributed."

"He did, and you're right, the alcohol didn't help." Paradiz cleared his throat uneasily. "I'm aware that you were the prosecutor on his case. He had made good progress toward ... an understanding of what he had done and the inability of such a young girl to make appropriate sexual choices. Chris did understand what a mistake he had made."

His words came out sounding wooden to her and Ilene felt her jaw harden at his bland clinical description. She'd heard it so many times from defense attorneys, and from where she stood, juvenile sex offenders who made that kind of "mistake" were future pedophiles.

"Did he understand the pain he caused *Heather*?" she asked somewhat brusquely.

"I think he did," the doctor answered sadly.

"Enough so that she took her father's belt and *hung herself* in the closet."

Paradiz nodded slowly. "You sound pretty angry at him."

Ilene bristled. "I'm sorry that he tried to kill himself, but it's not okay to be angry about the rape of a thirteen-year-old girl?"

"It was statutory rape; the sex was consensual."

"We both know the law disallows consent at that age, and for good reason. Heather is a perfect example; the guilt was too much for her."

"Is that what you think?" Paradiz leaned forward intently. He seemed to be trying to control his own anger. "That Heather committed suicide because of what she and Chris did?"

"You mean, what *Chris* did," Ilene challenged. "And frankly, yes, I've seen too many victims of sexual abuse to think otherwise."

Paradiz leaned back, lips pressed together and his brow furrowed. "Young victims can experience a great deal of shame and guilt arising out of their participation in sexual acts," he finally said. "But Heather's case, I believe, is different. She adored Chris. And he felt the same way."

"Puppy love does not give anyone license to have sex with a thirteen-year-old," Ilene asserted firmly.

"Of course not. But we're talking about her state of mind when she chose to end her life, in which case her relationship with Chris is important; and it was more complex than simply abuser and victim."

Ilene lifted an eyebrow, "I hear that 'Romeo and Juliet' defense quite often."

Paradiz acknowledged her position with a small nod, but held up a finger. "Let me finish. Because you have so much experience in this area, you know that sex offenders are moved to seek out illicit sexual contact for any number of reasons other than the sex itself; it might be to assert control or, in extreme cases, to inflict harm on their victims. In fact, most everyone has an array of emotional and psychological needs, albeit usually healthier, surrounding his or her sexual impulses, such as a desire for closeness or a need to be found attractive. Wouldn't you agree?"

"I suppose so."

"By the same token, I think that absent being physically forced or rendered incapacitated, victims of sexual abuse have their own backdrop that makes them more prone to be taken advantage of sexually."

"Of course. But I hope you're not implying that child abuse victims are *complicit* in the sex abuse."

"Not in the sexual conduct itself, but for what comes with it. You acknowledged as much yourself the other night when you described the kinds of children that pedophiles are likely to target – lonely kids with low self-esteem. Those kids don't seek out the sex, but they do respond to the attention and affection that their abusers give them in the process of the seduction. And aren't those impulses healthy in their own way?"

"How does this relate to Heather?" Ilene asked stiffly, unwilling to explore further a line of thinking she found dubious at best.

Paradiz explained. "Mr. McColl had a great deal of power over his daughter. As you know, Heather was his child by his first wife who abandoned them when Heather was quite young. Early on she and her father developed a strong bond. Too strong. I think he began to look to her as a kind of surrogate partner." He held up his hand when Ilene started to protest. "I'm not suggesting that Simon sexually abused his daughter, I have no reason to believe that. But I do think that despite his remarriage, he continued to seek emotional support from Heather that a wife might provide – with all the unconscious desires that go with it."

Ilene shifted uncomfortably in her chair.

"And when she reached her pre-teen years, it became suffocating and anxiety-producing for her," Paradiz continued. "She wanted out, and she turned to Chris. With him – and most particularly in a sexual partnership with him – she was able to simulate what she perceived as an 'adult' relationship for herself that excluded her father. Her actions were not mature or healthy, but the impulse to break from her father was, and it created for her intense and powerful feelings for Chris. So much so that she needed to protect him. I understand Heather refused to testify against him."

Ilene looked long at Paradiz. "That's right," she finally said hesitantly. "Initially, many victims are reluctant to testify."

"But there was a lot of pressure put on her to do so." Paradiz met her gaze.

"We don't *pressure* witnesses to testify," Ilene said quickly.

But she averted his gaze because it wasn't true; she *did* sometimes work on uncooperative witnesses. No one wanted to get up in front of strangers and give details about their sexual abuse. A certain amount, the right *kind* of prodding was often necessary.

Paradiz murmured a lukewarm assent and continued, "Even if you didn't, her father wasn't going to take no for an answer. Chris told me that he and Heather talked every day, even after he was charged and up until the trial began. They kept it a secret because both sets of parents warned them not to have any contact. But one day Mr. McColl found out, and he was livid. I don't know what he said to his daughter, but she stopped answering Chris's calls, and the next thing he knew she was on the witness stand."

Ilene remembered vividly. For two days she stalled the jury selection process and during breaks would run back to the office where she and Hector tried to talk the girl into taking the stand. Without her, they knew they had no case. Heather refused. But on the morning of the third day, when Ilene went across the street prepared to tell the judge that her witness would not be appearing, she got the call that Heather was on her way over – she was ready to tell all.

"Caught between Chris and her father must have been very painful for her," Paradiz was saying. "She had to feel responsible for Chris being convicted of a crime in which she willingly participated. At the same time, she must have felt powerless in the face of her father's ultimate control and quite angry with him as well. Kids have a way of turning that anger inward..." Paradiz didn't finish the thought. He didn't have to.

Ilene looked away. "You sound as though you might be angry with *me*."

Paradiz gave a small, sad chuckle. "I'm sorry," he conceded. "Perhaps I am and it's unfair to you. I'm having a difficult time with the knowledge of the suicide attempt right on the heels of learning about his murder. Chris was my patient, and I'd grown to like him and root for him, and to some degree under-stand the challenges he faced – though we obviously had not plumbed the depths of his pain." He sighed deeply and then said, "I don't want you to feel that I'm judging you or the choice to prosecute. Heather was a deeply troubled girl, and her desire to harm herself took root long before Chris. Likewise, his choice to act out by engaging in sex with such a young girl was wrong and he needed to be held accountable."

"I don't feel unfairly judged," Ilene said smiling thinly. "If someone commits a sexual offense and there's enough evidence to go forward, that's what I do."

"As you should," said Paradiz. "I just wanted to shed some light on what was a very difficult situation for both kids."

"I understand, and I'm very sorry about Chris."

All of sudden, Ilene had the same urge to run that had overtaken her in the waiting area, only now her legs didn't refuse to obey. She had long since forgotten why it was she had come to see the doctor in the first place. She thanked him for his time and made her escape, passing the emptied lounge where an ESPN sports commentator blared out scores to no one. But the sights and sounds of the flashing TV screen were replaced by another image that played over and over like a wide-screen movie in front of her eyes. It was the moment when the Owen verdict was announced and Heather erupted in sobs. At the time, all Ilene discerned was relief that the ordeal was over, but the desperation and self-hatred carved on Heather's young face was there for anyone to see – if they were looking.

CHAPTER TEN

SAM'S HEAD BOBBED happily in time with the rhythm of the squeaking sneakers and thumping basketballs on the court. Standing next to him by the bleachers, Ilene wondered again at the contradiction in her son's sensitivity to certain sounds. He hated the screech of metal chair legs in the computer room, he recoiled at the playground squeals of small children, but here in the Schoenberg Stadium at Hudson State none of the high-pitched noises seemed to bother him. He caught his mother's eye.

"You see that guy, number eleven?"

"He's huge."

"Six-foot-ten, Jerome Augustus Taylor, but everybody calls him JT. He's awesome," Sam said proudly. "Do you believe that his individual possession stats, so far, are nearly forty percent ahead of any other player in the whole division? He uses twenty-five percent of the team's possessions and has an offensive rating of a hundred and twenty. Nobody else puts up numbers like that, except maybe in the NBA."

"Wow," Ilene said. She had no idea what he was talking about.

The coach blew his whistle and Sam winced.

"That bother you?" she asked.

He shook his head and patted her tentatively on the shoulder. "It's okay, Mom. Sometimes there are noises that hurt a little. But if I turn them into visual images they go by quickly."

"Must be distracting."

Sam thought about it for a moment and replied, "For me, *life* is distracting."

Practice was over. Very tall, sweaty men in maroon and gray warm-ups ambled toward them, downing bottles of Gatorade like shots of water. A few stared unabashedly at Ilene, checking her out. And as they headed to the locker room, a few of the players acknowledged Sam with a towel flick, a "W'dup, Stat-Man," a playful jab that never landed. At the end of the line marched Coach Boone, head of the basketball program for Hudson State University, a Division II school hoping to make a run in the post-season, if not this year then the next.

"You must be Sam's mom. Nice to finally meet you. I'm Jay Boone," the coach said enthusiastically.

Ilene returned his greeting in kind, thinking privately that he looked far too small to manage a team of such giants; he had to be at least half a foot shorter than his smallest player. But as he herded them down the hall and got right to business, she realized that the imposing, powerful athletes she'd witnessed on the court were equally matched by Boone's energy and vitality. He shut the door to his office and leaned against the edge of his desk ready to spring into action.

"So I guess Sam told you," he began, "we'd like to make it official and invite him to be part of our Renegades staff. The pay's not much, but he'd have free room and board at the University, and I'm sure we can work out transferring his credits so he can graduate from Hudson."

Sam was beside himself with excitement. His hands tapped rapidly against his legs, an adaptation of his childhood hand flapping. After a moment he recognized what he was doing and self-consciously shoved his hands into his pockets.

"He would live in a dorm?" asked Ilene anxiously.

"If he wants to. He can always rent off-campus, but in this neighborhood, I'd suggest he stick with most of the other students in the dorm."

Ilene frowned. "Doesn't the team travel?"

"On the overnights we usually stay in the dormitories of the host campus. But if none are available we find a motel nearby.

Nothing fancy. Sam would probably room with Blakely, our equipment manager. He's a good guy."

Boone could see Ilene struggling.

"Mrs. Hart, I'm aware of Sam's..." He seemed reluctant to come up with a description.

"Asperger Syndrome," Sam filled in helpfully.

"Right. And I'm sure it'll all work out fine. We really need him. He's doing great work for us."

Boone's praise turned Sam into a grinning fool. No one had ever said they *needed* him before.

A heavy knock on the door interrupted. Boone sprung over to let in the indomitable Jerome Augustus Taylor who ducked through the doorway.

"Sorry, Coach. I didn't know you were with anybody," said the big man.

"S'okay, JT. I was just talking with Sam and his mom about taking Sam on full time."

"Cool," drawled JT. "Asperger Man, he da man wi' da plan." He reached out his long arm to knock knuckles with Sam. "Back wi' you later, Coach."

JT left, and Boone looked over to see if Ilene had caught the ease in their exchange. She had, but it didn't make her feel any better.

She turned to her son. "Can we have a moment?"

Not getting her meaning, Sam stayed put and looked expectantly from Ilene to Boone.

"Would you wait outside for a minute, please, Sam?" Ilene asked in a do-over.

"Why?"

"I'd like to talk to Coach Boone privately."

"Okay." He paused. "Now?"

"Yes."

Ilene waited until he had left before continuing. "As you can see," she said, "Sam has some difficulties processing subtleties in language."

"Believe you me," Boone said emphatically, "on the basketball court our language ain't subtle."

"That's not what I meant." Ilene was not amused.

The coach recalculated. "Sorry, I shouldn't make a joke of it. You're concerned about Sam, and undoubtedly you've made a lot of sacrifices to help him adjust. Look, I can't promise he's going to be on top of every situation. But so far he's doing well and I'll help him as much as I can."

"What do you know about the autism spectrum?"

"Not much. I do notice that sometimes I have to re-phrase what I say to him and sometimes things the players say go over his head. But he's incredibly bright."

"His IQ is not in question. I'm more concerned with his social adaptation."

"Well, college is a big transition for all incoming students," Boone suggested.

"But Sam is not your ordinary student."

Boone stared at Ilene for a moment, then said, "You don't want him to take this job, do you Mrs. Hart?"

"I'm not sure."

"Listen, I wouldn't be offering this position if I didn't think we had a good chance of making it work."

He looked earnest enough, but Ilene was conflicted. She knew how much Sam wanted this opportunity, but his deficient social skills could spell trouble in a big school like Hudson, and Boone was naïve about Sam's disorder. Could he cope with Sam's panic when he was beset by certain combinations of fatigue, confusion and frustration? And if the coach did have an awareness of the difficulties facing her son, was it trumped by his ambition and need for his unusual mathematical gifts?

Ilene gave Coach Boone a wary smile. "I'm going to have to talk this over with him."

"Oh sure. And if you have any questions, I'll be around and we can—"

Boone's voice was drowned out by an escalating war of words in the hallway outside his office.

"Fuck you, man," someone was shouting. "I was four for five last game!"

And Sam. "But your offensive efficiency rating has fallen below sixty."

"What kind of bullshit is that?! Four for five is fucking *efficient*, and don't tell me it's not."

Sam's voice became higher in pitch. "But the turnovers when you don't hit bring down your overall floor percentage."

"Don't *hit*?! I'm the best three-baller in this whole league! You just too blind to see it."

"And you're too stupid to understand how the rating works!"

Boone wrenched the door open to find Ricky Wilkens, his back-up point guard poking Sam in the chest. Wilkens drew back when he saw him, but if Sam also saw the coach, he couldn't stop himself. He swung at the six-three guard who ducked adroitly and now felt justified in taking a return shot when JT and another teammate grabbed hold of him.

"Wilkens!" Coach boomed. "Get your ass into the locker room and wait there." He turned to Sam. "And Hart, if you want a job here you better control your temper."

Ricky Wilkens gave Boone a barely disguised glare and trooped off down the hall. Her heart pounding, Ilene stepped between Boone and Sam.

"Sam cannot tolerate unwanted touches," she tried to explain.

Coach was having none of it. He dismissed the players who had gathered in the hall anticipating a real fight. Then he pulled Sam back into the office, abruptly shutting the door on Ilene in the hallway.

"Listen to me, Sam." He prudently waited while Sam got his breathing under control. "You ready?"

Sam nodded.

"Your analysis is important to the team, and most of the guys know that. They want to be the best they can be; they want to win. But don't talk to them about your stats or analysis. That's between you and me. Understand?"

Sam didn't look convinced, so Boone explained. "Most of these guys are not gonna get floor percentages and individual scoring possessions. I don't even understand some of the math stuff you do, but we're seeing results. So, there's two rules. Rule number one: we don't discuss any of the stats with the players, got it? We let them play – which is what they're good at. You and I will look at the numbers. And after that, *I* make the coaching decisions. And so it's very clear to everyone," he continued, "I'll lay down the law to the players and the rest of the staff."

"Lay down the law?" Sam wasn't familiar with the metaphor.

"I'm going to tell them about rule number one, okay?"

"What about rule number two?"

"They know that already. Rule number two: anyone who throws a punch in my gym is benched."

"Am I benched?" Sam asked nervously.

"No, because you didn't know the rule. But you do now."

* * *

By the time they got on the highway a cold, hard rain had replaced the earlier snow flurries. Sam was chattering nervously about a new formula he'd adapted to determine the weight for offensive rebounds. Ilene let him go on, hoping it would settle him after the fight with Wilkens and because she needed time to compose her thoughts.

"Sammy, we need to talk," she finally said.

"…but the improvement in efficiency is in the offensive rebounder's own ability to score–"

"Sam, be quiet. Please."

The rain beating on the roof hammered at the tension in the car.

"I have a lot of worries about you taking this job," she finally said. "Hudson State is a very different place than what you're used to. The city can be very confusing and sometimes dangerous."

"I've been to Hudson State eighteen times."

"Really? That many?"

Her question was foolish; Sam was nothing, if not precise.

"I only had a problem once," he said. "But that was because the man gave me bad directions. Now I know how to go."

"It's not about traveling to Hudson. It's about living there, and I'm more concerned about you getting lost academically and socially. It's got a huge student body, much bigger than Community College. And you may not be able to find professors who are willing to work out strategies to help you with organization and time management the way they do at CC."

Ilene took Sam's silence as a kind of acquiescence. Concentrating on the dark, wet road ahead, she didn't see him squeeze his eyes closed, a warning signal she had come to know well.

"And after the incident today, I question whether this high-pressure, competitive environment is right for you now. Am I wrong to think you might be nervous about it also? Maybe in a couple of years … I just don't think you're ready. If you had gotten into a fight with that player he might've really hurt you. And if you're constantly around people who don't understand you – or worse, you try to conceal some of your issues because you want to fit in–"

"Aaahhh!" Sam cried out.

His scream shattered the dark interior, and Ilene flinched. The front wheels swerved over the double yellow line.

"Okay, okay," Ilene backed off, righting the car again.

She remained silent, allowing him to regain control while she fought off the self-doubt that had been chipping away at her all day. The anonymous letter was deeply unsettling, and bearing witness to the Owens' pain still sat like a lump of cold, wet clay on her chest. Hearing about Heather and her father from Dr. Paradiz was even worse and she wasn't sure why. Now tonight – to have Boone shut the door in her face while *he* straightened things out with Sam! She had been so flustered by his easy dismissal of her that she turned her ankle as she paced indignantly in the hall. Limping back into his office she felt foolish and off balance in more ways than one.

After a few miles, Ilene tried again. "Do you agree with anything I've said?"

"No."

Ilene sighed in frustration.

"You want to keep me at home," Sam said. "You want to keep me at home to babysit for Frankie."

"Oh, Sammy, that's not true. I only want the–"

"Knock Knock Interrupting Cow!" yelled Sam. "You can't protect me from everything. I'm nineteen years old, I'm an adult. I want to have a life of my own!"

"And I want you to have a life of your own, too," his mother answered angrily. "But we've gotten you this far by making good choices about school, about camps, summer jobs, and everything else. This is not a good choice."

"You want to keep me home to take care of *you!*" insisted Sam.

Ilene was stunned and wounded; she could deal with his anger, but his contempt was intolerable. "That's insulting," she managed to say. Hearing her own voice crack, she clenched the steering wheel for support and took a few deep breaths before pressing ahead. "You're not thinking this through. But when you do, you're going to realize that this particular job is not feasible right now. Let's talk in the morning when we're both rested and won't say things to hurt each other."

But Sam didn't hear her. His eyes were clenched shut and his hands were clamped over his ears while he recited calculations to drown her out.

CHAPTER ELEVEN

THE DOG CHARGED out of the house, snarling and barking at the intruder approaching the front door. The assault was more like gurgle and yip from the little white terrier, but Ilene took a step back in case it went for her legs. A heavy-set woman appeared and scooped up the frantic animal, scolding him, "Bad boy, bad boy, no, no, bad Duncan." Finally, with the trembling Duncan firmly in her grasp, she allowed herself a better look at her visitor.

"Ilene!" she said in surprise. "Hello."

"Hello, Rebecca. I hope I'm not interrupting anything."

Simon McColl's wife tugged self-consciously at the gray woolen skirt hugging her hips. She had put on a fair amount of weight since Ilene had last seen her, but the haunted look in her eyes had diminished. After a moment's hesitation, she invited Ilene in.

"Would you care for some coffee or a cup of tea?" she asked.

Ilene thought that would be very nice and followed her into their small, spotless kitchen where Rebecca placed Duncan on a doggie bed in the corner.

"Stay!" she said firmly. He promptly scampered over to Ilene to give her a proper sniff.

Rebecca started after him, but Ilene waved her away. "It's okay, he's not bothering me," she lied.

"He can be a real handful," said Rebecca as she pulled out coffee and filters. "Simon isn't crazy about him, but I'm hoping they'll get along in time."

"He's … adorable."

"I've always loved terriers. Had them as a kid. Heather was allergic to dogs so we couldn't have one. Duncan is good company for me."

Rebecca continued her chatter while she set up a tray, moving randomly from one topic to the next: the right color to repaint the kitchen, the weather, the price of gas. Usually composed, she seemed edgy, and Ilene tried to put her at ease by interspersing exclamations of interest. Finally, Rebecca sat across from her guest at the kitchen table and passed her a steaming mug. The smile she gave Ilene couldn't mask her underlying suspicion.

"I'm surprised to see you," she said.

"Simon came to see me day before yesterday," Ilene began. "Did he tell you?"

Rebecca shook her head slowly.

"He was pretty drunk."

Rebecca's even gaze let her know that this wasn't news.

"I guess with it being Heather's birthday … it was pretty hard for him."

"It's still difficult," Rebecca agreed.

"Is his drinking bad?"

Rebecca blew on her coffee, took a small sip, and put it down.

"How are *you* holding up?" Ilene asked.

"I'm better. I joined a grief group which has been very helpful, and my church is a big support." Rebecca's words offered a glimpse into her emotional state, but her tone was still cautious.

"Look, I feel bad about not coming around or calling recently," Ilene said hurriedly. "And when I saw Simon the other day obviously struggling, I thought I would stop by and see how you were doing."

"That's kind of you. Simon and I feel as though you've done so much for us already." She paused and lifted her eyebrows. "Now, why are you really here?"

Ilene was taken aback, less by Rebecca's perception than by her own lack of it. She suddenly understood that she hadn't driven to the McColl's home at eight o'clock in the morning to check on them; her need to connect came on the heels of her conversation with Dr. Paradiz. Until then, Heather was the quintessential tragic consequence of sexual abuse and Chris Owen the cloaked, self-gratifying predator. She, of course, was the enforcer who would ensure that *justice* was done – as if justice healed all wounds. But from the moment Maggie Owen's scream pierced the doctor's inner office, the stock characters had begun to shift and assume different masks. It was no longer clear who was the victim and who the offender. And now, even Ilene was stumbling through her lines – Rebecca McColl could see that.

"I've been thinking about Heather," Ilene confessed. "I met yesterday with Dr. Paradiz because of what happened to Chris."

"Yes, I heard about it. Poor boy."

"He told me that Heather felt I coerced her into testifying and that she was in a … fragile place. And I can't help but wonder if–"

"… If you played a role in her suicide?" Rebecca finished for her.

Ilene nodded.

"Heather did feel some arm-twisting from your office," Rebecca replied candidly. "But Simon wouldn't have let you drop the charges. And to be honest with you, the trial was only part of it, perhaps a trigger, but it wasn't the loaded gun." She caught herself and sighed. "Sorry, that was a poorly chosen metaphor in light of Chris's murder. Heather was an angry kid," she continued. "I'm learning from my group that a lot of teens who take their own lives are quite angry inside. She hated school, struggled with grades and teachers all the time; she was angry at her father for remarrying and at me for being the new wife. There was also her mother. Heather was furious at her for abandoning them."

Ilene knew something about that. In one year her own mother's cancer had turned a spirited woman into a pale, bedridden wisp of smoke, and the burden on Ilene as the only child had become intolerably heavy. Rather than hang out with her friends after school, she came home to cook foods her mother would tolerate, clean out the bedpan, change the sick-smelling sheets and help her mother bathe. She had huge mood swings from grief to hope for remission. The middle ground was taken up with disgust for her tasks, fury at incompetent doctors, and hardest to bear – the quiet strain of trying to convince them both that she wasn't resentful.

Rebecca's voice brought Ilene back to the present. "It was quite natural for her to feel angry and take her feelings out on me," she went on. Her words sounded as though she had memorized phrases from a self-help book, yet Ilene had to admire Rebecca – she was obviously working hard to understand and accept her loss.

"I'm so sorry," said Ilene.

"I don't think we'll ever really know why Heather took her own life. I'm afraid that's just something we have to try and live with." Rebecca cleared her throat. "Can I get you more coffee?'

"No, thank you. I appreciate your talking with me. Where is Simon, by the way?" Ilene asked, knowing that he worked out of the house.

She almost heard a door slam shut across Rebecca's face. "I was curious," she stammered, wondering what she had said.

"Curious? That's all?" Rebecca rose so quickly that the dishes clattered on the table, and she snatched them up to put in the sink. "I already talked to the police," she announced stiffly.

At once, Ilene understood. Of course the cops had been by; they were trying to find out if Simon had an alibi for the night Chris was murdered. Now Rebecca thought that Ilene had come on the same mission and felt betrayed that her stepdaughter had been used as a pretext.

"Oh! That's not why I came," Ilene exclaimed. "I didn't know the police had spoken to you."

Rebecca glared fiercely at her.

"Please believe me, Rebecca, that's not why I came over."

"That Simon would be suspect is absurd!" snapped Rebecca. "He's the last person in the world to inflict harm on anyone. No matter what he might say – he turns everything inward. Why do think he's in such agony?"

Ilene hesitated, feeling slightly sick to her stomach. "What do you mean 'no matter what he might say?'" she asked warily.

Rebecca fanned angrily at the air in front of her face as if to wave away the words that followed. "He made some threats when he was drunk at an office party the other day. He was upset to learn that Chris was out of that rehabilitation place; he always believed the boy deserved jail time. And on top of that, he saw him with a girl that reminded him of Heather. It drove him a little crazy."

"What did Simon say at the party?"

"I don't know exactly. A co-worker drove him home that night and told me that he was ranting about the kid who raped his daughter."

"Did you tell the police?"

"No. They didn't ask."

"What *did* you tell them?"

"I told them I didn't know where Simon was, and it's the truth," she said defiantly. "I haven't seen him since Tuesday morning. He's done this before," she added too lightly. "I'm not worried. He'll be back tonight or tomorrow; he's never gone more than a day or two. He's just letting off steam some-where."

"He's disappeared before?"

"After Heather died, a few times, yes."

"And you have no idea where he goes?"

"He doesn't tell me everything."

An oppressive silence descended on the kitchen, the space between the two women thick with unpleasant questions. Ilene was used to asking them, but this next one was difficult.

"Do you think it's possible that Simon–"

Rebecca's mouth twisted. "Do I think Simon killed Christopher?" she finished, flushing with anger and surprise that Ilene had dared to ask. "No! No, it is not possible." She

76

turned her back and began to scrub the dishes under running water.

Ilene stared at the white knuckles of her own clasped hands. Sensing his mistress's upset, Duncan raced protectively over to Ilene where he stood growling at her shoes.

"Please go," said Rebecca, her back still turned.

Ilene rose slowly. "I apologize for the insinuation," she said. "But you obviously know the police are suspicious of Simon, especially if he's … gone with no explanation. It looks bad."

"I don't care how it *looks*." Rebecca squared around to face her. "My husband is not well. Heather was his life. He's in pain, he's an alcoholic, and he's lost his way. But he is *not* a murderer."

Ilene looked into her grief stricken eyes and nodded. "I don't think he is, either," she said.

Wearily, Rebecca dried her hands on a kitchen towel.

"The police will probably come back, you know," cautioned Ilene.

"I'm sure they will. But until I talk to Simon, I won't be able to tell them anything."

"Would you call me, or have Simon call me, the minute he shows up?"

Rebecca didn't answer, and Ilene let herself out feeling sad and uneasy. She meant what she had said – she didn't believe Simon was capable of murder. But she had detected a thin crack of fear underneath Rebecca's outrage and it was enough to give her pause. If the cops found out about Simon's threats, as undoubtedly they would when they interviewed his co-workers, they would also learn that Rebecca had withheld that information. It would make them wonder what else she wasn't telling them. Ilene had to wonder the same thing.

* * *

Hector saw Matt first and waved him over to their table in the corner. Chief Bingham walked purposefully through the lunchtime crowd. He was looking very dapper, Ilene thought, in a well-cut, navy suit and a sea green silk tie that she had given him for Christmas. Along the way, a few patrons attempted to waylay the Chief to say hello, but with the exception of a brief greeting to a superior court judge, Matt just nodded and stayed on course, eyes only for Ilene.

He gave Hector a hearty handshake then eased into the chair next to Ilene and under the table pressed his thigh into hers.

"You look too sharp for a cop," said Hector suspiciously. "Jurors are not gonna believe you if you're dressed better than the lawyers."

Matt grinned. "I make sure they see my gun."

"How'd it go?" asked Ilene.

"Short and sweet. I'm finished for the day, including cross. I was only there for some continuity." Like most police officers, Matt's job wasn't done once an arrest was made; there was always the ensuing prosecution.

A waitress came over to take his order. Without looking at the menu, he asked for the broiled fish and a baked potato, hold the sour cream.

"Aren't *you* good," Ilene exclaimed.

"I've been eating a lot of take-out at home by myself," he added, and then confided to Hector, "gotta watch my weight in case I see my lady some time. A guy gets lonely, and at midnight that half gallon of ice cream starts to look awfully tantalizing. It's no substitute, of course, for–"

"Okay, Cowboy," chimed in Ilene with a wry smile, "you can put your gun away."

"… For a good home-cooked meal was all I was going to say," said Matt innocently.

Ilene's garden salad entrée and Hector's grilled chicken arrived along with a promise that Matt's meal would be right out.

"Anything turn up on that letter?" Matt asked them.

Reminded of it, Ilene's stomach clenched.

Hector filled him in. "There were no prints just as Les thought, and the lab won't be able to test DNA for a couple of weeks; they're backlogged. Technically, there's been no crime committed and they gotta work on those first."

"But someone has threatened a crime," Ilene argued. "What he described about keeping a child 'hidden' is unlawful imprisonment, if not outright kidnapping."

"So far, we have no local reports of a missing child," said Hector.

"Have you run an Amber Alert?"

Matt frowned. "Can't without a name or a description, and not without a reasonable belief that an abduction has taken place."

Hector signaled his agreement. "I still think it could be a crank," he suggested.

"Maybe," Ilene said, poking at her greens. "But I can't stop thinking about it."

"And what about the Owen case?" Hector asked Matt, changing the subject. "Any progress?"

"It's a strange situation," replied Matt somberly. "There's convincing evidence that Chris attempted suicide not long before he was shot."

"I was waiting to see Dr. Paradiz yesterday when his parents were told," Ilene said.

Matt chewed on his lower lip. "How'd they take it?"

"Pretty bad."

There was a moment of silence while she remembered.

"I was told Chris left a note," Ilene said.

"In his locker at Westover High."

"In his locker?" Hector interjected. "That's an interesting choice."

"How so?"

"If he'd left a note at home, one of his parents could have found it in time to intervene. But he left it in his locker where no one would search until after the fact. Tells me he didn't want anyone to stop him."

"Well, the abrasions on his neck tell us he *was* serious," said Matt. "But something happened."

"You think the killer interrupted him in the process?" asked Ilene.

"We know that Chris drove to the park. He had been drinking, and he managed to get a rope up in a tree, get it over his neck and hang himself sufficiently to cause damage to his neck. There were scuff marks on the trunk and pieces of bark in the bottom of his sneakers showing that he climbed up. It's possible that he didn't tie the knot tight enough in a noose and it slipped. That can happen. Even if a person wants to die, the body instinctively fights off the strangulation."

The waitress arrived with Matt's order and overheard his last comments. She placed the dish in front of him. "Bon appétit!" she added brightly.

"How do you know that Chris isn't shot first, and then his assailant tries to hang the body?' Ilene probed. "Some kind of statement...."

"Because he wasn't moved after he was shot. Plus, the abrasions on his neck were consistent with a short suspension time and some struggle. If the body had been hung post mortem, they would have found deeper ligature marks, and we would have seen blood under the tree."

"Do they know what kind of gun?" Hector asked.

"Looks like a .357 or a .38."

"This may sound crazy," Ilene interjected, "but might Chris have hired someone to shoot him in the event he was unsuccessful in his attempt?"

"Like a back up?" Hector asked incredulously.

"I suppose anything's possible," Matt replied. "But I have a hard time believing that a teenage boy in Branford would know how to find a hit man. And despite his attempt looking pretty earnest, I learned that his cell phone stored the last call he made, or tried to make."

"To whom?"

"His therapist, Dr. Paradiz. The call didn't go through, but he might have been looking for Paradiz to talk him out of it."

"Then you have to ask – how did the killer know Chris was at the park?"

Matt nodded. "Someone either knew he was going to be there or followed him."

"That would mean that his killer *watched* him try to hang himself and then when he failed, *shot* him!" Ilene said in disbelief.

The three of them contemplated the cold-heartedness of that scenario until Matt broke the silence. "We probably won't really know what happened until we find his killer." Ready to drop the conversation and dig into his food, he tucked his napkin into his collar to protect the tie and then doctored his potato with salt and pepper.

Ilene plowed forward, frowning. "And what about the graffiti at the Westerly, Chief? The phrase 'one down, twenty-nine thousand to go'? It's obviously a reference to Chris in relation to the sex offender study Dr. Paradiz talked about at school. Whoever wrote that must have known Chris was dead. They might have read it in the paper, but they couldn't know that Chris was a Westerly patient."

"Why not?" Hector protested. "If one person in his high school knew he went to the Westerly, what with texting these days – they *all* knew."

"And his stint at the clinic was a motive for murder?" proposed Ilene.

Matt shook his head. "Just his connection to the clinic doesn't sound like a reason to kill him."

"Not unless he was targeted because he was a sex offender," said Ilene.

"I'm not dismissing anything, including the fact that Simon McColl doesn't have an alibi for the night Chris was murdered."

Inexplicably irritated, Ilene asked, "You're stuck on Simon? Why?"

"Because he *does* have a motive … and a strong one," answered Matt. He scanned the table, "Is there any butter here?"

"What motive? The case against him was over a year ago."

"From what you told me about your run-in with him, McColl still seems pretty emotional."

"Oh, well," Ilene bristled sarcastically, "you'd have thought he'd gotten over his daughter's suicide by now."

Matt wisely remained silent while Hector, head down, sawed away at his chicken.

"Do you have any other evidence?" Ilene pressed.

"I spoke to his wife. The night Chris was killed, Simon left the house after dinner because she was hosting some kind of group. Apparently he didn't get back until about four in the morning."

Ilene put her fork down, her appetite gone. She knew she ought to tell him about going to see Rebecca, but she remained silent, remembering Rebecca's sense of betrayal when she thought Ilene had come on behalf of the cops.

"When he woke up," Matt continued, "he told his wife he was going out again, and she hasn't seen or heard from him since."

"He's gone?" Hector asked wide-eyed.

"Hasn't shown up at work, neighbors haven't seen him, and his wife doesn't know where he is – that's *gone* in my book."

"You believe her?" asked Hector.

Matt gave it some thought, then said, "I believe she doesn't know his whereabouts. But she's not telling us everything."

"And she's not about to start," said Hector through narrowed eyes, remembering Rebecca from the trial. "That woman's a soldier."

Ilene pushed her plate away, still rattled over the visit to Rebecca. She had gone seeking some kind of assurance that she had played no part in Heather's suicide, and not only had she failed to get that assurance, she left feeling as though she had been pulled further into their squalid family secrets. It brought up murky, uncomfortable memories of her own family before her mother's death.

"Hello there!"

Ilene looked up to see a tall, handsome woman standing at their table. It was Lynette Kulik from Child Protective Services.

"How are ya, Lynette," said Hector.

"I'm well, thanks."

"Would you like to join us for coffee?" Matt asked.

"Kind of you to offer, but I have to get back." She hesitated. "I just came over to tell you that we've all been trying to squeeze in unannounced visits, but we haven't found anything that would shed light on that letter, sorry."

"Thanks for trying," Ilene responded.

"By the way, I thought it admirable of you to tackle the situation head on at the school the other day."

"You're in the minority on that one," said Ilene dryly.

"Well, we don't get the opportunity to educate people very often. And it's important to correct the misperceptions about abuse, especially in a town like Branford – that's where it's most likely to get brushed under the rug."

Matt concurred, "Frankly, I was surprised by the overreaction to the Westerly."

"Hey, no one wants to acknowledge abuse in his own backyard," Hector said. "It's easier to get riled up about the 'Attack of the Forty-Foot Sex Offender.'" He mimed a cartoon Godzilla. "The enemy without and all that."

Lynette broke into a smile that brightened her face. She had what Ilene's mother used to call "good bones," but she did nothing to accentuate her better features. Her dark blond hair was pulled back in a tight bun and she used little makeup or jewelry. When her name came up, even some of Ilene's staff drew a blank, she was that invisible. Some called her standoffish, but Ilene waved the criticisms away; she herself hated professional social functions, avoiding them like the plague. Ilene cared that Lynette was very good at what she did.

"I'd better be off," Lynette said, and then to Ilene, "I'll see you next week at the Destiny Bashe deposition."

"I thought Gillian was handling that case."

"She is, but she has a doctor's appointment that day and asked me to fill in."

"Good enough."

Lynette was about to turn away when she said as an afterthought, "I heard about Christopher Owen. Terrible thing."

"Yes," Matt concurred.

"Any idea who did it?"

Matt shook his head.

"It's probably nothing," she said, chewing on her lower lip, "but about two weeks ago I happened to see Christopher in Branford with a girl. She could have been in her late teens or early twenties, but came across as rather *young* to me. In fact, she looked sort of like Heather McColl, and I wondered if that might have touched a nerve with anyone."

"Thanks for letting me know," said Matt with a circumspect, thin-lipped smile.

"If there's anything I can do to help...." She stepped back nearly colliding with a waitress who was gliding toward the next table with a tray full of drinks. Lynette muttered her apologies and walked away, head bowed.

Hector turned to Matt and said grimly, "Wonder if Simon McColl saw them together."

Matt wiped his mouth with his napkin and raised his hand for the check.

"If he shows up, we'll ask him," he said.

Ilene didn't like the flint in his eyes.

CHAPTER TWELVE

B ACK IN HER OFFICE, Ilene studied the Bashe file and wrote out some questions for the upcoming deposition, but she kept having to drag herself back to the task. The whole business with Chris and Heather had stirred up a caldron of feelings. Finally, with some of them gnawing at, she picked up the receiver and punched in the number she knew by heart.

"Hello?"

"Hello, Brooke."

Pause. "Ilene. How nice to hear from you."

Brooke Caldwell, her father's second wife (Ilene refused to call her "my stepmother") didn't sound overly enthused, but they both made an effort at cordiality.

"How are you?"

"Terrific, and you?"

"Everything's good."

"That's great."

"Is my dad around?"

"Sure. Hold on." The sound of high heels clicking against the parquet floors in their Fifth Avenue apartment. "Bill? It's Ilene." It seemed forever until he came to the phone.

Her father had been floating at the back of her mind ever since Roz mentioned the publicity photo at the ballet fundraiser. Ilene didn't need to see it, she could picture the scene well – her father, elegant and smart, working the room with ease. People *loved* to give money to William Caldwell. He was connected all the way up to the Court of Appeals and the Governor. Even after all of her own successes as a lawyer, Ilene still felt like a substitute teacher next to her father's professorial dominance.

"Hello! How're you doing, sweetheart?" Her father's voice was deep and resonant, and he sounded genuinely happy to hear from her.

"Hi, Dad. I tried you at the office, but they said you'd left. You don't usually leave this early." Her office clock read five-oh-five.

"We're going to an exhibit downtown tonight. Do you remember Harold Schiffman?" he asked.

"Your partner?"

"*Ex*-partner as of Friday; he's leaving the firm to work at the Treasury Department. His son is an artist and has a gallery opening tonight. Harold has one of Stuart's pieces in his office. Absolute junk if you ask me, but I told him we'd be there. Just hope he doesn't make me buy anything."

"Be strong, Dad."

Ilene heard the clinking of ice against the glass as he chuckled and took a sip of his scotch.

"How're my grandsons doing?"

"Couldn't be better."

"Frankie's in fourth grade now?"

"Fifth."

"That's right, that's right. And Sam?"

"Doing fine."

"You better bring them down to see me, you hear?"

"Sure."

"We missed you at Thanksgiving," said her father with a slight edge to his voice.

"Sorry, we had a previous invitation to Frankie's best friend's house," Ilene said. It was a half-lie. Roz hadn't asked them about Thanksgiving dinner until after Brooke left *her* invitation on the answering machine, but the boys had no interest in a formal dinner with Brooke and her aging mother. Ilene thought she'd be liberating them all by declining Brooke's invite.

"You have to honor that prior engagement." Ilene could tell he didn't buy her excuse for a minute. "Some other time."

Her father took another sip of his drink while Ilene nervously clicked a ballpoint pen in and out. There was such a history of tension and disappointment in their relationship, Ilene didn't know where to start to heal the calcified rift and wasn't even sure she had the will to try. It hadn't always been that way. As a youngster, she had been the apple of his eye; he admired and nurtured his daughter's spirit, intelligence, and wit. And she adored him. But it all changed when Mary Caldwell was diagnosed with rapidly advancing cancer, as though its toxicity seeped into the bonds that held the family together. Out of sadness or denial, or both, her father threw himself into his work, leaving his wife and daughter to stare down the approaching train wreck. And instead of devoting her senior year in high school to SAT's and college applications, Ilene spent it in trips to Sloane Kettering or to the library to investigate alternative medicines. Toward the end, she felt crushed under the weight of her nursing responsibilities and the emotional toll of watching her mother die. She wanted desperately to flee to the University of Chicago where she had been accepted. But it was too late, she had already become her parents' caretaker, so she stayed and enrolled at NYU. A few months after her mother died, Ilene found a way to cut the umbilical cord completely – she got pregnant. In one drunken, crazy encounter she was able to thwart her father's patrician dreams for her and make him as angry at her as she was at him.

"Your picture was in the *Times* the other day. I didn't see it myself," Ilene quickly added, "but someone told me about it."

"Right, right. Terrible photo, made me look fat."

"Do you remember when we went to the opening of the New York City Ballet? The night it was snowing?"

"You and I? Sure, I remember."

"Mom was pretty sick then, wasn't she?"

"Is that right?"

"Yes," said Ilene, prickly at his lack of recall. "That's why I went with you, because she was too weak to go."

"There were a few events, weren't there?"

"I've been wondering why you took me to all those dinners and fundraisers."

Her father hesitated. She could hear him thinking, hear the lawyer in him trying to anticipate where she was going with her questioning. She also heard him walk to the sideboard in the living room and refresh his drink.

He answered lightly, "I guess because I always got two tickets and paid handsomely for them. The ballet tickets alone were five-hundred-dollar seats."

"How did Mom feel about it?"

"You loved the ballet," he said, "ever since you were a little girl."

"Was I like ... a date?"

"What? What are you talking about?"

"It wasn't just the ballet, there were the big dinner engagements, too."

In the background, Brooke called a warning to her husband, "Bill, we're going to be late." He put his hand over the receiver and told her to hold her horses.

"What's your point, Ilene?" he asked, uneasiness in his voice.

"We never talked about this, but I think it was hard on Mom."

"Sweetheart, there are many events I don't want to attend, but I have to. I'm on the board of three or four organizations and it's just something you have to do."

"But why take me? I was only seventeen."

"For Christ's sake, your mother was the one who said I should. She thought you were spending too much time at home and it would be good for you to get out of the house."

"She did?"

"Of course." Her father sounded so sure. But Ilene was haunted by one evening in particular, a moment that had stayed with her all these years.

Late one night, her father had gotten waylaid in the lobby trying to resolve a delivery problem with the night doorman. Ilene headed upstairs, a little tipsy; she'd had four glasses of champagne at the dinner, sneaking two of them while her father was table hopping. She opened the door to the darkened room where her mother lay in the rented hospital bed, the white sheets glowing around her. *Hello darling,* her mother whispered, *where have you been? The partner's dinner, remember? Oh, of course, how was it? Boring.* It wasn't at all. As a precocious teenager, how could she have been bored looking younger and more vibrant than any of the pampered wives? Limousines, champagne, the freedom to flirt back with their husbands because she was so off-bounds? It was grown-up and exciting. *Come closer, I want to see you. Oh my goodness, look how beautiful you are. Is that a new dress? Give me a kiss, pet, and get to bed, it's late.* Ilene tiptoed to her mother's bed and kissed her dry, soft cheek. Her lips connected with a tear that uncoiled slowly down her mother's temple and disappeared into the pillow. In that single tear Ilene tasted an ocean of yearning and jealousy.

"I don't know," Ilene said tentatively to her father. "Maybe it was a little ... inappropriate."

"What are you suggesting?" her father questioned indignantly. He didn't wait for her answer. "You know, Ilene, if we're going to look back, I'll remind you that you certainly didn't put up a stink about any of it. In fact, you were having a swell time at those events, maybe too good a time–"

Ilene grit her teeth and broke in, "Did you know how much I was drinking then?"

Huge sigh. "I don't remember, and anyway, you were a grown woman."

"I was still in high school!" cried Ilene.

"You were very mature for your age."

"If you say so."

"What do you want?" her father barked. "What do you want me to do over? What?! I'm not the one who walked out of *your* life. I tried to help you with Sam, but you wouldn't take any money. You don't approve of my life? You don't like Brooke? Fine. But I'm not going back to relive all your resentment again, so don't ask me to."

"I'm just trying to understand what happened." Ilene felt herself close to tears and swallowed hard to hold them off.

Brooke had come into the room and was whining that they had to leave. Her father's frustration crackled over the line.

"Nothing *happened*, Ilene. I took you to a few fundraisers. You couldn't have understood at that age, but I was lonely. I was suffering my own loss, you know, and I tried to take good care of her and you, too. Who was going to take care of *me?*"

William Caldwell took his daughter's silence as affirmation that the conversation was over. He brusquely pointed out that he had to go, said goodbye and hung up. Ilene closed her eyes and leaned back in her chair. She thought again about Heather and what it must have taken to choke out her own life in a dark closet; she thought about Chris and his sad attempt to replicate the act on a lonely winter's night.

And was still thinking about them when Anita poked her head through the door.

"Sorry to barge in, but your line's been busy," she said.

"What's the matter?" asked Ilene, seeing the anxiety on her face.

Anita held out a piece of mail pinched between her thumb and finger buffered by a piece of Kleenex. "I think you got another one," she said.

Ilene stared at the plain white envelope addressed to her in the now recognizable outmoded typewriter font. Her mouth went dry.

"I already called over to Les Dawkins," Anita added. "He's on his way down."

"Okay," Ilene managed to say.

CHAPTER THIRTEEN

D R. PARADIZ WAS waiting for her in the last booth at
the Route Seven Diner, easy to spot since most of the
breakfast customers had cleared out. Ilene hurried over to
where he sat stirring a small creamer into his coffee, and she
slipped into the red leather booth across from him. She placed
the manila envelope on the table.

"Thank you for meeting me," she said.

"I'm not sure how much help I can be," he said, "but I'd be
glad to take a look."

Ilene pulled out copies of both letters from the envelope
and handed them to Paradiz. "As I mentioned on the phone,
these were sent to me just a few days apart. My office and the
state police are working on it, but we sure could use some help
from a psychological standpoint."

While Paradiz examined the first letter, the one Dawkins
referred to as the "Beacon of Light Letter," Ilene ordered a coffee for herself.

"The second one I got yesterday," she said. "My secretary
told me it had been thrown in with the motions and decisions
we get back from the court every afternoon. No one knows
how it got there."

Paradiz spread the letter on the table. His face was grim as
he read.

She screams so loud he must put his hand over her mouth and tie her down to finish. He makes her say dirty words while her little lips do things to his body. He takes her hands and moves them back and forth. It makes him groan with pleasure and weep with guilt. Is this in my imagination? Or did it really happen? When I hear the child whimper in the night I refuse to believe it is real. But the sound is getting louder. And if it doesn't stop I will have to silence it.

He looked up. "Pretty troubling."

Ilene waited anxiously for him to expound, then prompted, "What's your initial reaction?"

Paradiz read through the letters again. "The first thing I'm struck by is a seeming identity confusion by the writer. Sexual abuse is definitely present, but there's a shift in perspective. In the first letter the writer is the abuser himself, and in the second there is an abusive third person, then it shifts back again."

"What does that mean?"

"It could be that the abuser feels so guilty about his 'urges' that he has to see them as belonging to someone else."

"But the guilt doesn't seem to be strong enough to stop him. Here he talks about how afraid the girl is and she's got bruises. It sounds as though something has already happened. And in this one, he goes further to describe the sexual abuse."

"It could be a fantasy."

"But it might not be."

"It might not."

"And if it's not, do you think he means that he'll kill the child if she cries again?"

"I don't know," Paradiz said uncertainly. "There's a lot that's unclear, even to the writer. I think he really wonders if the abuse is in his imagination – something he wants desperately to do, but perhaps hasn't done yet. And I also see an underlying message that it is the *writer* who is in trouble and wants you to find him before he commits acts that he will feel terrible about."

"Why me?" Ilene asked with a pained expression. "What am I supposed to do, especially if he doesn't give me any clues how to find him? I feel totally helpless and it's driving me a little crazy."

"And quite possibly meant to. He asserts his powerlessness to stop, yet he's exercising a great deal of power. There is obviously the power over the child, and by dumping the threats on you with no way to find him, he is asserting power over you. These aren't just cries for help, they're also intended to be disturbing."

The waitress came over with Ilene's coffee and when they both declined her offer to bring them anything else, she tore the top check off her pad and left it on the table.

Ilene touched the first letter gingerly. "Les Dawkins, who's heading the investigation, thought the letters might have been prompted by what I said at the school the other night when I talked about keeping an eye open for pedophiles who groom their victims. He thinks that's where someone might have viewed me as a kind of 'prophet.' I have to say the timing is pretty coincidental."

"That's interesting," agreed Paradiz. "Here we were trying to address the concerns of parents and teachers – two groups most depended upon by children – and you called that trust into question. Your investigator is right, it could well have sparked a nerve."

Ilene narrowed her eyes, trying to picture the crowd at Branford Elementary. Was it someone there? It seemed unbelievable; she knew many of the parents and most of the school staff. Yet emotions were running high. She heard again the clatter of a metal chair flung to the ground and pictured the man who stormed out – something else, too, and Paradiz saw it in her face.

"What's on your mind?"

"It's ... nothing, really," she responded hesitantly. "I mean, it can't be related to the letters...."

"What?" Paradiz prompted.

"The word 'Prophet.'"

"Go on."

Ilene sat back and laughed weakly. "I haven't even told anybody yet, because it's just conjecture, hardly even a theory."

Paradiz looked at her expectantly, and she simply blurted it out, "Two convicted sex offenders have been murdered in the past week. I think there's a chance it's the same killer."

About to take a sip of coffee, the doctor put his cup back on the table so quickly some of it sloshed over the side.

"Christopher?" he asked.

"And a man in Rockville City named Travis Buel. He was killed during a supposed armed robbery, and his assailant shot him in the back of the head, then again right through the mouth. I found out that the guy's underlying offense involved oral contact with a child. The manner of death to me seems symbolic. And I find it strange that the night Chris was killed he tried to hang himself, just like Heather. His murder may have nothing to do with that, but it made me think."

Paradiz looked shaken.

Ilene explained, "Yesterday, I ran a search through something called the NCAVC, the National Center for the Analysis of Violent Crime. It's a federal database that collects information on unusual or repetitive crimes, and I came across two other unsolved homicides of sex offenders. Out of curiosity, I called the detectives on both cases. In New York, a man named Victor Troy was stabbed to death in a public restroom. One of the wounds was a deep cut to his groin. It could have been inflicted in the struggle, but the killer was apparently interrupted by a couple of teenagers who came in to use the facility. What if the killer intended to do more damage and just didn't get to it?"

"What was the man's sex offense?" Paradiz asked, recovering.

"I don't have any details, but Troy was charged with attempted sodomy in the second degree, which I'm guessing meant some kind of solicitation of a minor. The detective in the city thought the murder was an anti-gay thing. Troy was killed in a park restroom that had a reputation for being a homosexual pick-up joint and the detective thought he simply chose the wrong person to proposition.

"And then there's a man named Niles Middleton, who was killed in Westover a couple of years ago. His body was thrown into a dumpster. In his case there wasn't any mutilation to a particular part of his body, but he was shot in the chest three times – and had been accused of molesting *three* girls."

Paradiz frowned as he thought and then mused, "If it's payback, that's very strict retribution. Sounds biblical in a way."

Ilene nodded in agreement. "I thought so, too ... certainly with Buel and Troy. 'If thy right hand offend thee–'"

"'Cut it off and cast it away,'" finished the doctor. "It's from Luke or Matthew, I think." He paused and then said, "And now you receive letters that call you a 'prophet,' which also is a kind of biblical reference."

Biting the inside of her cheek, Ilene said, "It's a pretty flimsy connection. After all, the letters are coming from someone who has committed or is afraid he is going to commit sexual abuse, and my murder theory centers around whoever is killing people like him."

"Ah! So it *is* a theory."

"No, it's not," Ilene laughed. "You simply asked me what was on my mind, and I told you. But let's say, it was an ... *idea*. What kind of person would go around killing sex offenders?"

The doctor pulled at his chin. "I suppose you might look at a person with a defense mechanism called reaction formation, which is like an obsessional neurosis that can become an integral part of the personality."

"How so?"

"Without getting too Freudian, we often see this with individuals who become strongly homophobic in order to counter their own deeply-buried homosexual desires. They become obsessive and can dedicate their lives to combating acts they consciously perceive as immoral or evil. It's a form of anxiety relief, but only short-lived. For example, if one is on a quest to eradicate homosexuality, it necessarily involves dealing with the subject constantly which only feeds the underlying arousal, which in turn, produces more anxiety."

Ilene looked keenly at the doctor and asked, "I suppose this obsession would extend to closet pedophiles?"

He acknowledged her insight with a tilt of his head. "Absolutely. It's quite common; a person overly aroused by child pornography and disturbed by his feelings becomes vehemently critical of others who engage in it. He may wind up sacrificing family, friends and his job to become the vigilante who hunts down the 'evil-doers.'"

Seeing her soak in his words, Paradiz cautioned, "Bear in mind that acting on a neurotic obsession doesn't, in itself, make a person violent. If you're talking about someone capable of premeditated murder, you'd need to look at *psychopathic* reaction formation."

"Could strong religious beliefs play a part?"

"Obsession is often driven by rigid principles." He hesitated and looked down at his cold coffee. Ilene sensed a wariness in his fixed expression.

"But what?" she prompted.

"There's another profile to consider," he said, raising his eyes to Ilene. "Someone severely damaged, quite likely as a result of being sexually abused and/or physically mistreated in childhood. Someone who kills in order to seek dominance in their own fractured world. They might have delusional thoughts or hallucinations that drive their behavior."

Ilene thought of the NCAVC printout sitting on her desk and said, "Niles Middleton was murdered eighteen months ago and Troy about a year before that. If it's the same person, what do you make of the fact that Travis Buel was killed less than a week after Christopher?"

"If – and it's a big *if* – the murders were the work of one person, it would tell me that Christopher's death did not..." Paradiz looked pained, "... provide the catharsis the killer needed. Perhaps he couldn't complete what he felt he needed to do, for instance, hang the body; or in some other way the act created additional anxiety that necessitated yet another violent act. Either way, the proximity would not be a good sign."

Ilene sat motionless for a moment, then reached out for the check.

"Thanks for your expertise – on all matters," she tacked on with a sheepish smile.

"Any time – on *any* matter," he responded. "I mean that."

When Ilene gathered her things and rose from the table, Paradiz put out a hand to stop her. "About your investigation," he said seriously, "a word of caution. Whether or not it is related in some way to the letters you've received, be mindful of what and whom you're looking for. The pathology of someone with a severe personality disorder might be difficult to spot and quite dangerous if you do. As you're probably aware, psychopaths often appear well-adjusted, sometimes even charming. Many are of above average intelligence. But under stress their impulse control tends to disintegrate."

"Thanks, but as I told you, it's not an 'investigation.' It's not even a real theory," said Ilene with a weak smile. "And I'm a big girl, doctor."

Paradiz's soulful eyes looked suddenly weary. "Even big girls can get hurt," he said.

CHAPTER FOURTEEN

CHIEF BINGHAM AND his men, all in full uniform, presented an unyielding front. On the stage with Matt was Sergeant Bill Blue, thumbs hooked on the gun belt cinched underneath his large belly, while Officers Joel Levitsky and Brad Collins stood at the back of the gymnasium, one at each entrance. A fifth officer was positioned outside the school, directing traffic while the bubble light on his cruiser sprayed colored beams across the road. The parking lot was already full, the auditorium overflowing, and the tension inside palpable.

It was the incident with Amanda Prince that galvanized the school community for yet another hastily-convened forum. Mrs. Prince, the mother of a child in kindergarten, had logged on to the state sex offender registry and downloaded photographs of three men living within a ten-mile radius of the school. She printed copies that contained detailed information about the men's home and work addresses, license plates and convictions, and she was distributing these flyers at the school's front door to parents and nannies picking up their children. Sergeant Blue, on traffic duty for the afternoon dismissal, radioed it in. Within minutes, Chief Bingham arrived on the grounds to warn Mrs. Prince to stop immediately – what she was doing constituted harassment and if she persisted he would have to arrest her. She persisted. Matt found her not five minutes later passing out more leaflets by the soccer field in the back and told her she was under arrest.

There were different versions of what happened next, but according to a couple of fifth-graders who watched in awe, Mrs. Prince told Chief Bingham to "go to hell," and started to walk away. He took her by the arm and she kicked him, at which point he went for the handcuffs. After that, it took him and Sergeant Blue nearly three minutes to drag the biting, screaming woman to the patrol car and push her into the back seat. And now, despite her husband having retained Westover County's leading defense attorneys, the class mom of Miss Bergenstein's K-3 class was still sitting in a cell at the police station, charged with harassment *and* the more serious resisting arrest.

Word had spread like wildfire, rivaling the breadth and speed of the Westover School Alert System that Sam had programmed. The current "meeting" had been assembled by an angry group of parents who notified the principal they were going to use the school gymnasium. They had not extended an invitation to the Branford PD, but Matt, looking formidable as he took the microphone, let it be known his department didn't need one.

"All right, folks," he said stepping forward, "we're going to do this in a civilized manner. Settle down." The group began to quiet itself. "I'll be happy to take some questions in a moment, but first I want to advise you all on the law. Any unreasonable disruption or use of abusive or obscene language in this public meeting is chargeable with disorderly conduct." His steely gaze passed over the audience. "Second, disseminating information about *anybody* which alarms or seriously annoys the other person and which serves no legitimate purpose is harassment. Both are violations of the penal law."

Ilene slipped in by a rear entrance, passing Officer Levitsky who gave her a quick glance and then resumed his watchful eye over the crowd. Matt had called her earlier.

"All hell's breaking loose," he said, the ringing telephones and police radio in the background confirming it. He told her about the arrest, but added that was the least of it. He'd learned that a group of residents was going door-to-door asking neighbors to sign a petition to enact a zoning ordinance that would

effectively shut the Westerly down. Their actions were height-
ening the tension. The clinic had received more threats, one of
which promised to fire-bomb the place, mandating a call to the
FBI.

"Listen, Chief," she said, "you don't want me to say a word
there. After the reaction to my speech on pedophilia last time,
you'd need riot gear and snipers on the roof."

"I don't want you to talk, I just want you to observe – you
and Hector," he said. "Unobtrusively, if possible."

"What are we looking for?"

"This witch hunt is not picking up steam all on its own," he
explained. "I'm pretty sure there are one or two people fueling
the engine. I want to know who they are. Be good to have two
more sets of experienced eyes and ears. I'd also like you to let
me know if Simon McColl shows up. My guys don't know what
he looks like."

"You're not going arrest him, are you?" asked Ilene.

"No, I just want to talk to him, and I'm hoping this thing
will draw him out of the woodwork."

Ilene thought he was wrong about Simon and nearly
declined his invitation to stand around at another heated griev-
ance-fest. But then she realized that a lot of the same people
from the last meeting would be there, and if Dawkins was right
and her letter-writer was in the audience, she might be able to
spot him.

Now, joining the standing-room crowd at the back, she
caught sight of Hector leaning against the wall by the gym
mats. He appeared relaxed but was eyeing the crowd keenly.

An outraged woman stood up and bombarded Matt with
questions. "How can you hold Amanda Prince in jail? Are we
turning into a police state?! Isn't she entitled to a lawyer?"

Calmly, Matt explained that Mrs. Prince had representation
and was being accorded due process. He did not say that she
would have been released hours ago had she stopped her verbal
abuse of his staff.

"How can alerting parents about predators be illegal?"
demanded another parent.

He explained that the registry information on the website was intended to promote general public safety, not to single out offenders, and that this message was clearly stated on the website.

Someone else called out, "We have a right to know about pedophiles living in our neighborhood."

"Anyone can log on to the website," Matt responded evenly.

"Yeah, well, if you were doing your job, *you'd* be handing out the flyers, Bingham." This retort came from a well-dressed, slick-haired man in the third row whom Ilene recognized. He and his nervous wife had come up to her the other night. She couldn't remember his name, but did recall his overly-aggressive approach.

Another called out, "Apparently the rights of molesters are more important to your department. How about the boys from Westover High who were picked up by police and questioned – no, *interrogated* – about the murder in the park? My God, they're just kids!"

"So was the murder victim, Ma'am," said Matt.

A strong male voice came from the other side of the gym, "Your alleged murder victim raped a thirteen-year-old girl! And all he got was a year of 'therapy' at the Westerly 'Country Club.'"

Everyone turned around to look at the speaker. All but Ilene and Hector, who locked eyes in surprise. Divulging the fact that Chris had gotten a year of rehab, he had just revealed the sentence given to a juvenile offender – information ascertainable only from his sealed file. Ilene took a closer look at the speaker. He was the same man who had stormed out the other day. While other crowd members chimed in to offer their personal opinions on what kind of sentence Chris should have drawn, Ilene sidestepped her way over to Hector.

"Who is that?" she whispered.

"Name's Jim D'Ambrosio," said Hector out of the side of his mouth. "He's a court officer in Family Court."

"Oh yeah. I thought he looked familiar. He has a boy in fourth grade. Seems to know a lot about Chris Owen, wouldn't you say?"

Hector nodded, "More than he should."

D'Ambrosio was standing now, red-faced. Although not tall, he was muscular, thick-necked and obviously very strong. The buttons of his shirt were strained as he swept his arm around the room. "Listen, we don't have to accept sexual predators living in our town; we don't have to be politically *correct* – give 'em love and understanding in a *clinic*, hold their hand, poor little pedophiles," he sneered. "We can shut the Westerly down! Sign the petition up front and come to the town board meeting next Tuesday!" Finally he sat.

Bill Blue looked over to Matt for instruction, and the Chief walked to the front of the stage.

"Okay everybody," he boomed with authority. "Time to go home. You folks can *think* what you want, *say* what you want, *work* with your town board, and you can *write* letters to your congressmen. What you *cannot* do is become vigilantes and take the law into your own hands. We will arrest those who operate outside the law. Do I make myself clear?" He looked around the room and worked to keep his expression neutral. But to anyone who knew him well, the clenching of his jaw muscles gave him away. He was fuming.

An uneasy silence settled in the auditorium. A few people looked at each other with embarrassment, others fiddled with cell phones or pocketbooks. One by one, the crowd started to disperse. Trying to speak over the scraping of chairs, the school psychologist, an earnest young woman, took the microphone and weakly implored parents not to express their anxiety about sex offenders in front of the children, explaining that some students were repeating things they were probably hearing at home. Her plea was lost in the hubbub.

Meanwhile, Ilene never took her eyes off Jim D'Ambrosio. If Matt was looking for someone fueling the fire over the Westerly, he was a good bet. But more important, she wondered if his theatrical outrage was a symptom of the disturbed pathology that Dr. Paradiz had described.

* * *

After the gymnasium emptied, Ilene and Hector joined Matt in the second floor computer lab where windows overlooked the parking lot and he could keep an eye out as his officers supervised the exodus.

"Things almost got out of hand this evening," he said over his shoulder when they entered.

"Jim D'Ambrosio was pretty heated," Hector said. "Don't know him personally, but he's got a reputation for mouthing off."

"There was another man, too," said Ilene. "The one who got on your case about handing out flyers. Ah, I remember now, Jason Schatz, kind of guy who likes to poke you in the chest for emphasis."

Matt stared out the window.

"But my vote's for D'Ambrosio," Ilene continued. "It bothers me that he has proprietary information about Chris Owen's case. It means he's seen the court file. What is he doing looking at that? It's supposed to be sealed."

"Doesn't mean he had the file in his hand," Hector said. "It just means he got information out of it."

"How would he do that?"

"Plenty of people have access to juvenile files. He ticked them off on his fingers, "the court, cops, probation, Social Services, DA's office. Any one of them is capable of leaking information – present company excluded, of course."

Matt perched on a child-sized desk, arms folded, still watching the last of the headlights below. "People like D'Ambrosio are screamers," he said matter-of-factly. "He's going to make a lot of noise, but he doesn't have the people skills to organize the kind of movement that's happening in town."

"I wasn't actually thinking of that," said Ilene. "I was thinking more about Les's suggestion that the guy who wrote the letters could be someone who heard me speak the other night."

"Les may have a point," said Hector. "But why Jim D'Ambrosio?"

"Well I showed the letters to Dr. Paradiz and he said whoever wrote the letters has a lot of conflict about his urges and may feel so guilty about them that he has to imagine it's someone else who has or will molest a child."

Matt and Hector looked at her skeptically.

"He also described a kind of obsession that a closet pedophile might have," she explained. "This person might become a crusader against the very impulses he senses in himself. Dr. Paradiz said these people can get very worked up."

Turning all the way around to face her, Matt asked, "Are you suggesting that D'Ambrosio could have a child chained up in his basement?"

"Look at what else has happened," she argued. "A week before Chris Owen was killed, another sex offender in Rockville County was murdered. I spoke with a Detective Marks."

"Steve Marks, I know him."

"You're aware of the man killed at the Queenie's Mattress store?"

"Yeah."

"The victim was a convicted sex offender."

"I thought it was an attempted burglary," said Matt. "They rifled the place."

"Oh? Answer me this: who tries to rob a *mattress store?*"

"Anyone who wants money?" guessed Matt, rubbing his cheek.

Ilene waved him off. "*Nobody* pays cash for a mattress, especially not at Queenie's. They're top of the line; you can't get a piece of foam rubber there for less than five hundred dollars. You put it on a credit card or pay in installments."

"Maybe the burglar isn't as savvy a home shopper as you," he offered.

"Chief, there was no cash floating around at Queenie's, and any mope on the street would know that. Besides, there's something else. This guy Buel was shot in the mouth," she went on, "which is unusual. So I asked Detective Marks to pull up Buel's old sex offense file. He sent over a copy of the indictment." She dug around in her purse and pulled out a piece of paper. "It was about seven years ago – a sodomy two," she read off the page, "eleven-year-old girl ... to wit: consisting of contact between defendant's mouth and victim's vulva." She looked up to get their reaction. Both stared back at her.

"The Queenie's guy got a .38 right through the *mouth!*" Ilene reiterated.

"And this was in retaliation for his sex offense seven years ago?" Matt wasn't buying it.

"He was only out of prison a year," Ilene maintained. "Maybe it took that long to find him."

"But you're bringing this up on the heels of Chris's death," he said. "Are you trying to relate the Queenie's case to Owen's murder?"

"The two victims in the sex offense cases were both preteen girls."

"Come on," Hector cajoled, "you know as well as I do that females that age are the most common targets of pedophiles. And Owen was shot – that had nothing to do with his underlying sex offense."

Ilene took him up on the challenge. "Wasn't Chris also killed with a .38?"

"Excuse me, Chief?" Joel Levitsky poked his head through the classroom door. "I need to talk to you for a sec." His eyes shifted briefly to Ilene.

Matt lifted himself up and went over to see the junior officer.

Ilene turned to Hector. "I know it sounds far-fetched, but there could be a connection. And I ran an NCAVC search; a few other unsolved murders of sex offenders came up as well."

Hector stared at her in disbelief. "Ilene, just about every homicide goes into that database. If you punch in a specific criteria like 'sex offender,' of course you're going to pull up that category of victim. But it doesn't mean a conspiracy is underfoot. And besides, the numbers may be elevated because of vigilantism against sex offenders. I've heard of cases where the victims were randomly picked out of the registry, the perps showed up with a small arsenal, blew the offender's brains out and then waited around for the locals to come pat them on the back."

"I don't think that Chris's sex offender status is irrelevant to his murder," Ilene insisted.

"I never said it wasn't. But there's not a shred of evidence that it's connected to an attempted burg in Rockville."

Ilene opened her mouth to tell him about Victor Troy and the two-year-old murder of Niles Middleton when she saw Matt striding angrily in her direction. Levitsky gave her another guarded look and then slipped out the door. If Matt had been angry before, he was livid now.

"Since when do you go off on your own to interview a potential witness in a homicide investigation – and do it without telling me?!" he demanded. His eyes were shooting sparks.

Ilene blushed because she knew what he was going to say.

"Simon McColl is a suspect and he's missing," he thundered. "He's wanted for questioning by the police, and you tell his wife she should call *you* as soon as he gets back?! Jesus Christ, Ilene!"

"Wait a minute!" She threw her head back and squared her shoulders.

Hector muttered something and made his getaway, leaving Ilene and Matt glaring at one another.

She broke Matt's gaze and went over to the window, pressing her forehead against the glass. "I wanted to ask Rebecca about Heather," she said. "I wasn't looking for Simon."

"What *about* Heather?"

"Something I learned from Dr. Paradiz about her and Chris, nothing to do with Simon – not really."

Matt took a deep breath to calm himself. "What did she tell you?"

"We mostly talked about Heather, but at one point I asked her where Simon was. She doesn't know. She said he's disappeared before, sometimes for a couple of days at a time."

"What else?" he asked sternly.

"That's it. She didn't want to talk about him."

"I'll bet."

Ilene turned back to face him defiantly. "Rebecca admitted to you point blank that she didn't know where Simon was the night Chris died, didn't she? Clearly, she's not trying to cover for him."

"Maybe not. But I think *you* are."

"That's not fair," Ilene snapped.

"No?" Matt stepped closer to her. "You acted in a highly unprofessional manner by going to the McColl house and not telling me. You knew he was a suspect. What were you thinking?"

She looked away, but Matt persisted. "I don't get it. Why would you want to protect Simon McColl?"

"I'm not protecting..."

"Let me talk, Ilene. For once." There was a perilous urgency in his voice. "You are protecting him, whether you know it or not. Because you feel it's your job – no, it's your mission – to advocate for anyone who's weak or has been hurt. You feel you have to be more than an attorney for kids who've been abused, you have to be their *champion*. And then the whole family gets wrapped up in this victimized cocoon. I'll tell you something ... this sicko writing letters has your number, challenging you to save a child you don't even know is *real*!

"And it's damn well invaded your home, too. Your whole life is about protecting Sam and Frankie, like the world's going to end if you don't provide order and routine every minute of every day." He closed his eyes and squeezed the back of his neck to relieve the pressure. "And everything *we* do has to be planned out. Hell, we don't even sleep together unless it's on the calendar."

"Don't make this personal, Matt," Ilene flashed angrily.

"Sorry," he replied sadly. "It is personal. Everything that happens between us is personal. The stuff I tell you about my cases because I trust you and value your input, our relationship, and my relationship with the boys – it's *all* personal."

The last of the headlights from the cars below flickered across their set expressions like an old movie reel as they stood close enough to feel the heat from each other's bodies. Finally, Matt broke the silence.

"I think we should take a break from each other for a little while. I need some time to think things out."

Ilene wanted to say something, tell him she was sorry, that she loved him, she needed him. But no words came. She struggled to understand why it felt like such a failure to admit she was wrong – just once. But long before an answer came, he turned and walked out. The heaviness in her chest kept her from breathing until the echo of his footsteps had receded.

CHAPTER FIFTEEN

J EREMY BELL AND Dylan D'Ambrosio scowled at the blank computer screen. Mrs. Grumman had just left the computer lab with a stern warning that if they didn't finish their research on the Algonquin Indians during this recess, they would stay in the next, and the next, and for as many as it took until they had their reports on her desk.

"Mrs. Grumman sucks," complained Dylan to his fellow fourth grader.

"You got that right. Sucks *big* time," agreed Jeremy.

"She's got a fat ass." Dylan hunched his shoulders peevishly. "Somebody oughtta poke something up her big fat ass."

Jeremy reddened, but grunted his agreement.

"And the freakin' Algonquin Indians have big, fat asses, too. They're all gay!"

From the far side of the lab Sam lifted his head above his monitor and cautioned the boys about using bad language. Technically he was "off-duty," but Mrs. Grumman asked him if he wouldn't mind sticking around while the boys worked on their projects, not to offer any help, just be an adult presence. Sam wasn't thrilled with the assignment; he preferred working on his stat sheets in solitude, but he thought that not letting the kids use bad words was an adult thing to do.

Dylan made a face at Sam who quickly looked down at his keyboard and told himself not to get involved with the disgruntled boys. He'd seen them around school, teasing younger children in the halls, acting up in the computer lab. Dylan was the leader and more than troublesome, he was highly unpredictable – a bad mix. He wanted to steer clear of them.

"Hey, Mr. Hart!" called out Jeremy. "How do you turn this stupid thing on?"

Sam looked up. "It's on already. It's just sleeping. Hit 'enter.'"

"Should I really *hit* 'enter,' or should I just press the button?" This wisecrack caused his buddy to break out in giggles.

"*Press* the button," Sam said. His pulse quickened. He sensed trouble and wasn't sure how to keep it from escalating. When the kids got too rowdy, Mr. Wright, the computer lab teacher, would tell them to "knock it off," and they would. But Mr. Wright wasn't here.

"But you *told* him to *hit* it," Dylan piped in. "I think I'll hit it." He raised a taunting fist over the keyboard.

Sam jumped to his feet. "No!" he called out. The boys laughed. "If you break any equipment," Sam said breathing heavily, "I'll report you, and you'll have to pay for it."

Dylan sing-songed back, "I'll report you and you'll have to pay for it."

Sam hid behind his monitor. For a few minutes he didn't hear anything and thought the danger had passed. He checked his watch: twenty-three minutes to go. Then he heard one of the chairs scrape against the linoleum floor – a sudden, screeching rasp that lodged in the space behind his eyes. He winced in pain. He'd asked the school several times to put something on the bottoms of the chairs' metal legs, but no one had gotten around to it. Then he felt a poke in his arm.

"Mr. Hart," Jeremy was saying, "I have to go to the bathroom."

"Okay," Sam said, rubbing his arm where Jeremy had touched him.

A minute later he was back, jabbing his finger into Sam's other arm. "I'm back."

Sam whipped around. "Knock it off!" he shouted.

He tried to regain his composure. All the kids had been given a talk about invading others' space, particularly in the computer lab where crowding could result in broken equipment. He was aware the boys were tormenting him deliberately, but had no idea what to do about it. He thought about looking for a teacher who could help, but he remembered the night he took a swing at Ricky Wilkens. His mother accused him of not being able to control himself under pressure – and here he was about to lose it again with two *kids*. He had to prove to her and to himself that he could handle it. Sam held his ground.

Dylan pushed his chair back and forth, going for the highest pitch screech the chair legs could make. Then he strolled up to Sam. "I have to go to the baaaathrooom, Mr. Retard," he smirked. He reached out with a pointed index finger to strike him in the chest, but Sam caught his arm.

"Hey, you can't do that," simpered Dylan.

Seeing his friend in a tussle with 'the retard,' Jeremy bounded over and began to pull Sam's hair, alternately yanking and prodding, calling out, "Mr. Retard! Mr. Retard!"

Sam's overloaded senses made his head feel close to exploding and his mind froze like a virus-infected hard-drive. He had to *do* something.

CHAPTER SIXTEEN

ILENE HAD DOWNED black coffee all morning, but it's only appreciable effect was to make her teeth feel like she'd been chewing on metal. She hadn't slept well, fitfully rearranging the pillows all night as she went over and over the fight with Matt. More than once she reached out to pick up the phone. Part of her wanted to hear his voice and pour out her feelings for him; part of her refused, dimly recognizing the same stubborn resolve she made twenty years ago to cut her father out of her life. Sadly, she couldn't remember exactly why. Yes, her father had treated her as some kind of prized thoroughbred he could mold into an image of himself, and maybe he had used her. But he did love her, even if he could only express it selectively. He had broken through the silence to offer her financial support with Sam, which she could have used, and it was Ilene who had turned him down to prove she could go it alone. When she thought about how she held Matt at arm's distance, it occurred to her that she was still propelling herself in that same direction.

Shaking off the self-analysis, she turned her attention to Hector's last note before he went on vacation. It was a Post-it that read: *FYI - McColl's car found in NYC, in a parking lot since Sunday, but he's still AWOL.* He had stuck it on top of the crime statistics printout on her desk, a not so subtle brush-off of her theory about a single killer of Owen and Buel. He was probably right. She had asked the computer for unsolved homicides whose victims were convicted sex offenders. Of course the group was connected. And to be fair, the majority of the deaths appeared unrelated to the victims' prior offenses. A fifty-six year old man shot while staging a holdup at a 7-11 store. He had previously been convicted of rape and in another case assault with a deadly weapon, clearly an all-purpose criminal. And then there was the Albanian national who had done four years on a sodomy one charge. He had been knifed in a boarding house which was then set on fire, following the pattern of rival drug dealers at war in that community.

But there were others that sat stubbornly mute on the page, particularly the two she had mentioned to Dr. Paradiz. It was these that spurred her to spend another hour on the phone.

She learned that Victor Troy's sex offense had taken place right here in Westover County. He was a teacher at Thornton River High School, about thirty miles east of Branford. Troy had been accused of soliciting a twelve-year-old boy to perform oral sex. Although he had been charged, the school administration succeeded in getting it dropped if he left the district. And he had; his last known address was in Manhattan.

And Niles Middleton. He lived in Grandin Falls, but his bullet-ridden body was found in a dumpster fifteen miles away at the County Zoo. There were no suspects. Ilene had spoken with a lieutenant in Grandin Falls who told her that Middleton had been a youth group leader at a local church. He said that the case got quite a bit of press because of the concurrent publicity about pedophile priests.

The church connection made her think again about Paradiz's comment that obsession was often driven by strict beliefs. She might re-ignite Matt's fury for interfering with his investigation, but she had to know.

Rebecca picked up on the second ring.

"Rebecca, it's Ilene Hart."

"Yes?" Her voice was strained.

"Are you alright?"

"Yes."

"Is Simon back?"

"No."

"I need to ask you a couple of questions about him."

"What kind of questions?" Rebecca asked suspiciously.

"Was Simon raised in a religious family?" Ilene held her breath, hoping the answer was no.

"What does that have to do with anything?"

"I'd prefer not to say right now. I'm trying to figure something out." She waited while Rebecca decided whether to hang up or to respond.

Rebecca coughed. Finally she said, "To the contrary. He's not exactly anti-Christian; he's an agnostic, I guess. He let me take Heather to church on holidays but he wouldn't come."

With a sense of relief, Ilene tossed off the next question. "And you don't have any reason to believe that Simon was abused or mistreated as a child, do you?"

The pause on the other end seemed to suck the air between them leaving a vacuum. "Why do you need to know that?" Rebecca snapped.

"But ... you and Simon never said *anything* to me during the trial," said Ilene.

"Why should we have?" Rebecca shot back.

"Because it would have helped me."

"Helped *you*? As I recall you got your conviction."

"I'm talking about ... understanding what Simon was going through."

"It was supposed to be about Heather, was it not?"

Ilene felt a stab of guilt in her chest. "A sex abuse prosecution always involves the whole family, especially because Chris was a friend and she had feelings for him. It was complicated."

Silence.

"He didn't want you to know," said Rebecca.

Ilene felt sweat bead her upper lip. "Was Heather aware?" she asked.

"No, no," Rebecca insisted, "I'm sure not."

"You'd be surprised what kids know about their parents. What happened?"

"He only told me once when we first met, and then he never talked about it again. His father used to beat him as a young boy, pretty badly I think. He beat the mother, too. They were both hospitalized at different times."

"Was there sexual abuse?"

"Yes. Once."

Ilene closed her eyes and waited.

"It was his father when Simon was about twelve ... and that's all I'm going to say about it. Simon ran away and moved in with an aunt. I have to go now."

Rebecca hung up. Ilene sat without moving, the receiver still clutched in her hand. Despite the McColls' blind wish to the contrary, Simon's own abuse long ago was inextricably woven into the prosecution against Chris. Was his need to seek reparation more for himself than for his daughter? Did he feel cheated when his daughter's 'rapist' was released from the Westerly and take matters into his own hands? Ilene's thoughts ricocheted to Travis Buel and the others: Buel was out after serving two-thirds of his time, Middleton had gotten probation only, and Troy had never been convicted. Did Simon, or someone else, feel that more punishment was in order? The questions radiated from the daunting fact that Simon McColl's history seemed to fit the profile of a killer described by Dr. Paradiz.

* * *

Elizabeth Grumman was in her classroom nibbling on a tuna sandwich and correcting homework assignments when the boys ran in, their faces mottled from crying. She jumped up in alarm.

"What is it, Jeremy? Dylan? What's wrong?"

Jeremy threw himself on the carpet in the reading corner, buried his head in a pillow and sobbed. Dylan clung to Mrs. Grumman.

"Boys, boys, calm down," she cooed. But when she saw they would not be soothed, she became frightened. She took Dylan by the arms and shook him gently.

"What *is* it, Dylan? You have to tell me," she said sternly.

"I can't," he said, choking back his sobs.

"Go ahead, dear. It's all right."

Dylan leaned in and whispered in her ear. When he pulled away, Mrs. Grumman sat back in her chair, stunned, her heart racing. She looked over to Jeremy who was sitting up, watching his friend.

"Is it true, Jeremy?" she asked softly.

He nodded sadly.

"Dear God!" exclaimed Mrs. Grumman, shutting her eyes to what Dylan had told her.

CHAPTER SEVENTEEN

WHITE-LIPPED BEHIND his desk, the principal of the Branford Elementary School held one hand over the other to keep it from shaking. As an educator, this was the nightmare he'd dreaded for the past twenty-five years. A dear friend of his, principal of Hampton Village Elementary, had been drummed out of her job by the school board, losing her pension and health care for failure to report an alleged incident of sexual misconduct by a teacher. Ultimately the claim was determined to be unfounded, but parents faulted her for not pushing the panic button immediately.

Chief Bingham stood in one corner of the small office trying to keep his own emotions under control. *His* personal nightmare involved a face-to-face with an armed, drugged-out, back-against-the-wall cop-hater. But right now he would've taken that over the situation in which he found himself.

Across from Principal Carle sat Lynette Kulik, knees pressed together and back straight. She held a small notebook and glanced at it occasionally for reference.

"I've interviewed both boys separately and they seem credible," she said. "Their accounts of what happened are consistent, and there is nothing in either boy's demeanor that leads me to believe right now that this is a fabrication."

"I know what they reported to Elizabeth Grumman," said Carle anxiously, "but what did they tell you?"

"The boys were in the computer lab working on a project. It was just the two of them with Sam Hart supervising. Jeremy had to use the men's room and stated that when he sought permission to leave, Mr. Hart asked him if he had a 'hard dick.' Then Dylan also had to use the bathroom. He stated that when he approached Mr. Hart to be excused, Mr. Hart reached out and rubbed the boy's genital area. Jeremy confirmed this."

Matt felt sweat darkening the underarms of his blue button-down shirt; the small office was suffocatingly hot. Christ! This did not sound like Sam. Yet a seed of doubt lingered; Sam wasn't a normally-developed young man who had been dealing with his libido since seventh or eighth grade. He had never mentioned a girlfriend, didn't talk about girls, guys, or sex at all, for that matter. Could he be frustrated to the point he'd act out like that?

"The boys were understandably confused and fearful," Lynette continued, "but they remained in the computer room at their seats. A few minutes later, Mr. Hart came up to Dylan and began to rub his shoulders. He then put his hand down the back of Dylan's pants and inserted his finger into the boy's anus."

Matt cleared his throat. "Did he use that particular language?" he asked.

"No," said Lynette checking her notes, "I believe he used the term 'butt-hole.'"

"What did the boys do?" asked Carle.

"According to Dylan, he ran out of the lab and Jeremy followed. The librarian says that she saw both boys running in the halls, clearly upset. They went directly to their classroom where they told Mrs. Grumman."

"Do you have any corroboration?" Matt asked.

"No one saw it happen if that's what you mean, but the teacher reports that Jeremy soiled himself, perhaps as a result of the digital penetration. It would be consistent with the trauma of being groped in such a way." Lynette pressed her lips together and turned to Carle. "Have you any reason to believe Mr. Hart has inappropriately spoken to or touched another child in this manner?"

"No. Absolutely not," he said emphatically. "I would have reported it immediately."

"Did you do a background check on him?" she asked.

"I ... uh ... his is a part-time position," stammered Carle. "He keeps our computers up to speed and occasionally helps out in computer lab, but he's not a teacher." Seeing that Lynette was expecting more information he added, "Sam went to school here as a boy, and I've known him and his mother for some time."

"And who *is* his mother?" Lynnette asked with a frown.

"Ilene Hart. She's an Assistant District Attorney right here in Westover County," Carle offered.

Lynette snapped her head up and looked at Matt, who returned her gaze unflinchingly, although his stomach rolled over.

"Sam Hart is Ilene's *son?*" Lynette was unable to believe her ears. "How old is he?"

"Nineteen," Matt answered.

Lynette couldn't put it together. "And the father?"

"Before Ilene was married."

"Oh," she recovered. "I'm sorry. This will be difficult for everybody."

Carle looked nervously at Matt. "What happens now?"

"The parents are adamant that Sam be arrested and charged," Lynette said.

"Hold on," Matt asserted, stepping forward. "Right now, all we've got are allegations. You haven't even spoken to Sam yet. And you may want to ask the boys' parents what their kids have been hearing about sex offenders. Things are pretty tense around here right now. In fact, Jim D'Ambrosio, Dylan's father, caused quite a scene last night. The boy might have been impacted by that."

"Of course," Lynette said tersely. "Where is Sam?"

"He's with one of my officers in the library. But before you talk to him, there's something you should know about him–"

Matt was cut off by a commotion outside the office – Ilene insisting on being let in and a secretary trying to hold her off.

"I have to speak with him right now!" she said in a commanding voice.

"I'm sorry, no one is allowed—"

The door swung open and Ilene stormed in. "Matt! What the hell is going on?" She spotted the caseworker from Social Services. "Oh, Lynette," she said in relief, "I came as soon as I heard. This is crazy!"

Lynette stood and adjusted her suit jacket uncomfortably. "I'll be in the library," she said, managing to leave without looking at Ilene.

"Matt," Ilene pleaded, "where's Sam?"

Harvey Carle scuttled around his desk, offering to leave the two of them alone for a few minutes, and they could hear him shooing away the secretarial staff on the other side of the closed door.

Ilene collapsed in the chair vacated by Lynette and put her head in her hands. "My God, this is insane!" she cried. "I got your message from Anita; all she said was that he was accused of fondling some kid. What is this boy saying?" She looked up, incredulous.

Matt told her what Lynette had reported. When he finished, Ilene's face had become a hardened mask.

"Who are these kids?" she asked.

Matt hesitated. At this point they had to be considered victim/witnesses in an ongoing investigation. "Jeremy Bell and Dylan D'Ambrosio," he finally relented.

"D'Ambrosio." Ilene's eyes blazed. "He's the guy from last night who was screaming about closing the Westerly. He's out of his mind, and his son is a conniving, bullying, little prick!" She jumped up, spilling her pocketbook to the floor. "Those goddamn, *lying* rat bastards!"

Striding over, Matt reached out to take her shoulders, but pulled back at the last second. "Calm down, Ilene," he instructed. "Just ... calm down. You're not going to help the situation if you don't control yourself."

She acknowledged his admonition with a nod and gave herself a moment to get her breathing under control. "They're lying," she said quietly, her voice shaking. "Sam would never do something like that. If he was sufficiently provoked, he might *hit* them – but not...not *that*."

Both of them became acutely aware of the strain of having been thrown together while supposedly trying to gain some distance in their relationship.

"Has Sam been told what they're saying?" Ilene asked.

"Apparently. He says it didn't happen."

"Of course it didn't. He's incapable of lying. It takes an imaginative skill he doesn't *have*," she insisted.

Matt nodded sympathetically.

"Does the school believe it?" Ilene immediately waved off any response by answering her own question. "Never mind, it doesn't matter if they believe it or not, they have to report. Who called Lynette?"

"The school contacted Child Protective Services, and I guess they sent her. I got here about the same time."

"What does she say?"

Matt told her only that she was conducting an investigation, omitting that she seemed reasonably convinced the allegations were true.

"Where's Sammy?" Ilene asked urgently.

"He's in the library. Lynette's gone to talk with him."

"Oh God, Matt! Does she know about him?"

When he didn't respond, Ilene jumped up. "She's got to know about his autism. She can't interview him without me. He'll get tripped up. If he gets confused, he'll panic!"

"Ilene, you can't be there right now," Matt said, his voice cracking under the weight of his own conflict. He loved this woman, he cared about Sam, but he had a job to do and couldn't allow himself or Ilene to jeopardize the investigation. Even if he was absolutely convinced that Sam was innocent, he couldn't take sides.

Ilene knew he was right.

"Go be with him, Chief," she implored. "They won't know how to talk to him. I'm not asking you to intervene, but Sam will feel better if you're there." Fighting off a surge of helplessness, for her an unfamiliar feeling, she looked into Matt's eyes. "I understand the position you're in and I respect your need to be apart from me for a while, but... Sam needs you. Please."

Matt shifted uncertainly, "Okay. Hang tight." He went to the door where she stopped him.

"Are you going to charge him?" she asked fearfully.

"I don't know," he said. "But if we have to, I'll talk to the judge. There's no reason not to release him to you."

"Please don't let him go to jail," she begged.

"Don't worry," Matt tried to reassure her. "It'll be okay." But he was unable to meet her eyes.

* * *

Sam painstakingly removed the pieces of cucumber from his salad and forked them on to a separate plate; he perused the greens looking for any wayward cucumber seeds that had escaped his inspection and finding two, removed them as well, using his napkin. Then he measured a few drops of dressing supplied by the take-out pizza place and was about to take a bite when Frankie, who had been watching protectively, pointed out he'd missed a seed poised on the tip of some iceberg lettuce at two o'clock. It was too much – Sam pushed the plate away.

Ilene put the remaining pepperoni slices into a tupperware container, crushed the large pizza box and stuffed it into the trash, wishing she could throw the entire afternoon in with it. After Matt left, she had signed Frankie out of school and tried to explain in age-appropriate, nebulous terms what his brother had been accused of and what was likely to happen next. Frankie's first question was, "Is he going to jail?" But no formal charges had been lodged. Not yet. Matt had convinced Lynette to broaden her investigation, mindful of the paranoia in the school. She agreed, but reluctantly; both Dylan's and Jeremy's parents were putting tremendous pressure on her agency to file criminal charges. The police were getting the same push, but she agreed to the forty-eight hours the Chief requested after persuading her that Sam could not be at risk to re-offend if he was not in contact with children. That, of course, had been taken care of by Harvey Carle, who had fired

Sam on the spot.

Frankie looked from his mother to Sam. In private he had told her that he thought Dylan and Jeremy were bad news, always making trouble. Now assessing he could add nothing more and wanting to escape, he asked to be excused. When they were alone, Ilene said to Sam, "You haven't said much tonight."

"I don't have much to say," he replied. He thought he'd sufficiently explained what happened.

"You know I believe you completely, don't you?"

The question required an ability to make a judgment about what she was thinking that Sam didn't have in his current emotional state, and she tried again. "I believe you, honey. I really need, however, to try and understand..." She caught herself. "Tell me what you were thinking when you put the boys in the closet."

Sam contemplated the request for a moment then answered, "I wasn't thinking anything. I had to bench them."

"Bench them?"

"You get benched when you throw a punch."

"You didn't tell me anyone punched you," she said, confused.

"The brown-haired boy poked me five times, very hard. That's as bad as a punch. The other one grabbed my hair and pulled it. They were screaming in my ear, calling me a 'retard.'"

"I'm sorry," Ilene said, her eyes filling with emotion. "What did you do then?"

"I told you already. I put them in the equipment closet and locked the door."

"How did you do that?"

"I pulled them by the arms. They didn't really fight me."

"Did you leave the computer lab?"

"No."

"Were you going to let them out?"

"Of course." He looked at his mother strangely.

"Did you mean to *scare* the boys?" Ilene asked.

Sam put his fists to his forehead and squeezed his eyes tight.

"No," he finally said. "I wanted to *stop* them."

"When the boys hurt you, Sammy," she said, leaning toward him urgently, "why didn't you go get help? Haven't we talked about strategies to use if the children were doing things that bothered you? The noises, running around and being mischievous, remember?"

He nodded his agreement.

"So why didn't you get *help*, honey?"

"I wanted to handle the situation on my own," he tried to look into his mother's eyes to impress on her the importance of what he was about to say. "I know you think that Hudson State is a bad choice, especially after what happened with Ricky. But Mom, the job is very important to me, and I can do it. I understand now that Ricky is just insecure, and I'm not going to talk with any of them about the stats." He sighed. "The computer lab was different. Those kids were extremely hostile, and when they started to hurt me, it was too late. I think if it happens again, I'll be able to cope."

Ilene bit her tongue. She thought he was minimizing the incident with Wilkens, but throwing a punch at an angry six-foot-three basketball player seemed minor in comparison to what he had done in the computer lab and was a vivid reminder of his need for point-by-point strategies in difficult situations. Drawing on her diminishing well of patience, she said, "It's never too late to ask for help."

"I suppose." He stared past the kitchen table at Frankie's empty seat.

"Those kids were very frightened," she pressed. "And they are much younger than you."

"They shouldn't have been frightened, I was going to let them out."

"But they didn't know that, and the experience scared and humiliated them."

"I won't do it again."

Putting her own head in her hands, Ilene agonized over the uncertainty of Sam out in the world. How could he think far enough ahead to assess the consequences of his actions?

"Don't be sad. I didn't do what they said," he offered gently.

Ilene looked at him and he met her gaze.

"I know," she said. "I know you didn't."

Sam's face lightened and the tightness dropped away from his shoulders. He pulled his salad bowl closer and began to eat. After he'd slowly chewed his third forkful he raised his head.

"There's a practice at Hudson tonight. So I'd better get ready," he announced.

"What?" Ilene asked dumbstruck.

"They're having a practice at Hudson," he repeated patiently.

Overcome with frustration, she challenged, "Do you understand what is going on here, Sam?"

Too vague for an adequate response, he chewed on his lower lip.

"This is not some kind of game!" said Ilene forcefully. "You are in serious trouble. You cannot leave this house! Not tonight."

Unbowed, Sam banged the table with his fist sending dishes jumping. "I didn't do what they said!" he shouted.

"It doesn't matter!"

"They are lying and I'm telling the truth. Why am I being punished?" he cried, starting to rock in his seat.

"Oh, Sammy! It's so complicated. I know how stressful this must be, but until it's resolved, you're going to have to–"

"I want to go to practice!" He hit the table again.

"Stop that!"

Sam stood up. "I'm going to practice!"

Ilene bounded from the table, her long legs taking her nimbly past him to the front hall where his car keys dangled on a hook next to hers. She snatched the keys and held them tight in her hand. When he came up behind her, she turned to stare him down. Flushed with emotion, Sam glared but made no move to take the keys, as she knew he wouldn't. Then, with a pained bellow, he ran up the stairs and slammed the door to his room.

After the sound retreated into the walls, Ilene went into the living room where Frankie was watching a reality show. He was accustomed to his brother's outbursts and didn't even turn his head. Scantily-clad young women on the screen were being dared to see how far they would go to seduce a panel of buff young men without physically touching them. Ilene squinted at the TV for the minute it took her to understand the premise and then switched it off in disgust.

"Go to bed, Frankie," she said.

"What?! It's only eight-thirty!" he complained.

"Just do as I tell you," she snapped. She was close to losing her temper, and Frankie recognized the thin line he was treading. Nevertheless, he took a chance on his way out and muttered, "You should've let Sam go to practice."

Ilene turned on her heels and marched back into the kitchen. Under her breath she cursed the two fourth-graders who were wreaking havoc on her family and railed against the school and social services system for buying into their lies so easily. She tried to calm herself with the routine motions of clearing dishes and wiping counters, but it was not enough to dissipate her bitterness and isolation. Matt's need for a break in their relationship felt like a restraining order, keeping her from reaching out to him. She really needed to talk with someone. And when the last damp dishcloth was finally hung to dry, she picked up the phone and dialed Roz's number. Her husband Terry answered. Usually he was friendly and would ask about Frankie, but not tonight. After a moment, he got back on the phone and announced that Roz would call her back. His brusqueness stung.

She rummaged through the stack of bills and coupons next to the phone looking for a pad. Grabbing a pencil, she sat down at the kitchen table to make a plan. When in doubt or when there's no clear answer, she'd tell the boys to make a list. Pros, cons, things to do, people to call; "there's always some way to attack the problem." Ilene tapped the eraser on the blank pad a few times and wrote: *sit down with Jeremy and Dylan's parents.* Bad idea. They probably wouldn't even speak to her, she thought, and might view an approach as harassment. She crossed it off and wrote below: *school, any other claims or complaints by J & D? discipline problems?* Of course, that would be something Lynette would do, or should do.

How many times had she sat in this same spot writing her lists of ways to help Sam when he struggled? She remembered his years at Branford Elementary where she battled and scraped for him like a tigress, arriving at special education meetings armed with binders filled with his test scores, psychological testing, notes from his classroom teacher, his occupational therapist, his speech and language specialist, the school psychologist. Ilene routinely passed out copies of new research on Asperger Syndrome. A class bully who tormented her son? Ilene was in the principal's office the next day making a case for how the situation should be handled. Never abrasive or hysterical, she'd smile and thank everyone for their time, but she was firm and impossible to get rid of.

Similarly, she was out in the neighborhood campaigning like a politician for her son's social needs. Unlike Frankie, who made friends instantly and everywhere, Sam did not connect with his peers. Ilene spent her weekends trying to work out play dates for him, most of whom didn't return for a second visit. She tried to ingratiate herself to their parents; she signed up for every event she could attend, every pancake breakfast, book fair, class trip. And each daunting Halloween, she would promenade with a wary, uncostumed Sam alongside the younger moms pushing strollers, while Frankie cavorted with his fellow Spidermen and Darth Vaders way ahead. Most of the moms were friendly and seemed understanding, but their kids didn't want to play with Sam. And who could blame them?

As a youngster he needed everything just so. Ilene recalled one disastrous day when she had convinced Daniel to take him on a Boy Scout camping trip. It would be good for the "boys" to spend time together. They returned at midnight, not speaking to one another, both of them sullen, uncommunicative, and covered with mosquito bites. Never again, Daniel vowed: Sam didn't like the feel of walking in the woods (too squishy under his feet), the food was inedible (cooked hotdogs that looked like giant charred worms), the sleeping bag intolerable (slimy and cold). Ilene fought on. Sam was worth fighting for. He hadn't asked for his disability. It had been bestowed on him, a gift from an uncharitable God as proof that life wasn't fair. And through most of it he remained a kind, generous kid with a great sense of humor. So if he gave the world a kick back once in a while it was understandable.

Ilene sat, tensed, pencil poised. She wracked her brain to come up with something she could do, someone she could confront, persuade, cajole, but in each scenario it seemed that her position at the DA's office only made things worse. The sense of impotence was alien and overwhelming. If it were her case, she'd have had witnesses lined up by now, case law printed out, psychologist interviews scheduled – but this? It felt cruel. She put the pad down and listened to the dull thudding footsteps of the boys in their bedrooms. She wished she could do the evening with them over again but all at once felt drained. When Roz called, she would commiserate, and perhaps her friend would have some ideas. Maybe Matt would have a change of heart and call to see how they were doing.

But the telephone never rang, and its silence became louder as the minutes went by. At nine-thirty, Ilene went up to bed, brushed her teeth and put her hair up, still listening, though less hopefully, for the phone. She lay in the dark waiting for sleep and fighting off the wave of emotions that crested but never broke.

CHAPTER EIGHTEEN

GERALD MALONE DISGUSTEDLY stubbed out a Newport Light in the tinfoil ashtray on his desk. "What a disaster," he groused, extinguishing the last spark with a final stab.

Deputy DA Tom Squires, who handled public relations for the office, inwardly agreed, but did his best not to show it. "May not be as bad as you think, Gerry," he said, tugging anxiously at a corner of his salt and pepper. "They're only allegations."

"Only *allegations*," Malone repeated bitterly. "For Christ's sake, the Chief of my Sex Crimes Bureau has a pedophile son living in her house."

"Special Prosecutions," Squires reminded him out of habit.

Malone swatted the correction away. "The press is going to have a field day with this. Especially with the Westerly thing going full speed."

They both turned at a knock on the door. "Come in," barked the DA. Bess Nadelson, who worked directly under Ilene, entered tentatively. Malone motioned to the chair next to Squires.

"Hi, Tom," she said to Squires. "Sir," she acknowledged Malone with a nod. She couldn't bring herself to call Malone by his first name when Squires was present since it made her think about the cartoon duo Tom and Jerry.

"Thanks for coming in, Bess," said Squires, hoping she didn't notice the tic that had started in his left eye.

"I gather Tom told you about Ilene," Malone said.

She nodded. "I can't believe it's true, sir. I've met Sam several times."

"He's retarded, right?"

"Not at all," she bristled. "He has Asperger's Syndrome. Look, I really think it's some wild accusation from a bunch of kids caught up in the furor over the rehab clinic."

"I certainly hope so," answered Malone glumly. "But for obvious reasons I'm putting Ilene on leave. Until the *allegations* against her son are cleared up I'm making you acting Chief."

Bess's shoulders slumped. Ilene was her friend, and she knew this would be very hard for her. "Starting when?" she asked anxiously.

"Starting now."

"She's in the office this morning doing a video deposition."

"Call Tom as soon as she's done and he'll go over to tell her."

Bess glanced over at Squires who looked miserable at the prospect of delivering the bad news.

Malone caught her checking in with Squires. "Do you have any problem with the assignment?" he quizzed irritably.

"No, sir."

"What is her case load like these days?"

"I have to talk to her and see what she's got. The most immediate, I think, is a grand jury presentation on the Destiny Bashe case."

"Where is Hector?" asked Malone, looking around the office as if he might be lurking in a corner.

"He's on vacation."

"Get him back."

"I'm pretty sure he's with his family in the Caribbean," piped in Squires.

"See if you can get him back early, then."

"I'll try," said Bess, already decided that she'd wait a day or two before tracking Hector down.

"And if you need to work with Ilene to get up to speed, do it at her house or over the phone." The DA looked squarely at his deputy. "After today, I don't want Ilene Hart to set foot in this office. As sure as shit there's going to be some reporter camping out to get a statement from her. Jesus!" he suddenly thought, "they haven't already gotten one from her, have they?"

"I don't think so," reassured Squires. "But they're downstairs waiting for one from us."

"Not from us, from *you*," Malone said. "I'm in meetings for the next few days. And Bess, you keep me posted about what's happening with her kid, what the school is doing, and what CPS and the cops are thinking."

"Okay."

"One more thing, Tom. Let Ilene know that the press release is going to say that *she* requested a leave to handle some pressing family matters. She got an issue with that, she can talk to me."

Bess glanced over at Tom and saw his left eyelid in spasm. The images she had tried to keep away surfaced and ran in full color – there was the mouse stuffing the cat's tail in a waffle iron, then beating him over the head with a club.

CHAPTER NINETEEN

"IT'S NOW TEN-FORTY-FIVE and we're concluding the interview with Mrs. Jane Bashe, the mother of Destiny Bashe," said Ilene, turning to the camera. "For the record, again, with Mrs. Bashe is her attorney, Stephen Piesecki, and also present is Lynette Kulik from Westover Child Protective Services." She gave the date and file number and then rose to turn off the video recorder.

After Mrs. Bashe and her lawyer left the conference room, Ilene refused to make eye contact with Lynette and silently willed her to leave so they wouldn't have to walk out together. Just eighteen hours ago her colleague from CPS was with Sam conducting her own inquisition, and Ilene hadn't forgotten the excruciating wait outside the library. Nor had she forgotten the rejection she felt when Lynette finally came out and walked past with barely a nod in her direction. Perhaps she felt as uncomfortable as Ilene, but couldn't she have stopped and said a few words, some hint of what she was thinking? No, she'd sailed by, eyes straight ahead, as though Ilene was just another disconnected, enabling parent of a child abuser. And now she had appeared at the morning's deposition greeting her as if the day before had never happened.

"She's an odd bird," Lynette commented about Jane Bashe.

Ilene kept her eyes averted as she folded the camcorder tripod and found its place in the equipment closet.

"I think she loves her daughter very much," Lynette went on, "but I have to wonder how capable she is of managing Destiny's limitations."

"We do the best we can," Ilene muttered tersely.

Lynette paused as she watched her jam the camcorder and its unruly wires into a case. At last acknowledging the awkwardness of their situation, she said, "I'm going to be as objective as I am with any other case."

Ilene wheeled around. "I certainly hope so."

Stung, Lynette examined her short, unpainted nails. "I'm sorry it was me on the in-take," she said. "But I have to do my job."

"And I have to do mine. So if you'll excuse me…" With a quick motion Ilene locked the closet, grabbed her notes, and left the conference room.

As she strode down the hall toward her office, her mind began to clear and she kicked herself for becoming so prickly with Lynette. The last thing she needed was to antagonize the investigator on Sam's case. Hell, it was just Lynette's way. She was organized and procedural to a fault; if she was on the schedule to attend the Bashe deposition, then she would be there. The complexity of her relationship with Ilene, not that they were close, might not register with her – ironically, the kind of social ineptitude that Sam displayed. Ilene made a mental note to give Lynette a call and apologize.

Anita waylaid Ilene as she passed the front desk. The secretary handed her a fistful of "while-u-were-out" messages and told her about a new intern who was expected in the afternoon.

Ilene bit her lip. "Can you pass her off on Bess? I'm pretty distracted today."

"No problem." Anita's manner was offhand, but her gaze stayed with Ilene a little too long.

"I guess everyone knows. About Sam," Ilene murmured.

Anita pressed her lips together and gave a small nod.

"It's not true, you know," Ilene said, feeling her throat close with emotion.

The secretary merely smiled sympathetically.

"Is Bess around?"

"The boss called her upstairs."

"What for?"

Anita said she had no idea and with obvious relief went back to answering the phones.

Ilene walked slowly back to her office and shut the door. While her computer booted up she wondered what her staff was thinking. She had come in early to set up for the deposition and hadn't run into anyone except Anita just now. But they all had to be talking about it. At the least, it was a huge embarrassment for her unit. At the worst? Ilene had to face it, there were going to be some who believed the charges were true.

Trying to brush away the painful thoughts, she turned to her emails and scanned the addresses. She wasn't sure she was ready to open up any interoffice communications, so she started with the one that looked least taxing – from the Westover Library. She had taken out a few books for Frankie in the vain hope that he would actually read if she insisted on an early TV cut-off time. They were undoubtedly gathering dust somewhere in his room and she opened the mail to see how much she owed in fines.

When the image loaded on to her screen, Ilene's stomach lurched. What faced her was a grainy photo, but explicit enough – a naked man with an oversized gut thrusting his groin into the backside of a young boy. The man's mound of naked flesh hid his genitals, but the photo was made to look as though he was in the act of penetrating the boy from the rear. The child wore only a tight Mickey Mouse t-shirt and had curly blond hair that framed his round face. From his size and build he couldn't have been older than seven or eight.

Ilene then registered the digital tampering that had been done to the photo, and she moaned out loud. It was proportionately wrong and clearly superimposed, but there was Sam's face on the fat man. Ilene recognized it immediately – his graduation picture, a big smile underneath the wild mane of hair. She had her finger poised to delete the screen, but realized she hadn't seen the whole image.

Her trembling fingers scrolled down. There were no more photos, but a caption in big, red letters that read: TWO

DOWN Twenty-nine-thousand-nine-hundred and ninety-EIGHT to go!!!

Rising on unsteady feet, Ilene braced herself on the wall and vomited into the waste basket.

CHAPTER TWENTY

T HE BACKGROUND SQUAWKING and hissing of the
police radio wouldn't stop, nor would the steady stream
of inconsequential calls that underscored how insulated Branford was from the real world. Dispatcher: *Woman says there's a
sick raccoon on her property*, squawk. Officer Brodsky: *A what?*
Dispatcher: *A raccoon* ... hiss ... *She wants someone to come and get
rid of it.* Officer Brodsky: *For the love of Mary!* Dispatcher: *Hold
on, do I have anyone near the Branford Pharmacy?* Car 408: *This is
four-oh-eight ... we could be there in about five. What's the call?*
Dispatcher: *Guy is missing his wallet.* Car 408: *Maybe the raccoon
took it* ... laughter, hiss, squawk. Officer Brodsky: *I did not go to
the police academy and do twelve years on the streets of East Harlem
to hunt for a flippin' raccoon.* Dispatcher: *What'll I tell the lady?*
Car 408: *C'mon Brodsky, suck it up. Go find that varmint and if
he's got any credit cards, give us a call* ... laughter. The radio waves
crackled in anticipation of the expletive on the tip of Brodsky's
tongue.

Ilene was ready to throw it against the wall when Sergeant
Blue poked his head into Matt's office. "He'll be back in a few
minutes," he said. "Can I get you a cup of coffee or something?"

"No thanks, Billy."

"You okay?"

She wasn't, but nodded her reassurance. Blue looked like
he wanted to say something, but after a self-conscious silence

withdrew, closing the door gently. Ilene wished he had stayed. She would have tried to explain about Sam, make him understand how unfair the charges were. But it all felt dirty and secretive. She had rushed to the station looking for Matt and in the parking lot crossed paths with a few of the Branford cops. While they were pleasant enough, she could feel the oily suspicion that lay underneath. When it came to sex abuse of a child, no one was innocent until proven guilty, and the mere accusations against her son appeared to taint *her* as well.

She heard Matt in the station before he blew through the door bringing the day's bitter cold with him. He hung up his parka and eased into the swivel chair behind his desk. The radio squealed and he leaned over to turn the volume down before facing Ilene.

"I guess you can't get rid of me," she shrugged weakly.

"I'm not trying to get rid of you," he said. "Quite the contrary. I've been trying to get closer to you for years." He paused. "We have to talk."

Ilene felt the back of her throat constrict.

"But not now," said Matt.

He took a deep breath as though the oxygen could immediately transform him back into a cop and only a cop. "Okay," he went on. "Tell me again about the email."

She did.

"Is Les Dawkins working on it?" he asked.

"Yes. He confirmed it came from the library. Anyone who uses a computer has to sign in, so he should have some names soon. But he may not be able to determine exactly which computer it was for a day or two."

"Did you bring a copy?"

"Yes."

"Can I see it?" When she hesitated he recognized how difficult it was for her to show it to anybody. "It might help us find out who sent it," he prompted gently.

Reaching into her purse Ilene removed a copy of the digital photograph. She felt violated just touching it – indeed, having the tech investigators take her computer, print the photo, blow it up, enhance it, and examine it was like watching the pictured sex act over and over. Matt studied the photo without expression. Ilene was grateful, even Dawkins had winced the first time.

He re-folded the paper and asked gently, "Are you okay?"

"Functioning."

"Sam hasn't seen the photo, has he?"

"God, no!" Ilene said alarmed.

"Somebody's fixated on that study Dr. Paradiz mentioned the other night," said Matt. "We find out who did the graffiti and we find out who sent this."

"Les thinks it may be connected to the letters."

Just then, her cell phone rang. It was Dawkins. Ilene told him where she was and asked to put him on speaker.

"Hey, Bingham," he boomed, his deep voice undiminished by the tiny phone speaker. "You still up there in the woods enforcing noise ordinances? Come on down-county where we fight real crime."

"Yeah, Tough Guy," responded Matt with a tired smile, "when's the last time a Mac Book pulled some heat on you?"

Dawkins chuckled and got down to business, "We're in the process of checking each of the computers, so we should be able to find the source. In the meantime, I got a few names. You have somethin' to write with?"

"Go ahead."

"Okay. There are ten computers at the library, eight of which have internet access. At the time the email was sent, there were two kids from Community College working on papers. Neither of them sound like our sender, but I'll give 'em to you."

Matt wrote down their names.

"Next, we've got Nell Jennings, a middle school teacher at Meadow Hill. It's her day off and we couldn't reach her. Frederico Copocci: one of my guys ran him down and says he can barely speak English, he's visiting family from Sicily. Ralph R. Wool: no driving record on him, we'll get back to you. Laurel Visi: that's the name on her license, but on her library card it's Laurel Visi D'Ambrosio; we'll give her a call later. And last we—"

"Run that last one by me again, Les," said Matt. Ilene's eyes were wide.

"Laurel Visi D'Ambrosio." He spelled it.

"You have an address?" Ilene asked.

"Fourteen-oh-eight Guilden Drive in Hanover Heights. Why?"

"Hold on a sec," said Matt. He sprung from his chair and yanked open the office door. "Billy, run a DMV check on a Jim or James D'Ambrosio, capital D, capital A. I want an address."

Dawkins' voice came back, "You think it's her?"

"Or somebody who used her card," said Matt, pacing behind his desk. "We'll know in a minute."

Dawkins recited the last two names he had gathered and Ilene added them to the list. He finished by reassuring them that it was a simple matter to track down the email. "As far as I can see, there's nothing sophisticated going on here. The sender probably pulled the photo from some internet porn, put it on a disc or flash drive, and thought the public library terminals would be untraceable – so our sender's either techno brain dead or he doesn't care if you find out."

Matt stopped pacing and ran a hand through his hair. "How does that square with the letter writer, Les? Whoever sent the letters made sure he didn't leave any prints or any other way to locate him. And now we've got a relatively easy trace on an electronic communication? It's not consistent."

"True. But he could be getting sloppy or for whatever reason he's decided to drop some bread crumbs for us."

"All right," Matt responded. He thanked Dawkins and promised to call him back once he'd gotten the information he was waiting for. And seconds later, Sergeant Blue came in with a perforated printout in his hand.

"There are six James D'Ambrosios in the state. Only one here in Westover – in Hanover Heights," he stated.

"Guilden Drive?"

"Yup."

"Thanks, Billy."

They waited until he left.

"There is no way *Laurel* D'Ambrosio sent that email," fumed Ilene. Matt didn't disagree.

"It was her husband!" Ilene spat. She grabbed the sickening photograph from the desk and ripped it into pieces. Some of them fell to the floor, shredded red letters scattering like drops of blood on the industrial carpeting. Her face flushed, Ilene quickly gathered them up and crammed them into her purse where they could not contaminate anything else.

"Why would he do something that stupid?" she asked in disbelief. "Disseminating child porn is a federal crime!" She suddenly twisted around in alarm to face Matt. "What he did is downright pathological. And if he wrote the letters, too, he's really unbalanced. Maybe he did kill Chris!"

Matt frowned. "D'Ambrosio's obviously got problems. But Chris's murder feels different to me. Someone followed him to the park, which means it's very likely that they saw him climb up that tree. Sonofabitch *watched* the kid, and then shot him up close. That's cold. D'Ambrosio? I still see him as a screamer, and if he did send this, the fact that he didn't do a better job disguising where it came from supports that." He leaned forward towards Ilene. "Look, I understand how the letters and now *this* could shake you up. They would anybody. But let's not get them confused with murder. This is a reaction to the charges against Sam, and I promise you I'm going to find out who sent it. But, let's just deal with this situation, okay?"

Ilene pulled herself back, realizing he was right. "What about Sam?" she asked anxiously. "What if he tries to hurt him?"

"We'll keep an eye on D'Ambrosio, but I don't think he will."

"*Think* isn't good enough, Matt. He could go after him." She looked up at him, her eyes pleading, "Listen, what if I could talk to Jeremy Bell's parents without the D'Ambrosios around, maybe I could–"

"No," Matt said firmly. "You know better than that. Let CPS handle it."

"I was ready to let them handle it," she flashed back, "but not now."

"Here you go again, Ilene, trying to control everything. You can't. Stay out of it!"

She got up quickly. "I can't sit around and do nothing. This insanity is killing Sam. He doesn't understand why he's being punished for something he didn't do."

Matt came around to block her exit and took her firmly by the shoulders. "The truth will come out," he insisted.

"Will it?" Ilene pulled herself away.

"Go back to work."

"Not an option," she said bitterly. "Malone put me on leave while the charges are pending."

"God, I'm sorry, Ilene." Matt sighed. "Then go home. I mean it. I won't let you interfere with the investigation, I can't let you do that." This last said as she stormed out the door.

CHAPTER TWENTY-ONE

B Y SUNDAY, THE kitchen clock seemed to be ticking in slow motion. Ilene listened to Frankie halfheartedly tapping the controls of his favorite NFL video game in the family room; Sam hadn't yet emerged from his bedroom. The last two days had dragged in the same way. Dawkins' investigation of the pornographic email was proceeding too cautiously for her. He wanted to interview the librarian at the computer stations again about Laurel D'Ambrosio before confronting her or her husband, and that wouldn't happen until Monday. Trying to push Sam's case along herself, Ilene had taken a chance and called Lynette. The CPS worker answered uneasily, but Ilene assured her she only wanted to give her some of Sam's medical documents relating to his Aspergers. After some hesitation, Lynette said that would be okay and offered to stop by to pick them up sometime over the weekend. So far, she was a no-show.

To fight off her own inertia, Ilene took to the treadmill in the basement and had just broken a sweat when Sam clomped down the stairs to use the machine. As soon as he saw her, he turned around without a word and went back to his room. That had been the pattern, each of them revolving in their own miserable, isolated orbits. Ilene had tried to get the boys to talk, but was met with dull silence from Sam and from Frankie more testiness than usual. In fact, she noticed he looked pale at dinner and had turned off his cell phone. She couldn't remember the last time he did that without being told and wondered if his friends were talking about Sam.

Another look at the clock revealed that barely a minute had gone by. She really ought to wash her hair and put on something decent but let the idea go. Somehow it felt right to clothe herself in old jeans and a pair of worn winter socks while she wandered unmoored around the house. Until he was totally cleared of the charges, their lives were on hold, a shower and a change of clothes seemed a pathetic attempt at normalcy.

The telephone rang shrilly. Ilene almost didn't answer – they had already gotten a few hang ups – but thinking it might be Dawkins, she picked up. It was Roz, and her sympathetic voice felt like a cool breeze on a hot, humid day.

"Hi, sorry I didn't get back to you, things have been crazy around here. Hey, I heard, of course. How're you guys doing?"

"We're okay," Ilene said uncertainly.

An awkward pause ensued and Roz was the first to break the ice. "Listen, you don't have to say a word. If Sam says he's innocent, I believe him."

"You do?" Ilene asked with enormous relief.

"Sure. Heck, I know those kids. Dylan D'Ambrosio is a bullying little shit, and his sycophant sidekick Jeremy is no better. I'm surprised Carle didn't boot them out of his office along with their self-righteous parents."

"How well do you know Jim D'Ambrosio?"

"We've had a few coaching run-ins with him in the past. Jim coaches his son's travel football. Some parents think he's great, but only because their kids get most of the play time on the team. I don't particularly care for him. He's too much of a holy-roller for me and has some anger management issues. Look at him the other night!"

Ilene was tempted to tell her friend about the email, but was afraid that once she started, she'd pour out everything. And if she implicated D'Ambrosio – wrongly so – it would not help Sam. Roz was a friend, but not the soul of discretion.

Instead, she probed further. What else had she heard about him?

"Well, one of the reasons he may have had a fit at the last meeting is his wife is good friends with Amanda Prince, the woman that Matt arrested at school." Roz sounded almost cheerful. "Now there's another piece of work. Amanda's husband made a killing in commodities. I don't even know what you do with all that money. Anyway, she's used to getting whatever she wants, when she wants. I, for one, would really like to see the Westerly shut down. I don't care if they are juveniles, they ought to be in prison. But that said, Amanda went overboard with those flyers, and then I hear she got physically abusive with the cops. That must have been a show!"

"How about Jeremy's folks?"

"They're nice enough. She's a little frayed around the edges, but both of them work full time, and I don't know what their childcare situation is like."

"Why would their kids make up a story about Sam? He told me they were taunting him in the lab, but to say that he *sexually* abused them?"

"Hard to say. But it's likely the boys were hearing stuff at home about sex offenders which made them incredibly anxious, and maybe they were acting out in their own twisted way. God knows, they must have been subjected to some real sanctimonious clap-trap from Jim and his wife."

"What do you mean?"

"Oh," breathed Roz, happy to be finally telling someone, "he and Laurel are like Super Christians, and not just your ordinary devout, churchgoing folk. Religion is big in their lives, and I mean BIG."

Ilene's pulse quickened, "Really?"

"Yeah, he and his wife go to the Episcopal church on High Street. Jim runs a youth group there that supposedly draws a lot of kids who wouldn't go to church otherwise, and supposedly he does a pretty good job. But last fall he was doing a little too much Jesus-rah-rah stuff at his football games because some of the parents got upset and petitioned the league, including – surprise, surprise – two families from our Synagogue. It was a big mishegas. You didn't hear about it?"

"Maybe," said Ilene distractedly, "I didn't know D'Ambrosio was involved."

"And one time," continued Roz, building up steam, "we all went over to the D'Ambrosios for pizza after a game. You wouldn't believe it, their house is an evangelical party store – crosses, pictures of the Mother Mary with eyes that glow, angels, you name it – all over the place. A little creepy, if you ask me."

This piece of information about D'Ambrosio sent a chill up the back of Ilene's neck and fired up her imagination again. *If thy right hand offends thee, cut it off and fling it away.* While Matt seemed certain that he was just a screamer, Ilene was getting a very different picture. What had Dr. Paradiz said about a person so fearful of his own arousal by child pornography it made him want to hunt down the perpetrators? Psychopathic obsession fueled by rigid religious principles?

Roz was carrying on about how weird Kevin and his friends had thought the D'Ambrosio home was when Ilene interrupted.

"Does D'Ambrosio's church have anything to do with the Episcopal church in Grandin Falls?" she asked.

Where Niles Middleton also ran a Sunday school youth group.

"I have no idea, but they're the same denomination and probably do retreats and maybe some mission projects together."

"So Jim D'Ambrosio would know some of the staff up there – for instance, his counterpart running the youth group?"

"I would guess. Why all this interest in his church?"

"Just curious," Ilene hedged.

It was more than curiosity. After a few minutes she rang off, grateful to Roz for the call. Two days of living in suspended animation and Ilene could feel her adrenaline and determination kick in. If D'Ambrosio was there, hiding somewhere in the pages of incident reports or victim interviews, she was going to find him. She gathered her hair up in a loose ponytail, padded hurriedly into the old pantry off the kitchen which she had converted into a home office and shut the door.

With the emergency number of CPS in hand, Ilene was able reach a real person on Sunday. The intake worker who had drawn the short straw for the weekend was helpful, and an hour later, her fax machine still whirring, Ilene was beginning to put some of the stories together. Fresh on her mind after the conversation about the church groups, she started with Niles Middleton.

Sometime in September, ten-year-old Dahlia Carty told her mother that the handsome and helpful Sunday school teacher at Grace Church asked her to sit on his lap while he touched her private parts under her dress. Dahlia's mother slapped her across the face and berated her for making up filthy lies. Niles Middleton was a saint. What he put up with from the disrespectful pre-teen boys and the giggly girls was enough to make anyone tear their hair out. Why, more kids than ever had signed up for confirmation classes! Mrs. Carty made Dahlia continue with the youth group even as her daughter's behavior at home deteriorated. Dahlia began to wet the bed and throw temper tantrums. Her mother chalked it up to hormonal changes.

Meanwhile, Mary Tessler, who was just thirteen, wrote to her older sister Eve at college and asked if it was a sin to let a man push up against you and rub your bosoms. Her frantic sister phoned home that night and screamed at their mother *did she have any fucking idea what was going on with her own daughter?!* In fact, it was Eve Tessler who drove down to Westover County and stormed into the police station the next day. It turned out Middleton wasn't a saint after all. On any number of occasions he had groped, kissed, fondled and rubbed against Dahlia, Mary, and at least one other girl willing to give a statement.

Ilene closed her eyes and drew up a mental image of Dahlia and the others. How many times had she seen kids like these, scared and confused, acting out in ways that landed *them* in trouble. Her heart ached for them, and a lot of these kids weren't easy to love – uncommunicative and often detached. But with patience, most of them came around and bit by bit offered their confessions, staring at the floor with sucked-in cheeks, finally looking up to see whether or not she blamed them.

Sam's loud footsteps trooping into the kitchen interrupted her thoughts. She poked her head out of the office as he opened the refrigerator to hunt for something to eat.

"Want me to make you a sandwich?" she asked, trying to sound upbeat to offset his mood.

"No, thanks. I'll make it." He took out a jar of mayonnaise, a loaf of bread, and a package of cold cuts and proceeded to line them up on the counter. Not one to slap a sandwich together, he carefully prepared the bread by slicing off the crusts. Ilene left him alone and turned to the next case. Victor Troy.

There was very little in his file since the charges had been dropped, but Ilene learned that Pat Meehan, the supervising case worker in Westover, had been the one to interview Troy's young victim and his family. She called Meehan at home, apologizing for the weekend intrusion.

"No sweat, Ilene. You saved me from having to clean the basement. Victor Troy, eh? Hockey man – I remember."

"I thought he was a teacher."

"He was. But he was also the ice hockey coach at Thornton River High School. Apparently he worked out once with the New York Rangers; it made him quite the celebrity at Thornton. There was a kid on the junior varsity named David Mullen. Troy thought David was good enough to play college and get a scholarship. Kid's parents were thrilled. They developed a close relationship with Coach Troy, inviting him over for Sunday meals and actively encouraging his attentiveness to their boy."

"Sounds like Troy groomed the family pretty well," Ilene commented as she jotted down notes.

"Sure, he fed right into fantasies about a pro career for their kid. To them it looked innocent enough. The year before, Troy had taken a keen interest in another boy."

"Mmm. What happened with David?"

"Troy's ingratiating performance didn't work. I think he had gotten away with a certain level of physicality, arm around the shoulder, play-wrestling, etcetera. But one day alone in the boys locker room he asked David to perform oral sex, and the kid freaked. He told his best friend who told a teacher who told the principal, and two days later Troy was looking for another job.

"And the other boy?" Ilene asked.

"I had my suspicions, but neither he nor his parents would talk to us, and once the school had fulfilled its duty to report, no one was terribly cooperative. I know Lynette pushed them hard, but in the end, Mullen changed his statement and said Troy had never touched him; we couldn't sustain the sexual abuse charge on hearsay alone. Why? What's up, Ilene? You got Troy on something else?"

"Not exactly. He was murdered in the city about two years ago."

"No shit!"

"He was stabbed to death in upper Manhattan. One of the wounds was a cut to what the cops called his 'groin area.' It was superficial, but there was speculation that the killer was going after Troy's genitals and was interrupted when a couple of teenagers came into the men's room. They couldn't provide a decent description of the killer because he brushed right by them and apparently was wearing a hat pulled down over his face."

"What did the cops say?"

"It was a public restroom in the park and had a reputation for being a gay hangout."

"And Victor Troy propositioned the wrong person?"

"That's the prevailing view."

"Well, David Mullen turned out to be a bad target, too," Meehan concluded. "Obviously, Troy didn't know how to pick 'em."

Ilene said she'd keep him posted and reviewed the notes she had taken. There was something about the two murders that nagged at her. She tried to capture the thought by pressing the heels of her hands against her eyes, but it drifted away and was lost. She turned to the most recent murder: the Queenie's victim.

Buel was a forty-six-year-old electrician who was on disability after falling from a roof and injuring his back. He met Sally Lane, a divorcee, at a Parents Without Partners meeting in Rockville, and they hit it off. He moved in with her and her eleven-year-old daughter Jessica a month later. A slim, reserved girl, it had been hard for Jessica to make friends with her mom changing jobs and moving as often as she did. So when Buel enthusiastically took on a fatherly role, Jess embraced him. She was captivated by his breezy, fun style. Travis would pick her up from school, buy her donuts on the way home, making her promise not to tell her mother. Soon their little secrets multiplied. On the evenings Sally worked late, Travis began a new game called "Princess." It started almost innocently by winning kisses instead of points. But it wasn't until the third or fourth time that he won kisses "down there" that Jessica confided to her mother. She really liked Travis, but that didn't feel right.

Unlike some parents who dove into denial, clinging to the barest of defenses that their child was misinterpreting adult affection, or worse, they were making it up, Sally Lane went straight to the cops. Buel pled guilty to second degree sodomy and was sentenced to fifty-four months at an upstate correctional facility.

A summary of the interviews with Jessica by Rockville County Child Protective Services revealed there had been some additional touching, but the indictment revolved around the sexual contact between the defendant's mouth and the child's intimate parts. And now six months out of jail, Buel had been murdered. The shot to the back of his head would have been fatal, but the killer had gone for that second bullet in the mouth. Echoes of Middleton and Troy?

A crash in the kitchen jarred Ilene into the present. Sam was standing at the kitchen counter with an empty plate in his hand staring guiltily at the glass of milk he had dropped on the floor.

"Sorry, Mom," he said. "I'm really sorry. It was an accident."

"It's okay, Sammy."

"I'll pick it up."

He kneeled down to clean up the mess and Ilene crouched next to him.

"Careful," she said, "don't try to get the little pieces, I'll mop the floor."

"Sorry, Mom," he said again.

He looked heartbroken, and she tried to reassure him that it was just a broken glass. But she knew he was trying to apologize for what had happened in the computer lab.

"It's not your fault, Sam." Ilene's eyes, clouded with tears, met his for the briefest of moments. He tried a game smile.

"Don't worry," he said. "Those boys will tell the truth and then we can get back to normal." He patted her gently on the shoulder.

"You're right. It's going to be fine."

Sam stood, and she watched him put his plate carefully on the counter and head back to the solitude of his room. For all his struggles he was an optimistic kid and she admired his resilience. Suddenly, his situation hit her in a way it hadn't before, and the ground underneath seemed to shift, tectonic plates sliding apart to create an enormous hole through which she tumbled. To the rest of the world, Sam was now that "pervert." He was the one to be reviled and feared – a monster that even the most well-meaning people wanted isolated, imprisoned, or worse.

Ilene tore off sheet after sheet of paper towel to wipe the floor. She went over and over every square inch where a sliver of glass could have escaped, trying to keep her hands busy, trying to keep the realization from becoming overwhelming. Sam wasn't "one of those." He couldn't be included in that dispassionate category she was accustomed to filing sex offenders: that of the defendant – valueless, colorless, a non-person. And why not? Because she honestly believed Sam was innocent? Or because no matter what he did she loved him? And what did that make Chris Owen? Ilene could not erase the memory of Maggie Owen's gut-wrenching cries when right after her son was murdered, she learned he tried to commit suicide.

When she was done, Ilene stood staring through the window over the sink, barely conscious of a red pickup with tinted windows that drove slowly past the house. For that matter, what about Travis Buel, Victor Troy, Niles Middleton? Innocent, guilty, loved, unloved, salvageable or forever damned – somebody thought they deserved killing. She wiped her hands and mentally reviewed the statements by each of the abuse victims, dimly aware that focusing on their plight was less painful and more manageable than thinking about her own child's.

Dahlia had said of Middleton, "He was so cool and nice, he taught us a lot of things." Mary admitted to having a crush on him, as did the third girl who added, "He was the only one who really understood me." There was Jessica Lane who initially flourished when Buel began to shower her with attention; and David Mullen, or at least his parents, seduced into believing he was going to be the next Wayne Gretzky.

They all revered their abusers. And maybe not all of the affection was undeserved or misplaced.

Ilene didn't need Hector in the room to hear his chiding voice. *Come on, Counselor. That's what grooming techniques are all about. Emotional seduction is the way they manipulate the victims and their families.*

But to these kids, the abuser was a kind of hero, and the emotional part of the seduction was positive for some of them.

Like I said, they were being groomed. Just a way for the offender to get what he wanted. And if you're looking for a pattern to these murders, Heather McColl doesn't fit. Chris was no hero, he was just the boy next door.

She loved him.

She was only fourteen!

Maybe, countered Ilene. But she was so tied to her father, perhaps she saw Chris as her way out.

Way out of what?

Her way out of being suffocated by her father, a way to grow up.

Well, Chris took care of that in short order, didn't he?

Ilene leaned on the counter feeling weak. Just days ago when Dr. Paradiz suggested that not all emotional impulses drawing children to their abusers were unhealthy, she utterly rejected the idea. Now here she was embracing the notion. Dammit. The thought was dizzying.

Out on the street, Ilene registered the same red truck that had gone by moments before, and it dawned on her that she had seen it yesterday, too. The truck coasted slowly and stopped in front of the house. No one got out. But then a woman sitting in the passenger seat rolled down her window and threw something on the front lawn. Without a moment's thought, Ilene tore open the kitchen door and bolted down the path on the side of the house toward the truck. She leapt in front of the vehicle, and the driver slammed on his brakes. He and his passenger lurched into the dashboard.

"Are you crazy?!" he yelled at Ilene. Jim D'Ambrosio got out of the truck, fuming. Ilene stood her ground.

"Get off my property," she commanded.

"What are you doing? I could have run you over!"

"Get out of here or I'll have you arrested!"

D'Ambrosio sucked air in and out of his widened nostrils, a bull ready to charge.

"I said get off my property!"

"What he did to my boy," said D'Ambrosio, shaking his head. "What he did to my Dylan." Color flushed his cheeks. "I will see your deviant son in jail if it's the last thing I do."

"Your Dylan is a goddamn liar."

"How dare you?!"

"He and Jeremy are lying, Sam didn't do anything like what they said."

"Don't you say another word about my son," he warned.

Ilene was unflinching. She took a step toward him. "I know it was you," she said furiously. "You sent that vile email. And you sent those letters, too. You're a sick man and you need help. But I'll be goddamned if you're going to get it from me!"

D'Ambrosio raised his arm as if to strike her, but continued upward until his arm was straight, his finger pointing to the sky. His breathing loud and guttural. "Strike her down, Lord! Strike the hypocrite down! And may her pederast son burn in hell!" All the while he kept pointing at the heavens. "Sinner!" he bellowed. "Sinner!"

"Oh, shut up, you idiot," snapped Ilene.

D'Ambrosio's passenger rolled down her window. "Jim?" she called out.

"Stay in the car, Laurel," he warned.

She obeyed.

Ilene wheeled around and ran to the object Laurel D'Ambrosio had tossed out of the car. Adrenaline pumping, she picked up a hard, plastic Ken doll whose face had been blackened with magic marker and whose naked body was painted with a crude cross. In disgust, she threw it through the open window at D'Ambrosio's wife. Her aim was dead on, and it hit her in the shoulder.

"Ow!" cried Laurel, recoiling. She threw it back toward Ilene and quickly rolled up her window as Ilene charged toward her.

"You leave my family alone!" Ilene cried, pounding on the glass that separated them.

Jim D'Ambrosio hesitated, not knowing whether to round the pick up and physically pull Ilene off his truck or get back in and take off. He scrambled into the driver's seat and with the engine roaring, he put the Silverado into gear and hit the gas. As he did, his wife turned around in her seat and shouted "Filth!"

Her breath coming in gasps, Ilene picked up the doll again and ran into the street after the speeding truck. She heaved it as far as she could and watched it skitter harmlessly along the wet pavement.

"Leave my son alone!!" she screamed after them.

The truck disappeared around the corner, and she didn't hear Lynette Kulik come up behind her. She jumped when Lynette put a hand on her shoulder.

"Ilene, what's going on?"

She tried to speak, but nothing came out. The next thing she knew, Lynette was guiding her gently but firmly to the curb.

"You can't stand out here. It's freezing."

Indeed, she was shaking all over, as much from emotion as the cold.

"Is this your house?"

Ilene nodded numbly.

"Okay, let's go inside." Lynette trailed Ilene along the pathway and into the kitchen where she sat her in a chair. Ilene put her head between her knees to stem the dizziness. She was aware only that her socks were soaked through and chilling her feet to the bone. After giving her a moment to collect herself, Lynette asked gently, "Do you want to tell me?" But before Ilene could form a response, she heard footsteps and looked up to see Sam and Frankie standing in the doorway, faces pale and stricken.

"What's going on?" Frankie asked, his eyes taking in his mother's shivering frame and the strange woman in their kitchen.

"Who was that outside?" echoed Sam.

Surprised by her own display of physical aggression, Ilene wasn't sure what to tell them. Lynette jumped in, "It's all right, boys. Everything's under control."

But they weren't going anywhere until they heard from their mother. She chose her words carefully. "It was someone who was acting out in a very irresponsible way because of the allegations against Sam. He's a little..." she was going to say "crazy" until she realized that the boys had just witnessed her own behavior outside.

"I got angry and went kind of overboard," she amended. "Sorry. I'm fine, really." She gave them a brave smile to prove it.

Without expression, Sam turned on his heels and headed back to his room. Ilene guessed he had seen the whole episode from there. What must he be thinking? Frankie stayed put, his eyes going back and forth between Ilene and Lynette.

"Who was the guy in the truck?" he asked.

"His name's Jim D'Ambrosio," said Ilene.

"Dylan's dad?"

Ilene nodded.

"What did he want?"

"He's … he's upset because he believes what Dylan has told him, so he's acting out," she repeated.

From the look on his face, it was clear that Frankie thought there was more to the story, but he was too guarded and too cool to say anything in front of a stranger. Ilene introduced him to Lynette.

He grunted a "hi" and then asked, "What did you throw at him?"

Ilene sighed, "A toy doll."

"A *doll?*"

"They tossed it into the front yard," she responded casually, as if people frequently threw things on their lawn.

"And you picked it up and threw it back at them?" he asked incredulously. "That was stupid."

"It was."

"It could have been evidence. Now it's got your finger-prints all over it." Frankie shook his head in dismay and left.

Ilene looked sheepishly at Lynette. "He watches too many cop shows," she said.

"Is Mr. D'Ambrosio harassing you?" asked Lynette. She had moved over by the door and still hadn't made a move to take off her coat.

"Yes, I don't know, probably," Ilene equivocated. She told Lynette briefly about the email sent from the library. "We don't know for sure that it was him, but you saw what happened out there."

"Do you want to call the police?"

"I don't know what good that would do. If I claim harassment, the D'Ambrosios could turn around and file counter charges because I hit his wife with that thing. I've done enough today to inflame the situation."

Ilene peeled off her wet socks and walked barefoot to the stove to fill the kettle. "Would you like some tea?"

"No, thanks. I just came by to pick up the medical documents you wanted me to look at."

"Sure," Ilene replied, disappointed. She had hoped Lynette would stay for a bit; some sane adult company would've been comforting. She retrieved the packet she had put together and handed it to the CPS worker. "Sorry about snapping at you the other day," she said. "I was out of line. I know you're just doing your job."

"I understand."

Ilene saw a little bit of an opening. "This is really hard for me and obviously for Sam," she said wrapping her arms around herself. "You can see how volatile Jim D'Ambrosio and his wife are. I'm sure that Dylan and Jeremy have picked up on his hatred of the Westerly, which prompted them to concoct the whole story. You see, they were upset because—"

Lynette put up a hand to stop Ilene from going further. "I'm keeping all of this in mind," she said firmly. "This, too," she indicated the packet of medical records. "Now I really should get back."

The kettle began to whistle.

"Thanks for coming by," said Ilene, and then unable to stop herself she blurted out, "Sam is innocent. He—"

"I'll keep you posted," Lynette interrupted with a tight smile. She went out the side door, got in her car and drove away.

Ilene suddenly felt unbearably lonely. She turned off the burner under the whistling kettle and opened the cabinet where she stored teabags and coffee. On the top shelf she spotted an unopened bottle of wine which she kept on hand for Roz. She reached for the bottle, uncorked it and filled the mug she was going to use for her tea. She drank half of it down, quickly, taking it as medicine. The heat spreading into her chest and face felt good. She filled the mug again and brought it over to the phone. There was a call she needed to make.

"Dad? Hope you're not in the middle of anything." Ilene knew her father had friends and business acquaintances in Westover and she didn't want him to hear about Sam from anyone else.

As simply as she could, she told her father about the accusations at school. He listened to the whole story without interruption, then asked, "Do you need a lawyer?" His solution to all problems. "I know a couple of topnotch guys up there. I could make some calls."

"No thanks, Dad. We're ... not at that stage yet. I just didn't want you to read or hear about it somewhere else." She drank more wine.

"It made the papers?" Ilene heard accusation in his voice.

"I don't know, I suppose. I haven't picked up the local paper."

"Is it true?" her father asked bluntly.

"No. It's a total lie!"

"Damn shame. This is what comes from too much sex on TV, it's everywhere you look, and these kids are watching that stuff twenty-four-seven."

"Well, it has more to do with a situation we have up here in Westover."

"Who are these kids anyway?" her father interrupted. "Where are their parents? What do the school officials say? This makes me very angry."

"Me, too."

"What are you going to do?"

"There's nothing to be done right now," Ilene said unhappily. "Just wait, let the investigation unfold."

"If I were you, I'd file a defamation charge, see what they say when they get slapped with papers. They start looking at losing the house, the car, the whole shebang, you'd be surprised how fast they change their tune."

"It's okay, Dad." Ilene had to lean on the counter. Either the wine or the possibility that she'd be hearing from one of her father's *topnotch* legal buddies was making her legs feel rubbery.

There was a long silence on the line. Her father finally spoke, "Is there anything I can do?"

Ilene was moved by the unexpected warmth in his voice and how quickly he had jumped to Sam's defense.

"Uh, no. Not right now, thanks."

"You want me to drive up?"

"No," she blurted out quickly. Accepting his help would mean breaching the distance she had worked so hard to maintain all these years and she wasn't sure she could handle further displacement at the moment. No, what she really wanted was to hang up, finish the bottle of wine and get silently drunk. Which she did.

CHAPTER TWENTY-TWO

THREE ASPIRIN HAD barely made a dent in her throbbing headache and her eyes felt dry and gritty; it was an effort just to keep them open.

"The thing is, I don't drink," Ilene was trying to explain. "Well, hardly at all."

Dr. Paradiz waited for her to continue.

"I did when I was younger, before I got pregnant with Sam. My father is an alcoholic, a highly functioning one, but an alcoholic all the same, and I refused to be like him."

When she didn't offer more, Paradiz interjected, "But you drank yesterday."

"Oh, yeah," she said glumly. "Do I look as bad as I feel?"

"Well, I don't know how you feel, but you do look pretty terrible. I'm not your therapist, so I feel free to say that."

"And if you were my therapist?"

"I would've kept my mouth shut." He smiled.

Ilene put her head in her hands. Her hangover was nothing compared to the emotional turmoil that she finally concluded was destroying her judgment and hurting her family, and which finally prompted her call to Paradiz at the clinic. He was kind enough to make time in his morning schedule.

"I didn't know where else to go," she said. "I'm falling apart and it's really bad timing because of the thing with Sam. I have to be strong for him." Tears began to leak from her already red and puffy eyes, and she knew that if she let herself go they would carry her away in a flood tide. Paradiz handed her a box of tissues.

"Why don't you start at the beginning."

She told him about the imminent charges against Sam and about his Asperger Syndrome; she told him of the email she was sure D'Ambrosio had sent and how she had chased his truck down the street without any shoes on. Finally, she admitted nearly finishing a bottle of wine out of the clear blue and stumbling around the kitchen trying to heat up frozen dinners for the boys as they watched her with more than a little anxiety.

"They have never seen me like that, and I think they were a little scared."

"And you?"

"I'm scaring myself, too," Ilene replied candidly. "In the middle of all this, I'm watching myself become fixated on Chris's murder and the murder of this guy in Rockville and ... others ... and reaching for a theory that they were all done by one killer, thinking that if I can figure it out, I'll be able to solve all the crimes."

"When the crime you really want to solve – and can't right now – is what you believe are false and hurtful charges against your son."

Ilene nodded sadly in recognition.

"I'm guessing that feeling helpless, for you, is particularly threatening," said Paradiz. "So I understand how unsettling this situation with Sam must be. But I have to say, coming as it does out of the overly-fearful environment that I witnessed at the school the other night and what you've told me about Sam, the abuse claim sounds far fetched. If they're lying, their story will fall apart without too much prodding. As they say, 'the truth will come out.'"

Ilene leaned forward intently. "I wish I believed that, but I don't. Last night I kept remembering all the times someone has tried to convince *me* that the victim was lying, and I ... I found the claim *repugnant*. It would make me angry actually, because I honestly believed that kids don't lie, not about sexual abuse.

"Until now," prompted Paradiz.

"Sam did not do this, but I'm afraid he's going to get crushed by the system. I know how it works: the cops, CPS, the DA's office. Our law enforcement culture gears us toward thinking that people don't report crimes unless they really happened. And believing you're right feeds on itself because you look at everything in a light that supports your position; then with that tunnel vision you overlook facts and circumstances that don't fit your theory. Take me, for example – once I'm sure I've got something, I'm like a bulldozer with no brakes."

"You seem to be questioning your ability to do your job. Is it all about Sam?"

"Not entirely," Ilene answered truthfully. "Ever since I left your office the other day, I've been haunted by Heather. Talk about narrowed vision; I missed something that was more important than whether or not I made the case against Chris. I wasn't keyed in to who Heather was and why she was so desperate not to testify." She paused, struck with sudden remorse. "Listening to myself, I make it sound like it was an oversight. But it wasn't. I arrogantly believed I knew better than Heather what it was she needed – she needed *justice*. And by God, I was bound and determined to get that for her. I had to make a case, and bottom line? Without her testimony I didn't have one."

"I think you're being too hard on yourself, Ilene," Paradiz said. "It's unlikely Heather's father would have let the matter drop. And you can't always be guided by an uncooperative witness."

"I should have recognized Simon's involvement."

"What do you mean?"

"Rebecca told me the other day that Simon was physically and sexually abused as a child. He must have been seeking his own sense of retribution that even Chris's conviction couldn't give him. Maybe somewhere inside Heather knew that and felt like in the end she'd let everyone down."

She lifted her head to look out the window behind Dr. Paradiz's desk. "You know, all this time I've believed myself to be such a champion for these abused kids. But I think if I wasn't so blind a prosecutor, I might actually be a better advocate."

He sat quietly taking in her silence and the subtle changes in her expression. She was getting to something else. Finally she continued. "It must have been very tough for Heather to go against her dad. I suppose that using one's child as a substitute for a spouse, even if there's no sex, might be a form of abuse. A child I'm talking about," she hastily added, "not a teenager."

When she did not elaborate, Paradiz leaned back to give her more space.

"Inappropriate certainly," he offered, "and in many cases as damaging to the child as sexual or physical abuse. But why do you limit your thinking to young children, why not include teenagers?"

"Well, teenagers can make their own decisions," Ilene said, flushing.

"Not always. It depends on the person. I think a parent can do even more harm by putting a teenager in the spousal role. At that age, the older child is trying to establish his or her own identity, including sexual identity, and is preparing for the major separation of heading off to college or a job. Asking a teenager to play the emotional role of spouse can create huge amounts of conflict and guilt for him or her, especially if the parents themselves have a rocky relationship."

"Or, as in Heather's case, one of the parents has abandoned the family," suggested Ilene.

"That puts even more pressure on the child and can create a world of hurt."

Ilene looked into Paradiz's sympathetic eyes and realized he already knew she was talking about herself. Rarely had she felt so vulnerable as she did just then.

"When I was eighteen my mother died of cancer," she confessed. "Before she got sick my mom was a dynamo. She'd hustle me off to school, jog around the park, and then dash off to work. She didn't have to work, but she founded a nonprofit that brought art and music to disabled children, and she was passionate about it. She and my father were always going out to functions and fundraisers together. That last year she was sick and didn't have the strength to go anywhere, so I accompanied my dad to all the events that my mom would've gone to – and been brilliant at. I started to feel like I was my father's date, and in lots of ways he treated me like I was. There was nothing physical going on, but it became my whole social life. I didn't have a boyfriend, I lost touch with my friends, I started drinking a lot."

"Sounds like you were unhappy," Paradiz said.

"I think I felt … I *feel* … so guilty for trying to step into my mother's shoes while she was suffering at home, dealing with her chemo and radiation hell, like I betrayed her while she was helpless." Ilene closed her eyes, recalling her mother's wasting frame.

"Certainly she went through a very difficult time," he said gently. "But your mother doesn't sound like she was a helpless person and she was still your parent. If she felt saddened or left out by you accompanying your father, it was her responsibility to work it out with him. And they both should have recognized that you were being thrust into an inappropriate role."

Ilene's brow furrowed, her mind reorganizing, trying to make sense of what remained when she let go of assumptions she never even knew she had.

"You were asking me about my confidence in my ability to do my job," she started. "All these years I've been angry at my father for making me his partner, if not physically, then psychologically. Maybe this focus on fighting for the victims has been, in part, about 'prosecuting' him and making up for trying to take my mother's place."

"Because you perceived her as being helpless, like young abuse victims," Paradiz suggested.

Ilene blew out a deep breath. "That's it? Just click my heels together three times and I'm back in Kansas?"

"It's a process." He gave a wry look at her worn sneakers, adding, "And you don't have the right shoes."

Ilene clenched her dampened tissues tightly in her hand and prepared to leave. She felt drained, but not on the brink of disintegrating as she had when she walked through his door. She would go home and try to establish some normalcy in her family's life; she might even call her father and take a chance on chipping away at the barrier between them. Dr. Paradiz stopped her at the door.

"Ilene, with this multiple murder theory, you thought you might be on to something."

"I did. But I think you were right about it. It's become a substitute for the crime I really want to solve – the charges against Sam."

Paradiz smiled. "Fair enough." He held the door open for her and watched as she made her way down the hospital corridor.

CHAPTER TWENTY-THREE

T HE DEN WAS sparsely furnished, but neat and clean. It smelled of room freshener. Against one wall was a worn loveseat covered in cheap muslin. Near it was a child-sized desk on which sat an Olivetti manual typewriter made in 1964. It still worked except for the malfunctioning "s".

What do you say now, High Priestess of Morality? How can you live knowing your seed has despoiled the innocent with his groping hands and his dirty mouth? The more you try to protect him, the more complicit in his sin you are. Soon, you will see your child's cold, white body lowered into the ground where his tainted flesh will rot and his bones become home to maggots, like the bodies of the others. Judas!

The gloved hand, shaking with fury, pulled the message out of the roller, folded it and slipped it into a plain, white envelope. Ilene's name went on the front in tremulous letters. Suddenly, the hand froze in mid-air. Somewhere from the back of the house came the sound of a whimpering child. A familiar sound – relentless, sickening. It had to stop.

CHAPTER TWENTY-FOUR

"TWO HUNDRED DOLLARS?!" shrieked Frankie. "Are you insane?"

"I own all four railroads, dude," Sam responded implacably. "Hand it over."

Frankie thrust the two hundred dollar bills he had just picked up from passing Go into his brother's outstretched hand.

Ilene studied the board. Both of them would be coming around the corner to her orange properties and she had a house on each one. They were slim pickings next to Frankie's haphazard collection of real estate and Sam's customary monopolies on the railroads and utilities which she always discounted and which invariably bled her dry by the end of the game. Nevertheless, if one of them landed on her, the seventy bucks rent on St. James or Tennessee might keep her in the game.

Her visit with Paradiz had brought up subjects she hadn't intended to explore, subjects difficult to share, but doing so seemed to ground her, and she was taking charge again. Clinging to the psychologist's confidence that Dylan and Jeremy's stories would fall apart, she showered and with her hair still damp, plowed through mundane household tasks. The kids were off from school on their winter break; in the afternoon they picked up Frankie's friend Kevin and all went to the Boys and Girls Club to shoot hoops. Sam threw in a few half-hearted shots, but wasn't in the mood for competition and finally took refuge in the last row of the bleachers with a book. Frankie, who made *everything* a competition, quickly organized a three on three half-court game with some older boys. He played with a frantic, near-hysterical energy that was a bit unnerving, but Ilene chalked it up to his anxiety about Sam's situation and let him play on, even after he aggressively challenged a much bigger boy, threatening to turn a friendly pick-up game into a grudge match. Luckily, the gym was taken over by a girls' volleyball program before things got out of hand. At home, they had a quiet dinner and she suggested Monopoly.

The telephone interrupted Sam's roll of the dice.

"I'll get it." Frankie jumped up and bolted to the kitchen with a warning that if anyone landed on him they had to pay even if he was out of the room.

He came back with the phone. "It's for you," he said, handing it to Sam.

"Hello?"

For the next thirty seconds, Sam listened. His face grew slack and lost color.

"Who is it, Sammy?" Ilene asked in alarm. She thought it might be D'Ambrosio.

He gave her the phone.

"Hello?"

"Hello, Mrs. Hart. It's Jay Boone – Coach Boone from Hudson State. Do you have a second?"

Ilene rose from her chair and walked the phone into the hall with trepidation. His subdued tone previewed bad news.

"I feel terrible about this," said Boone, "but I got a call from the dean. He told me about the, uh … the charges against Sam by the two kids. I hope it's not true. He seems to me to be a fine young man. But under the circumstances we feel the University can't offer him the statistician job we'd talked about. I'm sorry. I know how hard he's worked and how much he loves being with the team. Really, I'm sorry."

"But the charges are false …" Ilene stammered. "We're fighting this, and … in a day or two–"

"Mrs. Hart, there's nothing I can do. I'm sorry."

"Yes, me too," she managed to say. As she put the phone down, Ilene was overcome with anger. It wasn't going to stop, was it? The doubts, the persecution. And her heart broke for Sam. Until that moment – until it was taken away – she hadn't fully understood how much he needed the job, how much he needed the acceptance and independence it offered. Matt had been right all along. Hudson State was Sam's chance to take his first steps into an adult world that had built-in validation for him. Of course he'd make mistakes. But if he did, he'd learn; if he went too fast and stumbled, he'd have the support to get back up again. If the opportunity disappeared, he might stay buried in Branford forever.

She made it as far as the living room entrance. Sam had his back to her; he and Frankie were in the middle of an argument.

"Give me the dice," Frankie demanded.

Sam had them clutched in one hand pressed to the back of his head as he rocked.

"I'm allowed to roll again if it falls off the table," insisted the younger boy.

"No! You have to take the roll!" growled Sam.

"I do not! Give them to me." Frankie reached around his brother trying to get the dice from his clenched fist. Sam pushed him off.

"Cut it out, you sicko!" yelled Frankie as he stood and reached for Sam again.

Sam swatted his arm away. "I'm not a sicko, shitface."

"Oh yeah? What do you call putting your hand down a little kid's pants?!"

Ilene came to life. "Frankie!" she warned, but it was too late.

Frankie had grabbed Sam's fist in both his hands and was attempting to pry open his fingers. As they wrestled, they screamed obscenities at one another. In the fray, they knocked the Monopoly board off the table, sending the houses flying across the room. Later, Ilene would mentally replay the incident in slow motion, but in real time it was instantaneous. Frankie clamped his teeth down on Sam's forearm and Sam released the dice with a scream. As he did, he sent his brother flying backwards with surprising force. The crack of his head on the table edge was like a gunshot.

Ilene ran to where Frankie lay, struggling to get up. Blood oozed from a gash on his head.

"Oh, God," she wailed. "Frankie, don't move."

He obeyed, and she tried to see how deep the cut was. Then, she looked up at Sam with fire in her eyes. "What have you done?!" she cried furiously. But Sam barely heard her; he was in another place altogether. Standing with his arms straight at his sides, veins popping out of his neck, he threw his head back.

"Give me back the dice!" he bellowed.

"Sam, Sam…"

"Give me back my LIFE! Give—me—back—my—LIFE!!"

He stumbled up the stairs and slammed the door to his room. For one crazy moment Ilene had the urge to run after him, break the door down and shake him. If only she could physically wrench the autism from his body. A few times in her life she had had this same impulse and understood how some parents can become so unglued they hit their children. She had never done it, but she understood.

Frankie groaned, and she looked down to see blood seeping through her fingers. Fighting the panic that rose in her throat, she told him to stay put while she dialed 911.

CHAPTER TWENTY-FIVE

RANKIE'S EYES FLUTTERED open just for a second and then closed again. His mother sat on his bed and pushed a lock of hair off his forehead; a few strands caught on the bandage adhesive and with a gentle finger she freed them and pushed those back as well.

"Will you talk to Sammy in the morning?" she asked.

"Yeah, okay." Frankie's words slurred as he drifted off.

"Does it hurt?"

He was already asleep. Ilene pulled the covers up and slipped out of his room, leaving the door open in case he woke. At the top of the stairs, she looked over to Sam's door, but it was still shut, closing him off from her.

Two hours earlier, Matt called from the emergency room to assure her that Frankie was okay, they were going to stitch him up and send them home. With heavy feet, she went up to Sam's room and knocked on the door. No answer.

"Sammy, are you awake?' she asked. Light spilled through the crack at the bottom of his door, so she knew he was.

"Frankie's OK," she said. "Matt called. It's just a few stitches, he's going to be fine." Nothing from the other side. "Can I come in?"

"No."

"Please. I'm not mad. I just want to talk."

"Talk from there."

"Okay." Ilene sat down in the hallway, hugging her knees and resting her head on the door frame.

"I'm so sorry about Coach Boone's call," she started. "It's really unfair. But I think once this thing gets resolved, they're going to see it differently. They'll want you back."

Silence.

"I understand why you blew up," Ilene continued. "It's not your fault. Once this thing gets resolved..."

"This *thing* is not going to get *resolved!*" cried Sam. Something hit the wall on the far side of his room. Ilene flinched. "Everybody believes Dylan and Jeremy," he said.

"That's not true, Sammy."

"Yes, Mom, it is. Even Frankie believes them."

Ilene startled. "Oh, honey, no," she protested. "Frankie was angry, he didn't mean what he said."

"Yes, he did." Sam had come closer to his side of the door. He spoke quietly, but with conviction. "He looks at me in a different way now. Frankie thinks I'm a sex offender."

A sob broke from Ilene and she tried to choke it back.

"Please, Mom, go away. Just leave me alone. Please."

His footsteps retreated and the light went off. After a minute, when no further sounds came from within, Ilene put her head down and wept.

* * *

Now, with Frankie in bed and Matt waiting for her, she took a last look at Sam's impenetrable door and walked slowly downstairs. Matt had made a pot of coffee and handed her a cup as he led her into the living room. She stepped around the wet spots on the carpet where she had scrubbed out the blood, and then she collapsed at one end of the sofa. Matt eased himself down at the other.

"How's he doing?" he asked.

"He's asleep."

"The doctor said to check him a couple of times during the night to look for signs of a more serious concussion, but she thinks it's minor. Frankie was alert and sassy, his usual self."

"I'm not too worried about Frankie," she said.

"Sam?"

Ilene took a slow sip of her coffee and closed her eyes. "He's afraid Frankie believes Dylan and Jeremy. He even told me, 'Frankie thinks I'm a sex offender.' It's killing him."

"Has Frankie said anything to you?" Matt's expression echoed her anguish.

"No, but he's been unusually quiet. I get the feeling that his friends are texting each other about Sam, and some of the nasty messages are getting passed along to Frankie," said Ilene. "One minute he's turned his cell phone off, the next it's vibrating in his pocket but he won't answer it."

"You want me to talk to him?"

"And what would you say?" Ilene lifted her head. "I mean … do *you* think that Sam abused those kids?"

Matt met her gaze. He wanted to lie. He wanted to say 'absolutely not' and mean it – but that wasn't the way he and Ilene would stay together.

"It entered my mind," Matt admitted. "Not for long, though. I don't think it's something he would do, I really don't. But there are times when I'm not sure I understand Sam at all…" he struggled for words. "I'm sorry."

His admission made Ilene sad, but how could she fault him? There were moments when Sam felt like a stranger even to her. The time seemed right to engage Matt in the difficult discussion they needed to have about their future together, but with her emotions bruised from the past few days, she felt too vulnerable.

"Did you speak with Dawkins today?" she sidestepped.

"Yeah. He's going to present a photo array first thing tomorrow to the librarian who might have seen D'Ambrosio."

"What will you do if she identifies him?"

"Get a search warrant. We want his computers so we can find the doctored photo of Sam. But I think we may turn up more than that. There's a good chance he's the one who wrote the letters, and Dawkins agrees. I've been hearing stuff about his Christian fanaticism which would tie in to the whole 'prophet' and guilt thing in the letters."

"What about the child he refers to?"

"I don't know," said Matt frowning. "Dr. Paradiz could be right. Could be all in his head – a wild fantasy that he feels he must punish himself for. But, to be on the safe side, we want to keep the search warrant on the QT. We don't want D'Ambrosio to get wind of it, and we'll be prepared for anything when we execute the warrant."

"Speaking of surprises," continued Matt, "you told me he showed up here, but you didn't tell me the whole story. I got the details from Frankie while we were waiting. Do me a favor," he added sternly, "don't confront him. If he is the one who did write those letters, he's a lot more twisted than I thought. Hopefully, we'll get the warrant tomorrow. In the meantime, if he comes around again, lock your doors and call the cops."

"He's making us prisoners in our own house," complained Ilene bitterly.

"Don't mess with him," Matt cautioned again.

Sitting on opposite ends of the sofa accentuated the awkward space between them, but even Matt seemed reluctant to transcend the shop talk.

"We had some news about Simon McColl today," Matt was saying.

Ilene was all ears.

"Chris Owen occasionally dated a girl named Tara Briggs. She was helping him in a couple of his classes, and I talked with her. Lynette Kulik was right, Tara does look a little like Heather. Big difference in age of course; Tara is twenty-one, but they both have the same color hair, similar build. We have a couple of witnesses who say that after Simon saw Chris and Tara together, he showed up at an office party and was quite vocal about how was going to 'take care' of Chris before he could do more damage."

Ilene considered the implications. "I don't suppose Simon's checked in with you," she said grimly.

"No. His car turned up at a municipal lot in the city and the parking staff is supposed to call us if he picks it up. But he could be anywhere. We checked a few of the local bars to try and put him someplace between nine and eleven the night Chris was killed, but no one remembers seeing him."

"Are you going to make an arrest?"

"Right now, he's just a person of interest and would be strongly encouraged to turn himself in for questioning."

Matt looked curiously at Ilene when she didn't respond. "Have you changed your mind about him?" he asked.

"I may be stubborn, but I'm not crazy," she sighed. "It would be awful if he killed Chris, but I have to admit it's a possibility. Rebecca told me a couple of days ago that Simon was sexually and physically abused as a kid. He's got some kind of rage eating him up inside; Chris would be a likely target."

"I know. Mrs. McColl told us about the abuse."

"She did?"

"I guess she thought we'd find out one way or another, be better to get it out up front."

"The thing that still bothers me," Ilene continued, "is the obvious link between the graffiti at the Westerly and Chris himself. Let's say Simon did go after Chris. Would he go up to the Westerly the next night and spray-paint a reference to Chris's death with the *one down* thing? Why do that and draw attention to himself? And how would he have known about the sex offender study that Dr. Paradiz spoke about unless he was at the school meeting?"

"How do you know he *wasn't?* It was a big crowd that night."

"I would have seen him."

Matt shrugged. "I don't think he did the graffiti, in any event."

"I don't either."

"It comes back to D'Ambrosio again, doesn't it? 'One down, twenty-nine thousand to go' written on the Westerly wall and in the email a reference to *two* down." He put his coffee cup on the table. "By the way, just so you don't think I blew you off completely on the Travis Buel homicide, I asked for a ballistics comparison on Troy and Owen. I also checked to see if McColl has a permit for a .38. He doesn't. D'Ambrosio, on the other hand, is a gun guy."

"Why am I not surprised?"

"He's got a sidearm for work and no doubt a few hunting rifles at home. But no .38. Well, he did have, but he reported it stolen about four, five years ago."

In the silence that followed, their mutual avoidance of intimacy descended like a blanket of fog through which Ilene could barely see Matt. A spark of fear ignited in her chest.

"Why don't you give up on me, Chief?" asked Ilene sadly.

"How can I?" he said with a slight twinkle in his eyes. "Every five minutes a crisis erupts in this household and you come running."

"Hey, *I* didn't manufacture–" Ilene began to protest and then caught herself. "You're right. A lot's been happening in the past few days, and I do keep turning to you."

Matt searched her eyes. "Are we talking?"

"We're talking," she nodded.

"Okay. I am kind of serious about you running to me whenever there's trouble. It makes me feel as though I'm good for emergencies, but when life slows down and it's just you and me, you find ways to avoid being close. You do this push-pull thing, letting me in and then shutting me out. I'm tired of it."

"Yes, I guess I do," Ilene acknowledged.

"Why?"

"I suppose I'm conflicted," she said.

"That's obvious."

"Oh, Matt, I'm not conflicted about loving you." Ilene said urgently, emotionally. "I'm conflicted about how much it costs me to love you, to need you. The one time in my life I really needed someone – when my mom was dying – my father wasn't there for me. It was just the two of us, and he didn't leave or anything, it's just that he needed me to take care of *him* so much that I ... I felt *used up*. I wound up hating both of us."

Matt said nothing, waiting for Ilene to continue. After a full day of work he had raced over to help her with Frankie, brought him to the emergency room and stayed beside him while they stitched him up. And now, exhausted, he was ready to listen to her pour her heart out. So she tried. Sometimes haltingly, sometimes in a rush of feeling, she talked about the year her mother died, about losing Daniel and being left with the monumental task of raising two kids alone, one of them with autism. She acknowledged the walls she had erected to keep herself intact.

"I don't understand it all right now, but I'm trying," she finally said. "And I want us to be together." She reached out and took Matt's hand and kissed his calloused fingers. Tears slipped quietly down her cheeks. "I need you on the good days and the bad days, Chief – every day. Stick with me, please?"

He gently wiped the tears from her face. "You never told me you needed me before. Is it hard to say?"

"No, I can say it easy enough – *meaning* it scares the bejesus out of me," Ilene smiled, "but it's still true."

They sat without speaking for a while until Ilene squeezed his hand. "Come on, it's really late," she said. "Will you come to bed?"

He pulled her close and with his lips close to hers said, "I hope that means what I think it means."

Ilene gave Matt a long, promising kiss in response, then told him she'd be right behind him after she locked up and turned off the lights. She took a detour to check on Frankie, tiptoeing over to feel his forehead and listen to his breathing; it was lighter than usual, but steady and easy. When she entered her bedroom, it was dark. She called out to Matt softly, seductively, as she began to slip out of her jeans. But he didn't answer; he was lying on the queen size bed, taking up the lion's share, his shoes off, clothes on, mouth open – snoring softly.

CHAPTER TWENTY-SIX

ILENE JERKED AWAKE, her heart thudding against her chest. She sensed the empty space next to her and realized that Matt was gone. She glanced around, reconnecting with the things around her, her bureau, the photos on the wall, strewn clothes from the night before, taking them all in to replace the images from her nightmare. In the dream, she was taking the boys by train to visit Daniel's parents in San Diego when she suddenly realized that there was a killer on board who thought they were both sex offenders. Somehow she lost sight of them and ran through the cars asking if anyone had seen the boys; people kept telling her they were in the car ahead. But when she'd get there, they were gone and she'd be told the same thing. The train had no end.

Still groggy, but breathing heavily, Ilene turned to the bedside clock which read a few minutes after nine. She hadn't slept that late for months. Swinging her long, bare legs over the side of the bed, she looked up to see Matt in the doorway.

"Oh," she said startled, "you're still here."

He eyed her half-naked body appreciatively. "Unfortunately, not for long," he replied.

"Is Frankie up?" Ilene inquired.

"Not only up, but had breakfast and has happily assumed his captainship at the video controls."

"What about Sam?"

Matt shook his head. "I think he's awake but he hasn't come down yet. Guess what? Simon McColl showed up."

That woke Ilene. "Really?! Where is he?"

"At the station; they just called. Apparently he got home late last night and decided to come in on his own. I'm heading over."

Ilene bounded out of bed and reached for the jeans she had thrown in the hamper the night before. "Wait, wait," she said, hopping into her pants' legs one at a time, "I want to come."

"No, I need to talk to him first."

"Please. I won't say anything, I'll just sit quietly in the corner."

Matt stared at her in wonder. "You have never done that in your entire life."

"Really, I won't interfere." She pulled on a sweater and rummaged through the closet for shoes. "Besides, he might feel more comfortable if I'm there."

Stepping to her bureau to check herself in the mirror, Ilene combed her fingers through her auburn curls and with surprising speed applied some lipstick. Then she turned eagerly to Matt.

"What are we waiting for? Let's go."

* * *

Simon McColl nervously twisted a worn Red Sox cap in his hands while he spoke. Still wearing his coat, he slouched in the chair across from Matt's desk with his elbows planted on his knees, head down.

"As soon as I got home, Rebecca told me about Chris," he said, "and how you all were looking for me. So here I am."

Ilene leaned against a table in the corner. Simon looked a good deal paler than he had at their last encounter, but his eyes were clear and it changed his appearance dramatically, making his other features sharper, more noticeable. He looked up, first at Matt, then to Ilene.

"I didn't know about Chris. I swear," he said.

"You didn't pick up a newspaper? Turn on the TV?" asked Matt casually, leaning back in his seat.

"No. Like I told your guys out front, the first time I heard about Chris was from my wife. Do you know who killed him?" Simon asked anxiously.

"That's what I'm trying to find out. Why don't you tell us where you've been, starting on Tuesday evening."

Simon sighed. "Rebecca and I had an early dinner, around six or so. Then I went out and got wasted; it was Heather's birthday ... would have been her fifteenth birthday. Somehow I got home, I don't know what time it was, but I was still drunk the next morning."

"What did you do?"

"I worked a little, but I felt like crap. I quit early, had a few drinks. That's when I went to see Ilene," he nodded in her direction. "I guess she told you about that."

"I'm more concerned about the night before," said Matt. "You said that you went to the Blue Mill Tavern in Grandin Falls?" Matt asked.

"Yeah."

Matt had already asked Levitsky to check it out, but he thought McColl was telling the truth.

"Any place else?"

"No."

"Why go all the way to Grandin Falls to go drinking. You could've done that locally."

McColl's face lost more color, highlighting the broken blood vessels on his nose and cheekbones. Finally he said, "Most of the places around here know me. I didn't want to risk that they'd ... uh ... ration my drinks or cut me off."

"And you really wanted to get drunk."

"No. I wanted to die, but getting drunk was the next best thing."

After a considered pause, Matt said, "Okay. So the next day you decided to check yourself into..." he glanced at his notes, "the Samaritan House on West 103rd Street?"

"The next night, yeah. After I saw Ilene."

"You didn't go to the meeting at Branford Elementary that night?"

"What meeting?" asked McColl.

"The Samaritan House," Matt prompted without answering Simon's question. "What is that?"

"A detox clinic."

Matt looked keenly at McColl. "New York City? There are clinics here in Westover."

"I was afraid I'd run into someone I knew, a doctor, someone from my insurance company."

Matt nodded thoughtfully.

"Simon, why didn't you tell Rebecca where you were?" Ilene asked from the corner. "She must have been worried sick."

He dropped his head and stared at the floor without answering.

"Maybe you *did* tell her," suggested Matt. "And she lied to us."

"No, no," Simon sat upright, flustered. "She's totally innocent in this. She didn't know anything about it."

"Then why'd you keep your wife in the dark?"

He looked around the room for a means of escape. Then he said dejectedly, "I didn't want to disappoint her. I've been to that place twice before, the last time just a couple of months ago. But both times I left after a day; I couldn't take it. I thought if I told her where I was going and I failed again, I ... I just didn't want to do that to her."

His cap dropped to the floor; he let it lie there and took a deep, pained breath. "I don't know if I love my wife, but she's a good woman and she tries really hard with me, just like she tried with Heather. I think she and I know that my getting sober may be the last chance we have. I owe that to her." He picked up his cap and busily dusted it off to hide the emotion creeping into his voice. "I owe that to my daughter."

"Is that all you owe your daughter?" asked Matt sharply.

"What do you mean?" Simon looked up fearfully.

"We have witnesses who say that you made threats against Chris Owen, and that you were pretty upset about his leaving the Westerly. Maybe you thought you owed him a more *severe* sentence."

Simon colored. "Listen, I thought he'd gotten off easy, but that's not why I was upset. I saw Chris the day of the office party. He was with a girl that ... for a moment, I thought I was seeing Heather. It shook me bad. And yeah, I wished I could've killed him. But it was just talk, you know?"

"Just talk?"

"To tell you the truth, I don't remember half of what I said. But yeah, just talk."

Matt let Simon's last words hang in the air before shifting in his seat. "We're going to have to check all of this out, Mr. McColl."

"Sure, sure."

"Okay, you're free to go, but in cop parlance, 'don't leave town.'"

McColl got up slowly and headed to the door.

"One last thing," Matt stopped him. "There's more to getting sober than making it through a few days in detox," he said softly.

"Yeah, I know," intoned Simon. "One day at a time, right?"

"It's helpful to think in even shorter increments," said Matt. "At least in the beginning."

Simon looked at Matt in surprise, then said, "I'll keep that in mind."

He got to the door just in time to cross paths with Officer Levitsky, who waited until he was out of earshot before saying, "His story checks out, Chief, at least the part he remembers. On Tuesday night, McColl was at the Blue Mill from eight until about two, long enough to get shitfaced. And the rehab place in the city confirms that he signed himself in on Wednesday at ten-fifty-two p.m. To their knowledge, he did not leave until last night."

"Thanks, Joel."

The phone on Matt's desk buzzed quietly. He picked it up and heard Sergeant Blue telling him who was on the line.

"Put him through," he said, his eyes flickering to Ilene. "Chief Bingham."

Ilene caught Matt's look and stopped breathing.

"We'll be right there," he said.

Reaching for his jacket, he pointed at Ilene and said gravely, "This time you *are* staying in the hall."

"Where are we going?" she asked, eyes wide.

"The school. Harvey Carle is there – with Jeremy Bell and his mother. They have something they want to tell us."

CHAPTER TWENTY-SEVEN

"LOOK AT THE policeman when you speak to him," Teresa Bell urged her son.

Instead, Jeremy took the gum out of his mouth and examined it before popping it back in his mouth. Matt gave Mrs. Bell a lukewarm smile and lifted his hand in a gesture that told her to back off. They sat in kid-sized chairs around a Formica table in Mrs. Grumman's fourth grade classroom, Mrs. Bell and her son across from Matt, whose knees were somewhere up around his shoulders. He felt the posture might diminish his stature but wanted to interview the boy in his classroom where he would be more at ease than in the principal's office, a place he would associate with being in trouble and where Ilene was waiting. Harvey Carle himself stood over by the windows fidgeting with the shades. He didn't know whether to be relieved or horrified by what he was hearing.

"All right, Jeremy, so you were telling us that you and Dylan made up the story about Mr. Hart," Matt prompted. "Tell me in your own words what happened."

"We made it up," Jeremy mumbled and snapped his gum.

"I got that part," said Matt. "I need to hear what actually happened."

Jeremy stared at the floor, hoping it would provide some guidance or better yet, open up and swallow him whole. His mother was not so patient.

"Answer him, Jeremy," she said with irritation.

"It's okay, Mrs. Bell," said Matt, "I'm sure he's going to tell me because he knows it's the right thing to do." The boy chewed his gum faster but remained mute. "And because I'm the Chief of Police and we either talk here or we go *down to the station.*"

Jeremy had watched enough cop movies to conjure up visions of being shackled to a steel chair and being worked over by the bad cop while the good cop stepped outside the interrogation room to get a cup of coffee. Silent, hot tears began to stream from his eyes and drip to the floor.

"It wasn't my idea," he blubbered. "It was Dylan's idea because he crapped in his pants."

"I'm listening."

"We was in the computer lab—"

"We *were* in the computer lab," corrected his mother. Matt shot her a warning glance.

"And Hart grabbed us and locked us in the closet."

"Just like that?" asked Matt. "Out of the clear blue he pulled you into the closet?"

"Well, we were just foolin' with him. He's like such a dork. He's so freakin' weird," complained Jeremy.

"Mr. Hart told me that you and Dylan were taunting him, pulling his hair, and jabbing him with your fingers."

"Yeah, but that's all we did. And then he like freaks out and starts screaming. And he grabs me and Dylan and pulls us into the closet and then real quick shuts the door. We tried to get out, but that stupid weirdo locked it."

"Then what happened?"

"Well, it was dark in there and we couldn't see. Dylan started to cry. First he was mad and then he got really scared."

"You said before that Dylan had an 'accident' in his pants?"

"Yeah."

"How do you know?"

Jeremy finally raised his head and looked at Matt as though he was a complete idiot. "I could *smell* it. It was totally gross."

"So how long were you in the closet before Mr. Hart unlocked it?"

"I don't know."

" A minute? Ten minutes?"

"A few minutes, I guess."

"And where did you and Dylan come up with the idea of accusing him of sexual abuse?"

"In the library."

"I meant *how* did you guys come up with the idea?"

"I told you, it was Dylan's idea. After Hart unlocked the closet, we ran out. We held up in the library and Dylan told me he thought Hart was a pervert and wanted to rape little kids. I said no, but he said he was going to tell Mrs. Grumman that Hart did nasty things to us, and that would serve him right for putting us in the closet."

Matt thought for a moment and then asked, "If you wanted to get him into trouble, why didn't you just tell Mrs. Grumman that he locked you in the closet? That probably would've done it."

Jeremy shrugged. "I don't know. Dylan was talking all week about perverts and homos and what they liked to do to kids. He was kinda like obsessed on it. Said there was all these sex offenders who wanted to move into our neighborhood and do, like, bad stuff to us."

"Mmmn. So you go to your classroom and ... what?"

"Dylan told Mrs. Grumman that Hart put his hand down his pants and put his finger in his you-know-what."

Teresa Bell looked like she was going to be sick right there. She closed her eyes and swayed a little in her seat.

Matt looked evenly at the boy. "So you're telling us now that Sam Hart did not do that."

"No."

"He didn't touch you at all, is that right?"

"He did when he grabbed my arm."

"But other than that, did he touch you or Dylan?"

"No."

"Did Mr. Hart say anything of a sexual nature?"

"No," Jeremy sniffed.

Matt got up out of his miniature chair, none too gracefully; he shook out his legs and took Harvey Carle aside.

"I'm going to make a couple of calls," he said. "I want to get CPS over here and give Dylan D'Ambrosio and his folks a chance to come in."

"Sure," Carle answered. "What should I do?"

"Keep Jeremy and his mom here until I get back. And make sure he doesn't use his cell phone. I don't want him and Dylan talking to each other."

* * *

Sam moved in his methodical way around the kitchen as he constructed a celebratory batch of chocolate chip cookies. He had taken the news of Jeremy's confession as a matter of course. His innocence was a fact. The anomaly was that it took so long for everyone else to accept it. Still, he couldn't keep the cheerful bounce out of his step; even his frizzy curls bobbed happily in rhythm.

Ilene kept him company. Initially, she had been more guarded, especially after hearing about Matt's conversation with the D'Ambrosios.

"What do you mean Dylan is sticking by his story?" she asked incredulously. "Did you tell him what Jeremy said?"

"Of course. And he was given the opportunity to make his own statement. But they're claiming Jeremy's been pressured to change his story," shrugged Matt.

"*They?* You mean *Jim* D'Ambrosio. He's not going to let the boy speak for himself. He'd rather see his son a victim of sex abuse than a liar."

"Don't worry," Matt tried to put her at ease. "I've already talked with Pat Meehan. He and Lynette are going over tomorrow morning to meet with the family. They'll see right through the senior D'Ambrosio, if they haven't already."

Ilene's unease wasn't just about Dylan's refusal to recant his allegations, she was also sensing a continued edginess between Frankie and Sam. So when Roz called to invite Frankie over, Ilene welcomed the idea thinking it might be good to give them some time apart ... let the incident settle. She shuffled him off to the Wohlman household, but declined Roz's offer to stay for a glass of wine. "Everyone is talking about what Jeremy and Dylan did," Roz had said, "and here I thought only bad news travels that fast in Branford. I'm so sorry you've had to deal with all of this."

Finally, late in the afternoon, she allowed herself to relax. She offered to help Sam with the cookies, throwing in some vanilla extract as he beat the butter and sugar in a large bowl. But he quickly reprimanded her; each of the ingredients had to be precisely measured and mixed in their proper order. Sam's censure of his mother's free-style method of cooking was delivered with his usual touch of humor, which felt like sunlight flooding through the windows, erasing the dark and airless melancholy that had threatened to take over their home.

CHAPTER TWENTY-EIGHT

A SEVENTIES POP SONG played softly on a radio in the back of the mail room. Roddie Polenko whistled along, his lips pursed, yet another feature that protruded in high relief from his long, bony frame. His bulging eyes, his aquiline nose, huge adam's apple, even his arms and legs seemed to stick out from his torso as though he had been hurriedly assembled like a malnourished Mr. Potato Head. Blinking rapidly, Roddie sorted the mail into two piles on his desk: interoffice and outgoing.

A figure filled the doorway. The man was stocky and wide, and he was holding a piece of paper in his hand. Roddie eyed him closely. A day or so before, Les Dawkins had come by. He showed him a photograph and wanted to know if Roddie had seen this person near the mail room in the past week. Roddie looked at the picture of Jim D'Ambrosio and shook his head. Now, there was a man standing in the doorway; his face was in shadow, but damn if he didn't have the same body.

"I have a delivery to the District Attorney's office," said the man, stepping into the mail room.

It wasn't the guy in the photograph.

"The guard at the front told me we had to see you first," he continued and handed the mail clerk an invoice for six upholstered armchairs. "They're supposed to go in the conference room."

Roddie took the paper from his hand and read it while his mouth twitched. " I'll call up and tell them you're coming."

"Where are we supposed to go?"

"Oh, sorry. The conference room is on the third floor, in the back. Someone up there will help you. I'll show you the elevator."

He didn't bother locking the mail room door; it was just down the hall. But far enough. As soon as he left, a plain white envelope addressed to Ilene was carefully deposited on Roddie's desk on top of the outgoing stack of mail. He would have seen it and called Dawkins immediately, but while he was still helping load the chairs on to the elevator, the US Postal carrier arrived and, as was his usual procedure, swept the "outgoing" into his canvas bag. Later, in the Post Office, the envelope was thrown into the postage-required bin, and by the time it finally got to Ilene's office it was too late.

CHAPTER TWENTY-NINE

P AT MEEHAN AND Lynette shared a quick glance as Laurel D'Ambrosio ushered them into the living room, which was dominated by a large air-brushed painting of Jesus surrounded by children and lambs.

"Dylan and my husband will be down shortly," said Laurel flatly. "Can I get you something? Coffee? A glass of water?"

"Nothing for me, thanks. But I do need to use your bathroom, if I may," said Pat. He had downed his third morning cup of coffee on the way over.

Laurel pointed him to a doorway off a short hall to the kitchen. She returned to the living room to see Lynette studying a child's drawing displayed in an acrylic frame on a side table. It was simple and bold, a huge shape with a gaping mouth with sharp teeth that looked ready to gobble up a tiny stick-figure boy. The picture had energy and flow.

"This is very interesting," said Lynette.

Laurel beamed, "Dylan drew that last year. It's Jonah and the whale."

"Ah, I see. That's a scary whale."

"Do you know the story of Jonah? From the Bible?" Laurel asked.

"Vaguely," Lynette smiled in apology.

Laurel seemed unwilling to leave the topic. "Do you have a faith?"

"I'm sorry?" Lynette asked.

"Do you attend church?"

Lynette looked past Laurel at Pat Meehan, who had come back into the room and was rolling his eyes as he caught the last of their exchange. But before she could answer, footsteps sounded on the stairs, and they turned to see Jim D'Ambrosio. He strode into the circle where each one waited awkwardly for someone else to start.

Finally, Meehan cleared his throat. "Where's Dylan?"

"He'll be down in a minute."

"I know this is difficult, Mr. D'Ambrosio," Meehan started. "I guess you talked yesterday with Chief Bingham, but after what Jeremy told us, we need to—"

D'Ambrosio put his hand up to interrupt. "I think it would be best if we said a prayer first."

Meehan was taken aback, but gave a reluctant shrug. And D'Ambrosio started right in, lowering his head and intoning, "Dear Lord, bless all those who are here seeking the truth. Help us to find your light in the truth and to accept whatever comes from that light."

The CPS supervisor pulled at his bottom lip in irritation and sneaked another look at Lynette. She didn't see him; her head was bowed.

"Alright," D'Ambrosio clapped his hands together. "Let's proceed."

However, he had no intention of letting Pat Meehan or Lynette participate. As he motioned for them to take seats, he began his lecture right away.

"Listen, I don't know why you're wasting your time here," he said. "It's Jeremy Bell you ought to be talking to. Maybe the boy is embarrassed or afraid; we understand that. What these boys went through is ... is unimaginable. But I think – and it's better to get this all out on the table – that somebody got to him. Not naming names or anything, but you know that the Chief of Branford Police is the mother's boyfriend. He's been involved in this from the very beginning."

Meehan eyed him keenly. "Mr. D'Ambrosio, I appreciate that this is a hard situation for both you and your wife. But in light of what Jeremy Bell has told us, we have to get to the truth here. We won't punish your son for telling us what really happened, and I certainly hope you feel the same way."

"I'm not going to *punish* my son," D'Ambrosio was offended.

"Good," Meehan confirmed.

Further dialogue was interrupted by the sound of Dylan clomping down the stairs. All eyes turned in his direction as he entered the living room with a four-foot boa constrictor wrapped around his arm. His mother cringed, clearly unhappy that it was out of its cage.

"Dylan, put that thing back!" she cried.

With a glint in his eye, the boy headed straight for Lynette, anticipating her revulsion. But she held her ground and peered curiously at it.

"Are you afraid of snakes?" he asked, a hint of tease in his voice.

"Not really," smiled Lynette.

He thrust the boa close to her face. "You want to hold it?"

"Dylan, stop that," his mother protested. "Don't make her touch the snake."

Lynette swallowed, her mouth dry. "No, it's okay."

They managed the transfer of the boa, who began to curl its muscular body around Lynette's arm. She ran her other hand down its moist, glistening scales.

"He's beautiful," she said, appearing oddly serene with the large snake creeping up her arm.

"He likes you," Dylan said with obvious admiration.

"What's his name?"

"Isaiah."

"Like Isaiah Thomas, the basketball player?"

"No, Isaiah from the Bible."

Lynette seemed transported as she watched the boa. "'And the innocent child shall play at the hole of the asp,'" she said dreamily. "That's from Isaiah."

"What's an 'asp?'" Dylan sniggered, as though it might be something dirty.

"A snake." She straightened and worked gently to unwind the boa and hand it back to Dylan. "An asp is a poisonous snake," she said primly.

Lynette straightened her skirt, unaware that Laurel D'Ambrosio was staring at her in puzzlement.

"Have a seat, Dylan. You can keep Isaiah with you," said Meehan, noting with approval that Lynette had done a good job connecting with the boy before they began the interview. "Why don't you tell us what happened in the computer room."

Dylan petted Isaiah with great concentration. "I already told you," he said.

"You know that Jeremy said yesterday that you boys made it up because you were angry with Sam. Is that right?"

Jim D'Ambrosio stared at his son, his face a hardened mask. "No," said Dylan.

"No, Jeremy is lying to us now? Or no, the incident didn't happen the way you boys said it did?"

Dylan gave Lynette a dewy-eyed look as though she were the only friend he had in the world. But behind it was a glimmer of the same determined expression that his father wore. "Jeremy's lying," he said with a slight pout. "He's scared because of Chief Bingham – his girlfriend is Hart's mother."

Jim D'Ambrosio jumped to his feet to signal the end of the visit. "Okay, you have your answer. So I suggest you look elsewhere for the liars in the travesty of justice," he said with righteous indignation. Then he pointed Meehan and Lynette to the front door. "Good day to you."

* * *

Lynette buckled her seatbelt and waited for Meehan to start the car. He sat with the keys in his hand.

"This whole thing stinks," he said. "Put it all together – the sex offender talk around school, Jeremy, Dylan and his crazy father in that crazy house, with that hideous snake, no less…"

"Is that your *clinical* assessment?" asked Lynette with a little smile.

"Well, what do you think?" Meehan asked her.

"It's your call, Pat."

He turned the keys in the ignition. "Unfounded. Do up a report and close it out. You okay with that?"

Lynette took a last look at the D'Ambrosio home as they drove away. "Yeah, sure," she said.

CHAPTER THIRTY

T HE DIRECTOR YELLED "cut," the cameras rolled back, and the brute arc lights powered down. At least, that's how it felt to Ilene as she slipped off her shoes underneath the desk. The motions and the unanswered messages in front of her seemed blissfully mundane after the past week, and she relished the thought that they all might be getting back to a semblance of normal life. The horror movie was wrapping up.

There would be no charges pursued against Sam, and he was on his way that very morning to Hudson State to meet with Coach Boone. The job offer was back on the table, thanks to Matt's efforts. And Ilene had been warmly greeted by her staff; even Tom Squires came by to express the District Attorney's gratification that "this whole nonsense" was behind them.

"*Nonsense*? Is that how Gerry referred to it?" Ilene asked doubtfully.

Bess made a face. "The word 'shitstorm' would've been my guess, but Tom will never say, will you, Tom?"

Squires gazed at the ceiling.

"Tell Gerry I said thanks for his wholehearted support," said Ilene. "And make me sound sincere."

Before diving into her paperwork, Ilene picked up the phone and tried again to get through to CPS. She was anxious to find out when Lynette would complete the report officially identifying the claim as unfounded. She left another message and had no sooner rung off when she heard a soft knock at the door. She looked up to see Avery Flint.

"You have a minute?" he asked.

Ilene waved him in. The haggard Legal Aid attorney took a seat opposite Ilene, balancing his briefcase on his lap.

"I wanted to come by," he started, "and tell you I'm sorry I impugned your professionalism with my comment the other day about prepping Marielle. You're a good, fair prosecutor. *Tough*, but fair."

"Thank you, Avery."

"And by humbling myself as such, I wanted to see if I could re-open the conversation about the sentence. My client is very committed to treatment and counseling."

Chris Owen loomed in the back of Ilene's mind.

"He knows he's got to do jail time," Flint was saying, "but he's extremely worried about his aunt. She's got no income and can't work." Ilene listened while Avery described the older woman's health problems and his client's financial contribution to the rent and groceries.

When he finished, she asked, "What did we talk about before trial?"

Avery leaned forward eagerly. "One to three if he pled, but I'd take two to four with sex offender treatment at the Springdale facility where they have a halfway decent program."

Ilene picked up a pencil and twirled it in her fingers as she thought. "Can you get me a letter from the aunt?" she finally said. "And some kind of tax returns or other documentation to show that he's legitimately supporting her."

"Absolutely."

Ilene paused. "If I do this, you'd do well to remember that I'm still a hard-hearted, ruthless bitch in the courtroom."

"For goodness sake, Ilene!" Avery put his hand out to reassure her. "I would never not think that of you."

Ilene sniffed, "I'm not sure what you just said, but I'll take it as a compliment."

"By all means."

"I'm serious, though," said Ilene looking sternly at Flint. "If I find out your guy is not absolutely committed to sex offender counseling, I'll seek the max. Marielle Arroyo did not deserve what he did to her."

"I know. And he knows that, too. He's willing to do whatever it takes to get straightened out."

"No guarantees," Ilene finally said, "but I'll think about it."

"Thank you. Thank you very much." Avery bounded from his chair and then stopped. "Um ... I may be out of line here, but I heard about your son and the false claims and everything. I'm sorry."

Ilene nodded.

"How's he doing?" Avery asked with concern.

Ilene was speechless for a moment. In the last twenty-four hours, the relief expressed by family and friends was heartening, but Avery Flint was the only person who had asked about Sam. "I think he's going to be fine. Thanks for asking."

He acknowledged her with a lift of his briefcase and left. Ilene stared after him for a moment and then retrieved the defendant's thick file from the metal file cabinet. She found the sentencing folder and inside the front cover wrote in bold letters: *Recomm. 2-4, with sex offender treatment/Springdale.*

When she looked up, Les Dawkins was standing in front of her.

"I don't think it's connected to the letters," he said. "But I wanted to let you know before you heard somewhere else. The state police informed us this morning that a local girl has gone missing."

Ilene's heart stopped.

"But she's seventeen," he went on. "And this isn't the only time she's disappeared."

Every word of the second letter was burned into Ilene's memory: *I hear the child whimper in the night ... if the sound intrudes ... I will have to silence it. And there's only one way to do that.*

Dawkins read her mind. "The girl described in the letters is much younger. Got to be."

"Who's the missing girl?" asked Ilene.

"Her name's Tiffany Borelli. She's from Thornton River. And not likely to be voted Miss Teenage America; she's been truant several times and has a second DUI pending in the local court."

"Les, don't you think we should have gotten another letter by now?"

"What do you mean?"

"Well, the two we got came only days apart, and if we're right and whoever wrote them is someone who heard me speak in Branford, then he surely knows by now that my son was accused of being a child molester. That must have come as a huge shock when he believed that I was the person who could save him. I would have expected a reaction to the incident with Sam."

"But you *did* get another communication – that email."

"True," said Ilene uneasily. "But initially we all agreed it had a different feel to it."

"We're dealing with a *nut*, here, Ilene," Dawkins responded. "Consistency and lucidity don't come to mind. I think there's a good chance that D'Ambrosio sent all of them, but now that he's learned his kid lied about what happened, it's taken the wind out of his sails. In fact, that you haven't gotten another letter steers me even more directly to him. We're going in with the search warrant tomorrow morning. I am not going to be a bit surprised if we find that old typewriter."

Dawkins' pager went off and he asked to use Ilene's phone. She watched him as he took in the information he had been waiting for. He hung up and took a moment to fill her in.

"Okay. They traced Tiffany's cell phone to the motel on Route Four just outside of Branford," he said. "One of my investigators is over there with the manager. She came in yesterday with an older guy, and he thinks they're still shacked up. The manager described the guy as well-dressed, slicked back hair, platinum Rolex. He had to show a driver's license; name is Schatz, Jason Schatz. Apparently the two were looking ver-y cozy."

Ilene caught her breath, remembering him and his wife Mary Beth at the first school meeting about the Westerly. But Dawkins seemed not to notice; he was practically out the door.

"I'll call you," he said over his shoulder. It was clear her presence at the motel was not needed or desired.

The walls of the office seemed to close in on her, compressing the air in her lungs. Her mind was a constellation of elusive pinpoints of understanding. Imaginary lines seemed to connect them, yet constantly shifted, creating different shapes with each new thought.

Jason Schatz?! One of the more vocal advocates for shutting down the Westerly was now potentially looking at his own statutory rape charge if the girl wasn't yet seventeen. And if she did meet the age threshold, he was still in a heap of trouble. Suddenly it wasn't just Jim D'Ambrosio who had a reaction formation problem as Paradiz had described it: a mission that's the exact opposite of one's inner desire. Could Jason Schatz be the letter writer? What if Tiffany was not as consenting as Dawkins and the motel manager presumed? Ilene remembered, too, that Schatz's wife had said they'd recently moved to Branford from New York City – where Victor Troy had been murdered.

"Oh, stop it!" she chastised herself out loud. Obediently, the zigzagging lines in her thinking jammed. The notion of a serial killer was absurd, and she had rightly recognized it as a distraction from her turmoil over Sam and the crazy letters. She had let the obsession return as an excuse not to dive into the dull paperwork in front of her. Ilene donned her reading glasses and got to work. But not before Chris Owen reappeared in the montage of images that followed her everywhere – the boy splayed on the cold, hard ground, coming to, realizing the noose was gone and he was alive. What must he have felt? Remorse? Hope? The speculation was followed, of course, by the fiery blast from a .38 that put an end to it all.

* * *

Sam shook the car keys in his hand as he walked across the parking lot from the gym. Usually their jangling was an agreeable sound, the music that underscored the freedom and independence he had long awaited. But it did nothing to cheer him up today, even though he had his job back. It was the second incident with Ricky Wilkens.

It started when he stepped onto the court while the guys were warming up. Coach Boone was still in his office. Ricky spotted Sam, whispered something to one of his teammates, then pretended to be terrified, calling Sam an "ass-fucker" as he clutched his rear end and waddled down the court. The others had told Wilkens off, but not before laughing at his antics. Sam called after the attention-seeking point guard, stammering that it was all a lie, and then he got flustered and dropped his notes on the floor. He'd just made it worse, too, by telling Coach Boone what had happened. He thought he was doing the right thing seeking out an adult, but Boone had just gotten off the phone yelling at someone when Sam came into his office. Anyone else would've seen that Coach was in a bad mood and chosen another time, but Sam plowed ahead, describing what Wilkens had done.

"He's a jerk, what can I tell you?" Boone interrupted irritably. "The team knows the thing was a hoax. Let it go. I can't be running interference for you every time, Hart. You're going to have to find a way to get along with the guys on your own."

Sam unlocked his car. He had been so excited to return to the team, but Wilkens had dirtied the evening. And worse than the disappointment, he felt foolish, like he had tattled on a classmate. He took no notice of the car parked two rows behind that started up as soon as he pulled out of his spot. Nor did he see that it followed him out of the campus and stayed with him until he made the final turn onto his street. He never saw the driver's glassy eyes that stared at him with contempt. He didn't hear the bible verses that spewed like venom from the driver's lips. *Inflamed with lust … indecent acts with other men … due penalty for their perversion … wickedness … evil.*

CHAPTER THIRTY-ONE

I N THE REARVIEW mirror Matt recognized the unmarked
sedan that drew up against the curb a few yards behind him.
Les Dawkins eased himself out of the front seat and arched his
stiff lower back before he ambled toward Matt, who got out of
his own squad car.

"Hey, Les. Good to see you."

"Likewise, Bingham."

"I heard about Jason Schatz. Nothing you could charge
him with?"

"No sex-related charge," said Dawkins. "As far as the
statute goes the girl is a consenting adult. But the drinking age
is still twenty-one and there was booze in the room, so they're
going to get him for serving alcohol to an underage minor."

"Is he still in custody?" asked Matt.

"Nope, he had a lawyer show up before we even finished
interviewing him at the motel. But a couple of your boys
impounded his car, so he'll probably swing by to pick up the
wheels soon."

"Every day on this job brings something new," said Matt,
shaking his head. "Schatz was at a community meeting the
other day trying to shut down the Westerly Center because he's
afraid of *pedophiles* lurking around his children."

Dawkins nodded knowingly, "Yep, those are the ones you
gotta watch out for. Like *this* clown." He nodded in the direction of number 1408 Guilden Drive, a green-shuttered cape

with a rusted basketball hoop above the garage door and a plastic Virgin Mary guarding the small front lawn. "Thanks for helping out," he added.

"My pleasure," said Matt. "I don't mind being a thorn in D'Ambrosio's side. That photo and a drive-by he did at Ilene's shook her up pretty bad; and if he's been sending those letters to her, I want to nail the son-of-a-bitch."

"We'll see," nodded Dawkins thoughtfully. "Anyone would be upset if he thought his kid had been abused, but this guy sounds unglued."

"He is. Pat Meehan at CPS paid the family a visit earlier this morning. The son is sticking by his story, but he's got at least two different versions of it on record and Meehan is convinced he's getting big time pressure from the father. Anyway, CPS is fed up and Meehan told me he's closing the case. I guess D'Ambrosio is having a hard time with that."

Matt tapped on the squad car window and Officer Levitsky got out. He and Dawkins exchanged greetings.

"You think it's just the wife at home?" Dawkins asked the junior officer.

"Unless she's got house guests I haven't seen."

"Okay, here's what we got," said Dawkins as he pulled the search warrant from his back pocket. "We're limited to any computer and hard drive in the house or garage."

"Can we take them?" Matt asked.

"Sure. We're not spending time going through the hardware here." He handed the search warrant to Matt for review.

"Then it should be relatively quick," Levitsky noted.

"Well, that's not everything. D'Ambrosio probably used a flash key or disc to download the photo onto the library computer," Dawkins explained, "so we can search for any recording device as well. Oh, and be on the lookout for a manual Olivetti."

"What's that?" asked Levitsky.

"Oh, right," said Dawkins peering over his glasses at Joel Levitsky, "you're a digital-age guy. It's an old-fashioned typewriter – one of those things that has a keyboard, but not plugged into an outlet. Got that?"

Levitsky bounced on the balls of his feet, ready to go.

"One last thing," said Matt. "D'Ambrosio is a card-carry-ing NRA member."

"Any registered handguns?" Dawkins asked.

"Only the county-issued .45 for work," said Matt.

Dawkins narrowed his eyes at Matt. "This may be more fun than I thought."

"From what I hear, wait'll you get inside."

* * *

Laurel D'Ambrosio recognized Matt right away and she blocked the door with her body, thin and tight as a violin string.

"A warrant?" she asked, her eyes moving suspiciously from Matt to Lester Dawkins. "My son already spoke to you people. What do you need to search for?"

Dawkins proffered the document. "You're more than welcome to read it, Mrs. D'Ambrosio."

She ignored him and accused Matt directly, "You want Dylan to admit that he lied, is that it? Because of your girl-friend and her filthy son? Is that what you want?"

Dawkins jumped in. "This is not about your son," he said. "It concerns a communication sent to the District Attorney's office."

"I don't know what you're talking about," she snapped, but the color that came into her cheeks said otherwise.

"May we come in now?" asked Dawkins.

Laurel opened the door to let them in, her face a mixture of fear and fury. When she led them into the house, Dawkins looked around, clearly impressed with the home's ecclesiastical feng shui.

"I want to call my husband," said Laurel.

Dawkins responded, "Sure. And then you could make this a whole lot easier if you show us where all your computers are."

After she had done both, she perched stiffly on the arm of the living room sofa, arms crossed, and announced that she was not going to say anything or assist them further until Jim got home.

Matt let Dawkins and Levitsky conduct the search while he stayed with Laurel to wait for her husband's arrival. He was looking out the window, ignoring her silent outrage, when he got the radio call from Sergeant Blue. He stepped outside to the front porch.

"What's up, Billy?"

"Guess what? Looks like we got a double homicide on our hands. The lab came back with the comparison on the bullet retrieved from Owen and the ones from the Queenie's Mattress guy. Probably the same gun. Lab won't know if it's *definitely* the same gun until we find it and get it tested."

Matt closed his eyes. "Jesus," he whispered. He could almost feel it crawling out of the corner like a hairy tarantula – Ilene's theory that Buel and Owen were part of a pattern of murdered sex offenders.

"And another thing," Blue continued. "Did you call Steve Marks in Rockville to see if D'Ambrosio's name came up in the Buel investigation?"

"Yeah, it was a negative."

"Not so fast, Chief. Just got a call from Marks who says they ran a search through parking tickets issued to cars in a five-block radius of Queenie's the night Buel was killed. A Chevy Silverado registered to your friend James D'Ambrosio was one of them. Parking tickets – that's how they got Son of Sam. Anyhow, they issued a summons at eight-thirty-eight p.m., which puts him three streets west of the store about a half hour before the estimated time of death."

"You sure about that?"

"Yeah. Marks wants to know what the hell you have on D'Ambrosio."

Matt paused. He didn't *have* anything on D'Ambrosio – not that connected him to Travis Buel, anyway. He had just thrown a couple of darts in the dark because Ilene had a feeling that Buel and Owen were connected.

"Okay. Tell him I'm working on it and I'll call him as soon as I get back to the station."

A red pickup came squealing around the corner at that moment and jerked to a stop in the driveway. Jim D'Ambrosio threw the door open and marched up the front steps, eyes of fire focused on Matt.

"Thanks, Billy. I got it from here," said Matt before pocketing his radio.

D'Ambrosio faced off against the Chief. "What in God's name is going on?" he barked, slapping his hands on his hips.

"Good question, Mr. D'Ambrosio," Matt answered. "But why don't we take care of the search warrant first."

* * *

D'Ambrosio stood with his back to the mantel across from his wife where he could signal her if she spoke out of turn. The conflict between his desire to protect her and anger that she had already said too much was etched on his face. Right off, Matt had asked about her library card and she claimed to have gone to the library to use a computer, but then stumbled her way through a too-complicated explanation of why she had to go to the library when she had one at home. Ignoring her husband's advice to let him do the talking, she kept digging herself in deeper and deeper, just the way Dylan had. Dawkins was upstairs and Levitsky had gone out to search the garage when Matt veered his inquiry toward D'Ambrosio's whereabouts the night Buel was killed.

"Well, was your husband here with you or was he not? Which is it?" Matt was looking at Laurel.

"He was here," Laurel said evenly.

"Shut up, Lor'," interrupted D'Ambrosio. "Just ... shut up, okay?"

"I'm simply trying to understand why your wife is equivocating about where you were on the night of the seventh," said Matt.

"She's got the days confused. And besides, she doesn't owe you anything, all right?"

"Actually it's not all right. She could be charged with impeding a police investigation," Matt countered.

D'Ambrosio breathed out heavily through his nose. "Look. I'll tell you what I was doing if you leave her out of it."

Matt crossed his arms and waited.

"I drove up to Rockville to see a guy about a boat," D'Ambrosio offered. "He put an ad in the paper about selling it and I wanted to take a look."

"What's his name?"

"McPhail or McGee or something. I don't know, I wrote it down somewhere."

"Where did you write it down?"

"A slip of paper."

"Do you have it?"

"I threw it away. The boat was a piece of junk."

"Where'd he advertise?"

"First, I wanna know what's going on. Why are you asking all these questions about where I was on the seventh?"

Matt answered with another question. "Why do you think your wife was trying to cover for you?"

"Why do you think?" D'Ambrosio exploded. You people are all over my kid, accusing him of lying about being molested! And now you come into my *home* with a damn search warrant for who knows what! She's *scared*, she doesn't know what to say – that's why!"

Laurel began to cry. Matt ran a hand through his hair and held his tongue, waiting for both D'Ambrosios to compose themselves. Dawkins trooped down the stairs and carefully placed a Dell laptop next to the other two in the front hall. Then he tore off a copy of the list itemizing the computers and discs he planned to take back to his office. He handed the paper to D'Ambrosio, who snatched it from his hand.

"You won't find anything on any of those computers," he sneered. "This whole thing is a sham. When will I get my stuff back?"

"When I'm done," replied Dawkins.

Just then, Levitsky appeared and motioned Matt to follow him. He led Matt into the kitchen where he had left two cans of day-glo orange spray paint on the counter. Levitsky lifted one with a gloved hand.

"This one's just about empty, see?" He proved his point by shaking the can. "Same color as the paint used on the Westerly. I'll bet if we get it tested we'll find out it's the same brand, too."

Matt hesitated. "Pretty common in construction use and road repairs, and we can't take it because it's not in the warrant. Put it back where you found it, but make a note of the brand and color."

Levitsky looked disappointed, but then brightened. "We can take this, though," he said pointing to a shoebox next to the paint. Inside was a balled-up t-shirt which Levitsky pulled away to reveal a thick-barreled steel handgun with a wood grip.

"What's this?" mused Matt.

"It's a gun."

"I see that, Levitsky."

"One of the older Colt Super P models – a .38. I think I just recovered Mr. D'Ambrosio's stolen weapon," Levitsky grinned. "What a coincidence it should turn up in his own garage."

"Amazing." Matt stared at the piece for a moment. Given the information he had received a short time earlier from Detective Marks, he began to figure that if you throw enough darts in the dark, one of them might just hit the target. He turned and went back into the living room where Les Dawkins was suffering a more confident D'Ambrosio.

"So, arrest me, already. I'd love to sue you," he challenged Dawkins. "Name a charge, any charge. It ain't gonna stick."

"How about murder?" Matt asked.

All heads swiveled in his direction.

"I'm arresting you for the murder of Travis Buel in Rockville City on February seventh."

Dawkins' eyes widened a little, but D'Ambrosio was positively dumbfounded. He stood gaping, his jaw down by his knees.

Matt pulled out a printed Miranda card from his wallet and began reading D'Ambrosio his rights. Dawkins took a deep breath and rubbed his hands together.

"Oookaaay," he said. "I guess that about wraps things up here."

CHAPTER THIRTY- TWO

M ATT'S VOICE CAME drifting down the hall outside her office, and before she had gotten out of her seat, he blew through the door. She had been waiting all morning to learn what he and Les had found and held her breath expectantly.

"Okay," said Matt. "You were right and I was wrong."

Ilene grinned. "You didn't have to come all the way over here to tell me that – it's my working assumption."

"Very funny. We arrested Jim D'Ambrosio."

"He sent the email, didn't he?"

"Don't know yet."

"But you found the typewriter?"

"No."

"Then what?"

"We arrested him for the murder of Travis Buel," Matt said with a sly smile.

Ilene gasped, "Travis Buel! In Rockville?"

"And if the gun tests like we think it will, we're going to charge him with the murder of Chris Owen as well."

Stunned, Ilene clapped her hands over her mouth. "Tell me," she breathed.

"Well, on a whim – *your* whim, actually, I asked Rockville PD if D'Ambrosio's name had come up in their investigation. They said it hadn't, so I forgot about it. But they did a search through parking tickets around the area for the night Buel was killed, and there was our friend's red Silverado parked a few blocks from Queenie's." Matt unzipped his parka and pulled off his gloves.

"I asked him and his wife about where he was on the night of the seventh, and Mrs. D jumped on it like a lit cigar on the carpet, claiming that they were together at home," Matt continued. "He knew his wife wasn't pulling it off, so he interrupts and says, 'no, no she's confused.' Tells me he went up to Rockville to see a guy about a boat. But he can't provide a name or address, and he can't even remember where he saw the ad for the boat. And then, while we're executing the warrant, Levitsky finds the .38 Colt he reported stolen four years ago. He filed a false report so that he could use the gun without it coming back to him. I'd say that shows criminal intent."

"Is it the same weapon used on Buel?"

"We won't know for sure until it's tested which will take a day or two. But the caliber and size of gun are consistent with Buel's wounds."

"And Chris?"

"The bullets taken from Chris's and Buel's bodies match, and if they're from D'Ambrosio's gun, we've got him on both murders."

Feeling an electric charge go up her spine, Ilene grabbed a clean legal pad and began making notes.

"All right," she began, speaking quickly. "Ideally, we need to draw the link between D'Ambrosio and Chris to establish motive. I have to assume that it's his need to punish the offenders. But how did he know Chris? Through his church? If not, let's find out if he was on duty during Chris's trial. I don't remember him being there, but he could have been working any of the proceedings on the third floor. He might have seen Chris's file or heard details from one of the other court officers. Now, Buel's more problematic. What's D'Ambrosio's connection to Travis Buel?"

"He could have found Buel through the sex offender registry," Matt said.

"In the end, he might have tracked him down in Rockville that way," said Ilene shaking her head. "But look at how Buel was killed. D'Ambrosio knows too much about Buel's sex crimes, and in Chris's case, too much about his juvenile sentence."

"I've seen court officers from Westover go up to Rockville if they're shorthanded, and vice versa," Matt offered. "We're in the same judicial district."

After a pause, Ilene said bluntly, "It's not a lot to hold him on."

"There's work to do," he conceded. "But we have a few days before we have to present anything at a felony hearing; by then we should have the ballistics back."

Ilene bit the inside of her cheek, her mind racing. "The ballistics are crucial," she said.

"Yes, but not definitive. He could have another .38 someplace. We're getting a warrant for his home, vehicles and his locker at the courthouse."

"The typewriter may still show up," Ilene suggested hopefully. She was decidedly relieved about D'Ambrosio, but the authorship of the letters continued to prick at her, and she would have felt better had that mystery been solved as well.

"We think it will."

"Thanks, Chief. Is there anything I can do?"

"I'll let you know. But I've got almost everybody working on it. In fact," he said, checking his watch. "I want to see how Billy is doing on the warrant application. I'll keep you posted."

Ilene walked him to the outer office and watched him leave. The more she thought about it, the more she thought that a judge might see the arrest as premature. Matt's instincts were good and he knew the law. But if was looking for another gun, did he also have doubts about the .38 they did recover? Had he been too hasty? After all, he was protective of her and the boys, and if D'Ambrosio was a potential threat to them, Matt would err on the side of getting him off the streets. Hell, she wanted to put the creep away, too. But from a legal standpoint, they didn't yet have a triable case and even the probable cause for holding him wasn't rock solid. To make matters worse, a cynical judge might view Matt's actions as a payback for Dylan's accusations.

Anita disrupted Ilene's thoughts when she handed her a folded computer printout.

"What's this?" asked Ilene.

"It's from the NCAVC."

Ilene opened it; she had already gotten the National Center matches, hadn't she? Donning her reading glasses, she expected to see a duplicate of the search that had pulled up Troy, Middleton and the others.

This was new.

Buel, Troy and Middleton were on there, but so were about twenty other names she didn't recognize. She remembered that the national search usually took a few days longer, and as she walked back to her office, she scanned the list of convicted sex offenders who had become murder victims in other states. There was one that caught her attention immediately. It wasn't in New York, but it was close enough.

* * *

An unsolved homicide in New Jersey – a seventy-three-year-old man named Chester Gilbaugh had been strangled. The cause of death, however, was not the whole story for the convicted sex offender, nor did it hint at the grizzly details.

Ilene phoned the local police department in Gilbaugh's home town of Crawford. The desk sergeant was more than happy to talk about the case which had caused quite a stir in their little town. He told her that Grandpa Gilbaugh thought himself quite the thespian, while folks in the community generally dismissed him as a narcissistic, flamboyant nut who dyed his thick, wavy hair jet black, winked at every woman under sixty, and wore a red beret and cape in the winter.

According to Gilbaugh's wife, one afternoon in May, Chester had gotten all decked out and told her he was going to audition for the part of Leonato in *Much Ado about Nothing* at the Crawford Playhouse. When he didn't return by late evening, she phoned the police who found Gilbaugh's contorted body in the empty barn theater. No one was able to figure out why he thought they were holding auditions; the theater manager told the cops that they weren't due to open for two more weeks and *Much Ado* wasn't even one of the scheduled productions.

Gilbaugh had been garroted on the stage with only minimal signs of a struggle. Strangulation was the official cause of death. But the killer had gone further and dragged his body to the wings. There, the victim's right hand was secured in the electric winch that raised the heavy stage curtain. With one flip of the switch, the killer activated the winch which systematically pulled Gilbaugh's entire arm into the frame until it jammed.

Ilene worked to keep her voice steady when she asked the sergeant if Gilbaugh had a criminal record. He did indeed, although the sergeant couldn't give Ilene many details, just that Gilbaugh had been accused of, "puttin' his hands where he shouldn't." The victim was Gilbaugh's six-year-old granddaughter.

"As far as that goes," continued the Sergeant, moving a toothpick around his mouth. "The old son-of-a-bitch had it coming. But we're keeping the file open anyways."

"That's reassuring," commented Ilene.

"Hunh?"

"Never mind. Listen, I may have something for you in a few days."

"Okidoke. Send it down and we'll take a look-see." He couldn't have sounded less enthusiastic if Ilene had offered to share a favorite tofu recipe.

"Do you happen to know the Social Services agency that handled the sex abuse allegations?"

"The folks in Secaucus would've gotten it."

"And that would be?"

"DSS, Youth'n Family. I'll give you the number."

* * *

Ilene spent an exasperating fifteen minutes getting to the right office, but was finally patched through to Janice Pickel, a supervisor at Child Protective Services.

"A bureau chief from New York! I'm honored," Janice boomed.

"Secaucus isn't exactly out in the sticks," Ilene replied.

"I wish you'd tell that to our Governor. When it comes to funding, he must think they're gonna re-introduce the gray wolf right here on our streets."

"Ah-oo," Ilene howled softly in sympathy.

Janice chuckled. "And what can I do for you this fine day, Ms. Hart?"

"Call me Ilene, please." She expressed her interest in the Gilbaugh matter, adding only that she believed it might be related to something she was working on. Janice recalled the case.

"It was a sexual abuse?" asked Ilene.

"That it was. Lots of touching of intimate parts according to the victim. She was a sweet kid, smart. Hayley Martin."

"How did it all come about?"

"Hayley and her family used to visit the grandparents in Crawford. Then, her parents became estranged when Hayley was five. It was an ugly divorce. The girl and her older brother started staying with the Gilbaughs for longer periods while their mother was working things out."

"Did Gilbaugh deny it?"

"To the bitter end. But we got corroboration from Hayley's brother who was about nine at the time. He saw them through a window, spoke up, and that about nailed ole' Chester."

"Where is Hayley now?"

"I wish I knew. Afterwards, Mrs. Martin and the kids moved out west. I'd like to know how Hayley is doing; she'd be close to twelve now."

"You mentioned Hayley's family," Ilene said. "How did they take it?"

"As you would imagine, pretty angry. There were brothers and in-laws around for the trial. They were unhappy that he wasn't charged with a more serious felony and only got a few years of prison time. But I didn't hear anything from them after Gilbaugh went in. And he was killed shortly after his release."

"About two years ago," confirmed Ilene. She took a stab. "Does the name D'Ambrosio ring any bells? Jim or James D'Ambrosio? Could that have been one of the in-laws?"

"Oh, honey! I have trouble remembering where I put my car keys. I do remember that little girl 'cause she was a cutie-pie and because of what happened later to Gilbaugh. Names, though, are out of my range. Be happy to pull out the file for you."

"Would you be able to fax it to me?"

"Now that's a bit of a problem," Janice clucked. "We've only got two fax machines in the whole building and they're both down, par for the course around here. It'll probably take legislation to get a new one."

Ilene hesitated. Everything about the Gilbaugh case sounded like the others: a semi-ritual and gruesome killing that mirrored the sexual abuse.

"I'd be happy to have someone copy the file and send it along by mail," said Janice.

And Gilbaugh was a piece of the puzzle, Ilene was sure of it. There could be something in his file that would connect him to D'Ambrosio, and maybe to Buel, Chris and the others.

"Could get it to you by the end of the week," Janice was saying.

If she left now she could be in Secaucus in under two hours, depending on traffic. Later, she didn't recall making a conscious decision. The words just popped out of her mouth, binding her inexorably to them and fixing the nightmarish course of the next few hours.

"Thanks. I need to see it today. I'm going to drive down and get it," she said.

"Goodness! It must be awfully important."

"It is."

"You sure it can't wait? We're in for some snow I hear. They're saying anywhere between two and four inches, depending on who you listen to."

Ilene looked out her window. The sky was blue with patchy clouds. "I'll be all right," she said.

"Come on up and see me then," said Janice. "I'm on the ninth floor. And you drive careful now."

Ilene wrote down the address and within minutes, after telling Anita she was heading to Jersey and wouldn't be back, she was out the door.

CHAPTER THIRTY-THREE

JOEL LEVITSKY GAVE a cursory knock on the Chief's door and continued in without an invitation. Sergeant Blue was seated at Matt's desk minding the store.

"Hey, Billy," said Levitsky, adjusting the creaking gun belt on his lanky frame. "There's a 'briefcase' out here to see you."

"Who?" Blue snapped his head away from the computer screen.

"Don't know him. He's not from around here."

"What does he want?"

"He wants to see Matt, but I told him the Chief's not here, so he asked for whoever's in charge. I figured even though you're in here playing solitaire and picking your nose, that'd be you."

"Up yours, Levitsky."

"He's representing Jason Schatz."

"Mmmn," Blue murmured in understanding. "I'll bet I know. Did he say anything?"

"No," Levitsky said in exasperation. "He'll only talk to the person *in charge*."

Blue thought about it for a moment and then said, "All right, send him in."

Levitsky ambled out and a moment later held the door for a sleek, silver-haired man who breezed in sporting a custom-made suit and a razor smile.

"Seth Ferris," he said, handing a business card to Billy.

"Have a seat, Mr. Ferris. I'm Sergeant Blue. What can I do for you?"

"I believe you impounded my client's automobile and that it is now sitting in the parking lot out back." He produced a document from his briefcase and handed it to Billy. "Signed this morning at the Branford Court authorizing release of the car to me." He sat back confidently.

In the outer room of the station, Levitsky and Phil Gianelli were making coffee and laughing over a Bud Lite commercial that featured a talking hippo. Dave Cahone, the newest member of the force and a recent graduate of the police academy, sat at a desk outside Matt's office writing up his timesheet and straining to hear so he could join in the fun. The veteran officers like Blue and Levitsky treated him okay, but Gianelli was all over his case. He called him 'Depraved Cajones' and made him do all the drudge work when they went out on calls together, like moving the dead deer off the road. Cahone thought that if he could be funny like Levitsky, he might get a little respect. Just then the phone rang and Cahone lowered his voice to sound properly official.

"Afraid the Chief's not around at present. Can I help you?"

"My name's Bart McFee. I was asked by Laurel D'Ambrosio to call him." He sounded fairly put out by the request.

"You want me to put you through to Sergeant Blue?"

"Can't I just leave a message?"

"Sure." Cahone heard power tools in the background.

"I'm supposed to tell him that her husband was up to see me about my boat the other night."

"Okay." Cahone reached for a message slip and took down the information, but had no idea what McFee was talking about.

"At least I'm assuming it was her husband. Guy looked like a bowling pin with boots and was a real a-hole. So if that's the guy, he was here like I said."

Cahone had just finished writing *bowling pin* when McFee said, "That's it."

"Whoa, whoa," Cahone stopped him. "Gimme a number where you can be reached in case Chief Bingham needs to call back." McFee gave him a number and hung up.

Just then, the door to Matt's office swung open and Billy came out. He went over to a wall cabinet and retrieved the keys to Jason Schatz's 2009 silver Mercedes SLR. He handed them to the attorney who followed him out and said, "You're all set, Mr. Ferris."

"Oh no!" Gianelli groaned in mock grief. "Don't take it away. I just wanna be able to look at it for a couple more days."

"*Look* at it?!" Cahone hooted. "You told me you wanted to *marry* it."

Cahone's attempt at humor was met with silence. Gianelli gave him a disgusted glare and shook his head sadly. Then he turned to Ferris.

"How much somethin' like that go for?" he asked amiably.

"It's the McLaren – about four hundred ninety thousand."

"You have got to be kidding!" exclaimed Gianelli, clapping his hand to his head. "That's more than my house is worth."

"How would you know? You can only count to twenty," Levitsky chided him.

"Mr. Ferris," Sergeant Blue stopped the attorney as he went out the door, "why didn't Mr. Schatz pick up the car himself?"

Ferris hesitated, then flashed his porcelained white teeth. "All in a day's work, Sergeant."

They all watched through a window as he drove away in the Mercedes.

"Son of a gun," Levitsky finally said. "Lawyer's probably making seven, eight hundred bucks an hour – that's one expensive valet service."

Sergeant Blue shooed everyone away from the window, including Dave Cahone, who had jumped up to join the crew. "Okay boys, the excitement is over," Billy called out, his arm making windmill motions as though he was rounding up horses. "Weather Channel is predicting three-to-five for rush hour, so get your time sheets in 'cause you're all going out on the road!"

The phones started up again, and with Gianelli at his back complaining he had never said anything about wanting to *marry* the car, Cahone swept all the paperwork on his desk aside, forgetting completely about the message from Bart McFee.

CHAPTER THIRTY-FOUR

THE SKY HAD turned steel gray and the moisture rolling in from the southwest intensified every toxic smell the New Jersey Turnpike had to offer. The traffic moved well as the New York City skyline whizzed by to the east. She'd made the trip to Newark Airport a few times and had no trouble until she got off the highway. Getting to Municipal Boulevard proved more complicated than she anticipated. So did finding the parking lot entrance to the Government Center, a block-wide stone edifice seemingly with no access. Finally, she spotted an underground garage entrance, which she had driven by twice.

On the ninth floor at Youth and Family, a sleepy-eyed secretary asked her to wait, leaving Ilene time to take in the all-too-familiar leaflets strewn on the plastic tables advocating Alcoholics Anonymous, drug counseling groups, nutritional guidance for children, as well as anger management classes. Waiting with her was a young woman with a hyperactive toddler who crawled precariously on the lobby chairs under his mother's disengaged watch.

A few minutes later, the secretary sent Ilene down the hall to Janice Pickel's office. The DSS supervisor was exactly the way she sounded on the phone: large, forthright and approachable. Wearing a red flowered blouse that complimented her umber-brown complexion, she glowed.

"Hope you didn't have any trouble," she said, standing to shake Ilene's hand and offer her a seat. "Everyone drives around the neighborhood a while before they find the secret entrance to the parking lot. Is it doing anything out there yet?"

"No," said Ilene, "but soon."

Pickel glanced anxiously out her small window. "Be good if the rain held off until later tonight," she said. "The temperature drops just a couple more degrees it'll start to come down ice. I'll drive in anything but Northeast sleet. *That* makes me nervous."

Since Janice Pickel didn't look like she'd be intimidated by anything, for the first time Ilene questioned the wisdom of making the trip. Jim D'Ambrosio was safely in custody, what harm would it have been to wait another day?

"I have a copy of the Gilbaugh file here for you," said Janice handing over a thick manila envelope. "Should all be there: police reports, statements by family members, and usual department stuff."

"Did you happen to see the name D'Ambrosio in there anywhere?" Ilene had to know.

"I know you mentioned that name before, but I didn't scrutinize the file, just made sure it was in order for you. I have to run down the hall a minute if you want to take a look now."

Ilene opened the envelope and began to scan the account of Hayley Martin's visits with her grandfather, from the first hesitant call to Youth and Family Services by her mother to the post-conviction report after Gilbaugh was sentenced. The intake caseworker had recorded an interview with Hayley's brother, Tim, and then with little Hayley herself. Ilene slowed, not just to take in the facts, but to listen for what the child might not be saying. It took time and patience to elicit information from a six-year-old, but Janice had said Hayley was smart, and it came across in the transcript.

You liked coming to visit your Grandpa and Grandma? *At first.* What kinds of things did you do when you visited? *We went apple picking. And Gramma made apple pie. I helped her.* That sounds fun, I'll bet the pie was delicious. *'Cept one time we forgot the sugar and it wasn't so good. But then we put ice cream on it so I liked it.* Oh, yeah, I love ice cream with pie.

The interviewer, undoubtedly a woman who would be less threatening to Hayley, had done her job well, interspersing casual, non-threatening questions to keep the conversation from becoming too painful for the child, but at the same time bringing out details that added credibility to her account.

Do you remember the first time he touched you in that way? *I don't know.* Where were you and your grandpa then? *In the playhouse.* That he built for you? *Unhunh.* I bet that was a neat playhouse. *Yeah, it had real windows and curtains.* Wow! Where was it? *In back near the garage.* Could anybody go in there? *No, just me and Grandpa.* So it was kind of a special place for you?

Ilene read on – the statement by Tim about how he had gone looking for Hayley one afternoon and heard whimpering coming from the little wooden shack. He peeked in the window and saw Grandpa Gilbaugh cooing to his granddaughter with his hand underneath her clothing. There were investigative reports from the District Attorney's office corroborating the times that Hayley and her brother had visited the Gilbaughs, interviews with Jane Martin about her bitter divorce and the need to deposit the children someplace "safe," and statements by Jane's two sisters about the behavioral changes they had noticed in Hayley after the abuse began. They were furious with their father. But neither one was married to a D'Ambrosio. His name appeared nowhere in the file, and Hayley Martin's case seemed devoid of any police or court connection to Westover County.

When Janice returned, Ilene rubbed her eyes and tried to shrug off her disappointment. It was not lost on the supervisor.

"Didn't find what you were looking for?" she suggested sympathetically.

"Not really," admitted Ilene, "but I'll give it a closer read this evening."

Knowing her mission was finished, if unfulfilled, Ilene's thoughts turned to her return trip and home. "Do you mind if I make a quick phone call?" she asked.

"Go right ahead," said Janice offering her the landline. "Just hit '9' to get a line out."

Sam picked up before the answering machine.

"Oh, hi," said Ilene surprised. "I thought you'd be at prac-tice. I was going to leave a message."

Pause. "I decided not to go today."

"Why not?"

"It's no big deal," Sam answered woodenly.

"Okay. Listen, I'll probably be a little late tonight. Frankie is at Kevin's."

"I know. When will you get home?"

"I'm not sure, it depends on the weather. But if I'm not there before dinner, why don't you order pizza for all of us?"

There was silence on the line while Sam contemplated the idea. She could hear him breathing.

"I'll make dinner," he finally said.

"You don't have to."

"I'll make a chicken dish from *The Joy of Cooking.*"

"I don't think we have any chicken," Ilene said guardedly.

"Yes we do. We have frozen chicken in the freezer – pardon the redundancy."

"Well, do you have the other ingredients that you need?"

"I haven't picked a recipe yet. I don't know," said Sam with an uncharacteristic edge to his voice.

Ilene rubbed the tension from her forehead. Why hadn't he gone to practice? Was he coming down with something?

"Are you feeling okay?" she asked.

"Yeah, I'm fine."

She glanced over to see Janice holding back a smile. "I'll see you later, Sam," she said, and hung up.

"Sounds like someone has a mind of his own," said Janice, her eyes twinkling.

"Yes, a singular mind," agreed Ilene. "My oldest son has Asperger Syndrome."

"I have a nephew with Aspergers," Janice offered. "He wasn't diagnosed until he was an adult so he's had some diffi-culties. But he's doing well now."

Ilene met Janice's eyes. "That's good," she said.

"Let me ask you something," Janice leaned back in her chair. "What was so important that you came all the way down here today?"

"There's a case out of Westover County that I thought might have some connection." Since she was about to leave, there seemed no point in telling her more.

"To Hayley?" Janice asked, nonplussed.

Ilene hesitated. "I thought maybe to the grandfather. But I think I'm mistaken."

"Well, I wish you luck," said Janice heartily.

"Thanks."

Ilene gathered her belongings slowly. "The really young ones are hard to take," she said.

Janice nodded sadly. "Yes."

"Well, I have to say your caseworker seems to have done a great job with Hayley. You're lucky to have her."

"Not so lucky. Lynette left us a couple of years ago."

Ilene stopped breathing. "Lynette?" she repeated.

"She wasn't with us long, but she was good."

Ilene thumbed quickly to the last page of the interview with Hayley and scanned the bottom of the page where it was date and time stamped. Next to the imprint were the initials "LK".

"We have a Lynette at CPS in Westover County," she said looking up at Janice. "Lynette Kulik."

Janice's eyes widened. "I wondered where she went."

CHAPTER THIRTY-FIVE

THE LIGHT CHANGED and Janice proceeded cautiously through the intersection.

A cold drizzle beading on the windshield of her car fragmented the flickering neon signs in downtown Secaucus. Pedestrians along the way stepped quickly, hunching their shoulders to keep the freezing rain off the back of their necks.

"I hope I'm wrong about this," said Ilene.

"Honey, I hope so too." Janice looked somber.

Lynette's personnel file lay on the seat between them, the letter loose on top, held down only by the edge of Ilene's coat. She picked up the pink stationery, read it for the umpteeenth time, and put it back down.

"Her job is to work with abused kids," Ilene rationalized. "She can't be the only Social Services employee to transfer or move."

"True."

"And I don't see any connection to Jessica Lane, the little girl Travis Buel abused. She was up in Rockville County, not Westover."

"Who was the intake worker in Rockville?"

"A woman by the name of Sandra Sheinbaum. I know her, but not well. I see her at the occasional conference or seminar."

"Where Lynette would see her as well?" asked Janice.

Ilene nodded in recognition, "Sure."

"No inter-office confidentiality I'm aware of. Heck, your Jessica Lane could have been a case study."

Janice spun the steering wheel to the left to avoid a van that had pulled out of a parking space without warning. "Lord, get me outta this neighborhood without some jackass hittin' my car! Sorry," she held up her hand, "I don't normally curse."

Ilene looked at her incredulously. "Jackass?"

"I'm raised a Baptist," said Janice, her only explanation.

"When all is said and done," said Ilene chewing on a fingernail, "Jim D'Ambrosio is logical for this. He lied about his gun, he lied about being in Rockville the night Buel was shot. And he's a pathological, religious zealot obsessed with satanizing sex offenders."

"You're probably right," said Janice tersely. "Maybe we should just turn around, forget the whole thing."

"No, I'm sorry."

"Relax. We don't know anything yet."

Ilene tried, but she was tight as a drum. Early on, when she suspected a pattern in the murders of Chris and Travis Buel, and then in the killings of Troy and Middleton, she thought they might be motivated by a need to punish their sex crimes beyond what the law and the courts could do. But she also sensed the children were in there, too, dictating the killer's choice of target. After all, there were hundreds of registered sex offenders in the states' databases. Why were these men targeted? The ritualistic motive throbbed in the background, but couldn't be detected by separate police investigations. Not unless you looked at them together. For all the reasons she had just laid out to Janice, D'Ambrosio was logical. But his arrest, rather than wrapping up the cases in a neat package seemed to scatter them in disarray, because no matter how she bent and worked the facts, Ilene couldn't find his connection to the *children*. Even for psychopaths, there still had to be a motive.

Now, here was someone who had actually interviewed three of the young victims: Heather McColl, David Mullen, and Hayley Martin. Interviewed them, been drawn into their pain and their sense of betrayal. Here, too, was someone who had access to the accounts of the other abuse victims, perhaps even the files themselves, in Rockville and Grandin Falls through collegial association with fellow CPS workers. Yet, the idea was unfathomable.

Janice drove purposefully, her eyes glued to the road, her mouth set. After a moment, she said, "It makes me think…"

"What?" Ilene's stomach clenched.

Taking a deep breath, Janice proceeded, "When Lynette first interviewed, I was impressed. She came with solid recommendations from her last position in Baltimore or Philly, wherever she had done her Bachelors in Social Work, and she aced the New Jersey licensing exam. At the time, we had just lost two of our best caseworkers; one got pregnant, the other just gave up. We were strapped, the entire crew overloaded. Lynette turned out to be a hard worker. She took on more and more cases without letting her paperwork slide. But I began to notice things.

"To be honest with you, I thought it had less to do with *her* than the environment in our office. You see, I began weekly meetings for all the caseworkers, kind of informal get-togethers where we'd share all the craziness we see every day. Sittin' around the table, we laugh and cry, complain or toot our own horns, anything goes. My boss said it was too new-age, touchy-feely, but I insisted – still do. Anyway, Lynette never caught on to our sessions. You'd expect some discomfort initially, but she was still … awkward after a few months. Actually, *awkward* is the wrong word. She was *studied*. I could see her trying to relate to some of the others, but the way she'd express things … I don't know, her emotion seemed pasted on. I didn't look on it badly at the time because some people aren't comfortable with their own feelings."

"She is pretty reserved, at least with adults," Ilene posited. "But she does let her hair down with the children; her instincts are great and they really open up to her."

"They do," conceded Janice.

"Why did Lynette leave?"

"I don't know," Janice shook her head. "Just gave her notice one day and I wished her the best. Of course, everything I just told you is Monday morning quarterbacking. Like I said,

I recall seeing the letter, but didn't give it much weight. Who had the resources to go firing people because they had some quirks?" Janice gave Ilene a hard, honest stare. "Hey, she was good with kids and she didn't let the system get to her."

"Can't ask for more than that."

"I could. But I'd never get it."

Each woman became lost in her own thoughts as the windshield wipers ticked off the seconds and minutes. The letter on pink stationary kept drawing them forward.

* * *

The Secaucus landscape began to change. The fenced-in yards between row houses grew wider and a few young trees sprung up in their allotted squares of dirt along the sidewalks. Still, it wasn't Branford, no Wall Street commuters and Pilates moms here. These homeowners worked in the New Jersey factories and struggled to keep their small, local businesses alive. On Ferry Street, Janice slowed and squinted at the house numbers painted on the mailboxes. She stopped in front of number thirty-four, a pint-sized version of all the other houses but with a conspicuous lack of decorative touches, bikes, hoops or swing sets.

When Ilene and Janice stepped out into the frigid rain, the slats on a pair of Venetian blinds in an upstairs window parted. Janice shouldered her enormous pocketbook and led the way up the front steps. She gave a series of sharp raps on the front door, but they drew no response. She tried again.

"Was she going to meet us here?" Ilene asked, peering around the side of the house.

Janice frowned and prepared to knock once more when the door opened a crack. A slight, elderly woman stood eyeing them suspiciously. She had thin, white hair with a bluish tinge and pinched features made more severe by her sour expression.

"Mrs. Plant? Helene Plant?" Janice inquired.

"Yes," she answered slowly.

"We're from Social Services. I spoke to you about an hour ago," Janice reminded her.

The woman examined Janice first and then Ilene, taking her time; she knew who they were. She took a crumpled handkerchief from her sweater pocket and carefully wiped a bit of yellow crust from the corner of her mouth.

"It took you long enough," she said acidly.

Janice paused and then asked patiently, "May we come in, Mrs. Plant? We're getting awfully wet."

Lynette Kulik's old babysitter made no move to widen the door, but she stepped aside allowing Janice and Ilene to enter.

* * *

"We tried for many years," explained Mrs. Plant, even though neither Ilene nor Janice had inquired. "And I did get pregnant twice, but miscarried both times. Lawrence was working at Dow Chemical which is what finally did the poor man in; he died of kidney failure before he could retire. Of course, I wanted to donate one of my own, but it wasn't a good match."

Ilene's mass of auburn curls was nearly dry and she had finally warmed up. Helene Plant, however, hadn't yet de-iced. As soon as she ushered them into the starched living room, she made it clear that hospitality was not on the agenda. She stood stiffly by the doily-covered arm of the sofa, consciously positioned above her seated guests, hands clenched at her waist, yet incongruously poured out personal – and unbidden – details of her life story. Ilene and Janice listened as patiently as they could, both recognizing that Helene was a woman whose life had been one episode of helplessness after another. Now she jumped on any opportunity to assert some control. Speaking slowly, she seemed almost to enjoy the discomfort and restlessness building in her guests.

Janice coughed. "Tell us about Lynette, Mrs. Plant."

"Of course," she said after a pause. "You both must be very busy and I'm sure have better things to do with your time."

Ilene wanted to shake the old woman.

"The Kuliks lived down the street," Helene continued. "Leila Kulik was a decent sort, but always in poor health. She smoked like a chimney and died when Lynette was around eight. That was when Mr. Kulik hired me to look after the children. I was to be at the house when Lynette came home from school, and I usually made dinner and then left as soon as he came back from work. He had a machine shop on Route 19, about a mile past the old tire factory. I rarely sat for Lynette in the evenings because by that time her older brother had generally turned up from wherever he was gallivanting after school. Lynette was a raggedy, little thing, who–"

"Mrs. Plant," Ilene implored, "you wrote a letter saying that Lynette was ill-suited for a position at DSS because of her past. What did you mean by that?"

The small woman pressed her blanched lips together disapprovingly. "That was a long time ago."

"But you recall writing the letter?"

"Certainly I recall." She fussed with her fragile coiffure and mused primly, "Interesting you're in such a hurry now."

"What is that supposed to mean?" questioned Janice.

"You didn't concern yourself at the time."

"We did contact you, Mrs. Plant. According to Lynette's file, someone from Human Resources called you, but you refused to clarify your letter over the phone."

"I thought your organization should do its own investigation," Helene said.

"Lynette's background check was clean and her references excellent. How could we investigate further if you wouldn't tell us what you meant?"

"It was never my intention to share details about the child, certainly not in a telephone conversation. I thought that after you read the letter you would speak to Lynette directly and she might tell you."

Sighing deeply, Janice said, "Well, she did not."

"I really don't know if it's my place."

Janice had had enough. It was getting late and the roads were sure to turn treacherous. She went on the offensive. "Ma'am," she said, pushing herself to her feet, "I don't have time for this. If you have information to share about Lynette

Kulik, do it now." She picked up her coat and thrust an arm into the sleeve.

Helene's upper body seemed to collapse and she stared forlornly at the carpet. Her visitors got to the door before she asked softly, "Can I make you ladies some tea?"

CHAPTER THIRTY-SIX

S AM SQUEEZED HIS eyes closed in concentration, having a tough time with the words. The formula itself was easy:

$$\text{Stops} = \text{STL} + \text{BLK} + \text{FMwt} \times (1\text{-}1.07 \times \text{DOR\%}) + \text{DREB} \times (1\text{-FMwt})$$

Steals, blocks, and defensive rebounds were analyzed to determine a portion of the approximate stops each player contributes. That much Coach Boone could understand. What Sam had to do was explain to him how the difficulty of forcing a missed shot compared to the difficulty of getting a defensive rebound followed the same logic as the offensive rebounding weight. Without Coach fully grasping the concept, he couldn't move on to the next stage.

Pushing the pages of notes away from him, Sam became aware of a sound like tiny beads spilling to the floor. He looked out the window into the twilight and finally registered that the noise was coming from icy rain spattering against the glass. He decided to go downstairs to prepare the dinner he had promised. It was good being in the house alone, the emptiness was comforting in a way, a space he could navigate all on his own terms without any miscommunication.

At the bottom of the stairs, another sound halted him in his tracks. He listened, but it had stopped. He was about to take another step when he heard it again. What was that? Suddenly, being by himself didn't feel so good. The house was cold down here, and he couldn't identify the sound or where it was coming from. It stopped, then started up again. A kind of buzzing. Now he tracked it to the living room. Cautiously, he shuffled over to the sofa where he located Frankie's cell phone stuffed between the cushions. The phone whirred with news of an incoming text message. Sam bit the inside of his cheek. It wasn't right to look at other people's messages, but it might give him a clue about what was on Frankie's mind.

Ever since the fight over the Monopoly dice, his brother hadn't been the same. At first Sam thought it was because he had gotten hurt. Frankie told him to forget about it, no big deal. But it was a big deal. He seemed to look at him differently, and he stopped joking around; he wouldn't watch Knicks games together like they used to, analyzing how they would have set up the defense and who should come off the bench. Frankie was like a boat drifting away; and the harder Sam tried to pull it back to the dock, the farther it disappeared into the mist. Sam missed him – it was lonely without his brother.

Sam picked up the phone and read the screen. The message was from Frankie's friend, Eric. *Cant come ovr – Mom sez b/c yr perv bro.* Sam stared at the phone. Because of your pervert brother. So that's what it was. It didn't matter what Mr. Meehan or his mother said; it didn't matter that Jeremy admitted they lied. Frankie and his friends, Ricky Wilkens, and probably a lot of people still thought he was a sex offender. The thought made an ache in his chest that was as bad as any sharp sound. Finally, he tossed the phone back on the couch and headed into the kitchen to make dinner.

As Sam rolled up his sleeves, the lights flickered and dimmed. The brownout lasted just a few seconds before the electricity came back on and started the refrigerator humming again. Unfazed, he retrieved the chicken from the freezer and set it in a dish of warm water to defrost. Then he trooped back up to his room to take another stab at how to explain approximate stops. When he got into his room, he shut the door, more to keep out the accusatory buzz of Frankie's cell phone than anything else.

* * *

The three women were crowded around a small table in the kitchen. Helene had put out her good china and a plate of stale Fig Newtons on the plastic checkered tablecloth, but no one touched them.

"Vashni was…" Helene struggled for the right word and spooned another sugar into her cup, "…a bad man."

Who?" Ilene asked, confused.

"Her father. Vashni Kulik."

"He's European?"

"Vashni?" She looked surprised. "No, he was from Kentucky. Vashni is a Biblical name, a son of Samuel. He came from a strict religious family," she explained. "They used to follow the Pentecostal practice of handling poisonous snakes. He made the children go to some of those sessions. Lynette was terrified, but also fascinated by the whole thing."

Ilene winced, and her feeling of dread deepened. She had heard of the dangerous snake handling ritual but thought that even among the most ardent practitioners, children would be discouraged from attending.

"What else?" she asked.

"To many people, Vashni came across as virtuous and hard-working. He made the most out of being a single father, always talking about how much he sacrificed for his children and how he wanted to give them the kind of life he never had. But in private," Helene lowered her eyes, "he hit her, he hit them both. I only saw him do it a couple times, but they often had bruises."

"He physically abused his children?" Janice glowered.

"That was the least of it," sighed Helene.

Ilene and Janice looked at one another, sharing the sinking feeling about where she was headed. The ticking of the kitchen clock punctuated the silence. Janice nodded, and the old woman seemed to take it as permission to continue. "You have to understand," she said defensively, "the real Vashni was a violent man, overpowering. And the drinking made it worse. He came very close to striking me once. I was afraid of him. I didn't want to leave her there, but what was I supposed to do?"

Leaning forward with a dark intensity, Ilene demanded, "Tell us about the *sexual* abuse."

"I don't know for a fact," backtracked Helene.

"I think you do," Ilene insisted.

The elderly woman's eyes fluttered around the kitchen, but unable to escape Ilene's fierce gaze, she capitulated.

"I used to find things he left in her room: a jacket, a belt, a pair of boxers one time. I convinced myself it was just laundry that Lynette hadn't put away. But one day when she was about twelve, I had forgotten some medicine that I needed and I went back later that night to get it. Vashni was coming out of her room. I didn't say anything, of course, but I knew what he was doing. He fired me the next day. About a week later I went to see Lynette at school and I asked if her daddy was hurting her." Helene's voice shook. "She wouldn't say. I begged her to come with me to tell someone. But she said Ray would protect her."

"Ray?"

"Her brother."

"How old was he?"

"Seventeen, I suppose."

"And did he?" Janice spoke up.

"Did he what?"

"Did he *protect* her?"

She shook her head sadly. "He was a big boy and fought with his father all the time, but—"

"Go on," Ilene pushed.

What Helene Plant said next was delivered to an invisible spot on the window behind their heads as if her painful memories might seep through the glass and be washed away by the streaming rain. "Vashni got liver cancer, and he was in and out of the hospital. I thought with him not home as much, Lynette would be okay. But one afternoon, I came home to find her curled up in a ball by my back door. Ray had an accident in the machine shop, she told me. He slipped trying to cut a board and his arm went under the circular saw. It got cut off at the elbow. He went into shock and was unable to call for help. He bled to death."

Ilene and Janice stared at her.

"And Lynette was there?" asked Ilene, horrified. "What happened? Who found them?"

"No one found Ray until later."

Ilene tried to piece together what she had just heard.

Helene continued, "Lynette was quoting the Bible to me, scripture from Matthew, which her father made her learn word by word. Where it says that anyone who looks at a woman with 'lust in his heart' has already committed adultery."

"And 'If your right hand causes you to sin," Janice finished grimly, "cut it off and throw it away; it is better to lose one of your members than for your whole body to go into hell.'"

Helene nodded.

"My God!" Ilene exclaimed, suddenly understanding. "Her brother was sexually abusing her, too."

The obvious and sickening thought that followed hung like a bitter stench in the air: *what if Lynette hadn't just watched her brother bleed to death, but had, in fact, pushed him under the saw?*

"What did you do?" prodded Janice.

"What could I do? The poor child was in shock – there was blood all over her clothing. I cleaned her up and told her not to say anything."

"You didn't call the police?" Janice asked in astonishment.

Helene lifted her chin in defiance. "Why would I? The girl had been through enough hell. She should be punished further? Vashni was dying, and what with Ray doing dirty things to her it was a blessing he was dead, too."

"What happened to Lynette?"

"Right after Ray died, Vashni went into the hospital and never came out. She moved in with one of his relatives until she finished high school, and I didn't see her much after that. When I did, she seemed fine. In fact, I heard she did well in school and gave no one any trouble."

Ilene could scarcely believe her ears. "How could you think she was *fine*? She was brutalized by her father – then sexually abused by the brother she thought would *protect* her!"

Helene shrank before Ilene's anger, and Janice put out a restraining hand. "If you thought she was fine," she asked more evenly, "what prompted you to send us the letter?"

"When I heard she was applying for a position at your agency, I ... I thought working with abused children was probably not the right profession for her," said Helene.

"Not the right *profession?*" Ilene was aghast.

Dr. Paradiz's words came back to her with deafening clarity. *There's another profile – a severely damaged person, quite likely as a result of being sexually abused and physically mistreated in childhood – someone who kills in order to regain power in a world where even the people she loved savaged her.* Especially *the people she loved.*

How about *serial killer* as a profession?! Ilene nearly screamed. Lynette's victims suddenly crowded the small living room: Chester Gilbaugh – doting grandpa; Travis Buel – surrogate father; Niles Middleton – respected Christian leader; Victor Troy – supportive coach. All were in unique positions of trust. Even Chris Owen who, in Heather's naïve mind, offered her the chance to escape her father's inappropriate attachment. To Lynette, all had betrayed the children they were supposed to protect – like Ray.

"I have to go," Ilene stammered. "I have to get back."

"What has she done?" Helene asked fearfully.

Ilene briefly covered the old woman's ice-cold hand with her own. "I don't have time to explain now," she said. "You've been very helpful, thank you." She jumped up and ran into the living room where she had left her coat and bag, her mind reeling. It wasn't Jim D'Ambrosio. He may have done some despicable things, but he didn't kill Chris or Buel, or any of the others.

Behind her, Janice promised Helene she would be back, omitting the likelihood that she'd be bringing the police with her. Then she hurriedly donned her coat, snatched up her belongings, and ran after Ilene.

* * *

Oh my God! Sam!

In her haste to call home, Ilene's fingers fumbled the buttons on her cell phone, but finally got through. The ringing, however, went on and on, repeating its indifferent pattern until the answering machine picked up. *Hi, you've reached the Harts. No one is around to answer your call right now, but–*

"Sam? Are you there?" Ilene tried to keep her voice even. "If you're there, please pick up." Nothing. "Okay, listen. I need you to do me a favor. Just make sure all the doors are locked and don't let anyone in. Do you understand? No one. I'll be home in about an hour and a half. If you get this message, call me on my cell."

Janice jammed her key into the ignition and pulled away from the curb. The rain was coming down harder now, icy droplets sounding against the windshield. She risked a quick glance at Ilene.

"What's going on? Why are you so worried about your son?" she asked.

"Sammy," Ilene breathed.

"Is it Lynette? I don't understand."

Ilene closed her eyes and pressed the back of her head against the headrest. "Sam was accused of fondling two boys in the elementary school," she said. On the way to the Plant residence she had told Janice about Jim D'Ambrosio and his arrest, but whether she thought Janice wouldn't understand, or she still carried a sense of shame about the incident, Ilene had said nothing about the accusations against Sam. Now she poured out everything. "She knows where we live," she finally said.

"Why would she go after Sam?" countered Janice. "She's got a retraction from one of the kids; the claim is unfounded. She's probably doing up a final report as we speak."

Ilene flipped open her phone, dialed the main number for Westover Department of Social Services and asked for Lynette. She was put on hold. Fifteen seconds later, Lynette answered.

"Lynette, hi. It's Ilene Hart." She looked over at Janice who nodded encouragement.

"Hi, Ilene. How are you?"

"Fine … uh, fine. Listen, do you…" Ilene suddenly realized she hadn't prepared anything to say, "…do you have the deposition, uh, the one Dawena Fischer gave the other day?"

There was silence for a moment. Ilene felt her heart thudding against her chest. God, she'd almost flubbed that; could Lynette hear her heart over the phone?

"Fischer? I'm pretty sure I do, why?"

"I've looked all over my office and I can't find my copy. I want to review it before I see Judge Sanderson."

"You want me to email it over to you? I'll probably be here for another two or three hours."

"Staying late again?"

"What else is new?"

Ilene withheld an audible sigh of relief.

"I'll get it over to you ASAP. Give me a call to let me know you got it."

"Well, with the weather and all, I'm going home in a little bit."

"Okay. I'll tell you what, I'm meeting Bess tomorrow around lunchtime, I'll just bring a hard copy with me. Oh, and by the way, I'll have that report on Sam for you soon. I'm so sorry about all this."

"Thanks, Lynette. I appreciate it."

Fearful she had sounded false on the phone, a rush of heat flooded Ilene's chest and face as she ended the call. But she tried to reassure herself. Lynette said she'd be at her desk for at least two more hours, and she had sounded relaxed, normal – as if that was a word that remotely applied to the woman Ilene was now sure had murdered several people.

"What did she say?" Janice asked.

"She's doing the report on Sam."

"Good. Okay, good."

For the next few miles neither Ilene nor Janice said anything. Each was re-living encounters they had with Lynette, peering into the hazy past to recall moments when she might have exposed her pathology. *Was it there all the time and I missed it?* Ilene railed at herself, knowing she had noticed some peculiarities – awkwardness around adults, her dull and often unreadable affect – yet had brushed them aside because they shared an emotional bond with abused children. It was something Ilene was coming to understand, that this type of entanglement could go too far. Indeed, in Lynette's twisted psyche her identification with sexually abused children had turned her into a killer.

Ilene picked up Lynette's personnel file which lay on the seat beside her. While Janice drove, she flipped through the glowing supervisory reports and the letters of recommendation from her previous job. She got to Lynette's application for a position at Youth and Family and her heart stopped. Always neat and concerned with presentation, Lynette had typed her application. Name, date of birth, education, previous experience:

Four years at Department of Social Services in Princeton, NJ, working with unwed mothers...

The line swam before Ilene's eyes – the plain typewriter font with a malfunctioning "s".

"Oh my God," she breathed.

"What is it?" Janice asked.

"Please ... hurry."

The meaning of the mysterious letters and their cries for help began to take shape. There was no child being held captive. No child except in the writer's imagination. The horrendous violence done to her as a little girl had split her in two. She was the author *and* she was the wounded, terrified child she heard in another room, another part of her mind. Her last letter had said: *when I hear the child whimper in the night I refuse to believe it is real. But the sound is getting louder ... I will have to silence it. And there's only one way to do that.* Killing the offender silenced the whimpering. But clearly, the relief didn't last.

Ilene said a little prayer that the imaginary child would remain quiet for a little while longer.

CHAPTER THIRTY-SEVEN

LYNETTE PUT THE receiver down and pressed her palms into her eyes until she began to see red. Pethen began his slow ascent up the curve of her back. She stiffened, feeling his flicking, forked tongue tickle the hairs at the base of her neck. Usually she didn't mind his touch, but now she needed to concentrate. She reached around, took the snake by its head and dropped it beside her; its oily, meaty body made a small thud on the office floor before slithering underneath the credenza. The telephone jangled again. Lynette shook herself and willed the identity back over her face and into her voice.

"Lynette Kulik, how may I help you?"

"This is Judy Bromberg over in Family Court. The judge wanted to see if you could reschedule the Fischer hearing for next Tuesday. Apparently, the girl has chicken pox and has to stay in bed for a few days."

"Poor thing," said Lynette. "I hope she's okay. Let me take a look." She flipped through her desk calendar and saw an opening for the date mentioned. "Judy? Next Tuesday is fine, what time?"

Lynette wrote down the appointment in her careful handwriting. When she hung up, she sat staring at the notation and thought, *Has Ilene forgotten? Dawena Fischer was transferred to Family Court – the case isn't before Judge Sanderson anymore.* Lynette's eyes narrowed as she lifted the telephone receiver again and punched in the number for Special Prosecutions.

"Hello, Anita. It's Lynette Kulik, I was hoping to catch Ilene before she leaves."

"She's in New Jersey. I doubt she'll come back. And anyway, I just heard they're closing all county offices. Now they're saying we could get up to eight inches tonight. I'm surprised you're still there."

"Oh." Lynette saw movement under the credenza. "I thought she just called me from the office."

"No. She left before lunch. I haven't heard from her. I'll leave her a message, though."

"Why, thank you, Anita."

"No problem. Drive careful now."

Lynette clutched the edge of her desk for support. She knew it! Ilene Hart wasn't really calling about Dawena Fischer, that was a deception. Otherwise, she would never mistake which court her cases were in. And she'd called from New Jersey. New Jersey? Did she *know* something? The sickly smell of cheap vodka inevitably followed by the heavy scent of diesel oil crashed over her and dragged her into its undertow. She felt the rough, sweaty hands paw at her chest. And then she heard her father's voice coming from underneath the credenza. He was still alive in Pethen's hissed warnings. *That she-devil lied to you! You simple-minded fool – how could you think that Judas witch was going to save you?*

A knock at the door as it opened. "Hey, Lynette," said a co-worker. "They're closing all County offices. We can go home. Hallelujah!"

Lynette's outside self was slipping; she called it her "identity," the face she worked so hard to control and present to the world. From underneath the credenza, Pethen cautioned her to look in the direction of the co-worker's face and smile. He was always there to guide her.

"Listen, you and I are the last ones. If you stay, will you make sure the office is locked up before you leave?"

"Of course," replied Lynette mechanically.

"See you tomorrow, then. Get home safely."

The door shut in the nick of time. Lynette broke out in a sweat and felt her identity become unglued and slip silently to the floor. The sound of a crying child came from somewhere down the hall and she felt her body begin to crumple. Pethen lifted his tail and admonished, *Don't listen to that girl. She cries because she is weak and dirty, the way she entices men. You are strong, do what you must to silence her.* Lynette watched the snake weave its upper body back and forth and found herself swaying in rhythm, a calming dance. When she felt ready, she moved slowly to the coat closet where she stood in front of the mirror mounted on the inside of the door. She watched herself pull her thick brown sweater over her head followed by the yellow linen blouse; the skirt and nylon slip came next. She folded the garments and placed them on an upper shelf. Then she reached for her other clothes: the light blue stretch top that showed every contour, the tight jeans, the shiny, heeled boots. Harlot's clothing. It's what men liked.

The snake watched with hungry, glittering eyes.

*   *   *

Red brake lights ahead winked on and off as though connected to a widescreen circuit board; traffic had slowed to a crawl. After Janice dropped her off at her car, Ilene made decent headway up the turnpike until she neared the toll for the George Washington Bridge. The sleet had turned to snow. At this rate it would take her twenty minutes just to get across the bridge and another forty-five to Branford. She kept repeating to herself Janice's assurances: Lynette was working on the report that would establish that the charges against Sam were without foundation, and she was staying late at the office. Surely, Ilene would be home in time to contact the authorities.

The traffic was maddening. Ilene looked over her shoulder and seeing a slight opening, tried to ease her way into the next lane. Off to the right was a shortcut that would bypass most of the red sea ahead of her, but no one was giving an inch as the testy, frustrated commuters bucked forward. Undeterred, Ilene muscled her way across two lanes and turned on the radio to see what other traffic problems lay ahead. The weather, of course, was the story.

What have we got, Bob? Is this going to be the BIG one that takes us all by surprise or will it move through quickly? Well, Sally, the storm is certainly making for a nasty commute. That's because there's a low pressure system that's bringing in moisture from...

Just then a bright thought dawned, tuning out the chirping newscasters. The weather was a blessing, actually! Sam *hated* snow. When he was little, he used to call snowflakes "knife-feathers." In order to get him the short distance from the front door to the school bus she had to bundle him from head to toe so that not a single flake could reach him. He certainly wouldn't leave the house in this weather.

Right you are, Sally. With anywhere from four to eight inches expected, there are problems everywhere. Let's go to the bridges and tunnels...

Come on, people. Come on.

So far, there are only minor delays reported at the airports, but check your airlines for possible cancellations...

Ilene's right foot began to cramp from having to maintain a light, ready touch on the accelerator and the brake.

...and of course, a number of state and county government offices have closed up early. Here's a list that just came in: the five boroughs, Westover, Rockland and Nassau. There are a couple of major accidents to report, including an overturned tanker on six-eight-four...

Westover County?

That meant DSS and Child Protective Services. The knot of fear already present in Ilene's gut twisted on itself. If CPS was closed, where was Lynette? With one hand, Ilene fumbled for her cell phone and frantically punched in her home number. *Come on, Sam, pick up!* But he didn't.

Just then, Ilene saw her chance. She cut across the last lane and then gunned the car up the exit ramp. A Lincoln Navigator with the same idea came within an inch of her rear bumper and had to slam on his brakes. Behind him, drivers leaned on their horns and cursed them both. At the top of the ramp, Ilene made a left, then a quick right onto a side street that ran parallel to the highway. Seconds later, she entered the bridge traffic again, with only fifty yards to go. Then, she was through the toll and on her way.

Not for the first time, Sam's unnatural distaste for telephones exasperated her. Weren't they supposed to be a lifeline for teenagers? Not for Sam. He insisted they gave him headaches and didn't even own a cell phone. With one hand on the wheel, Ilene thumbed the number for the Branford Police station where Dave Cahone was by himself, fielding calls.

"Dave, it's Ilene Hart. Listen, I'm worried about my son at home. Could you send a car over to check and see that he's there? He should be, but he's not picking up."

"Is he in some kind of trouble?"

"I'm sure he's home," she sidestepped, unwilling to take the time trying to explain the whole situation to the junior officer. "I mean, he has to be, and I'd just feel much better if I knew."

"You say you know he's home. Um, maybe try him again," he offered hesitantly. "He could be in the bathroom or something."

"I will. But I'd really appreciate it if you could get someone over there."

The station radio squawked and Cahone left her hanging as he responded.

"Where's the Chief?" Ilene demanded when he came back on the line.

"An oil tanker flipped on 684; he's over at the site with the State Police."

"I need to reach him as soon as possible, okay?" She was working to keep her voice controlled. "When do you think you could get someone over to my house?"

"Is this an emergency? 'Cause we really don't have anyone to spare." Cahone was getting frustrated. "They're all on the road dealing with accidents."

"There must be somebody," implored Ilene.

Cahone rolled his eyes. They didn't have the manpower to babysit anyone right now, but she was the Chief's prosecutor girlfriend and he was still too new to know whom he could or could not piss off.

"I'll see what I can do," he said. "Give me the address."

* * *

Cahone dabbed at the sweat on his upper lip. He'd been in difficult situations during training, but handling the pressure of competing demands on a small police department on a night like this – forget it. He picked up the radio mike. "This is Bravo Thirty-Two to Unit Four, I need you get over to…" He searched on the desk for the slip of paper on which he had scratched Ilene's address.

"Shit, Cahone," the radio squealed impatiently. "We just got over to the Toyota on Post Road."

"Leave it. I need you to–"

"No way, Dave, we got our hands full here. There are kids in the car and there's a power line down. Find someone else."

"Got it. Unit Three, where are you?"

The telephone was ringing again. Some woman had gotten stuck in her Mercedes trying to make it up her winding, gated driveway. She whined that she didn't have the proper footwear to trudge a quarter of a mile in the snow, at which point Cahone assured her not to worry, he'd have a squad car there before morning. The woman tartly reminded him that she was a tax-payer, but he had already hung up.

"Unit Three, do you copy?"

Not answering. They were probably out of the car.

"This is Bravo Thirty-Two to Unit One. Chief, are you there?"

There was only crackling through the small speaker. Where the hell was everybody?

CHAPTER THIRTY-EIGHT

REFLECTED IN THE mirror, she was a different person – taller, full of confidence, and quite attractive, although anyone else would've thought her make-up too heavy, giving her a doll-like appearance. After going over her lips one more time, she pulled the bobby pins from her chignon and shook out her hair so it fell softly on her shoulders. There! She wasn't a little girl anymore; she was grown up and pretty. The snake at her ankles squirmed in anticipation.

Lynette took down a red handbag from the top shelf of the closet and reached inside for the .38 Smith and Wesson. She checked that it held the full five rounds, not that she would need them. The gun had been Vashni's "insurance," the only possession of her father's she had kept. During one of his hospital stays, she scoured his room and found the gun. She knew better than to try hiding it in the house, so she buried it by the rusted chain link fence in the backyard. As expected, when he came home he accused Ray and beat him with a belt to get him to confess. Her brother had a pretty good idea who had taken it, but never said a word. Later, Pethen encouraged her to make use of the Smith and Wesson, and she came to love how perfectly it fit into her hand. The steel didn't feel cold at all; it was warm and pulsed like a living thing.

She went to her office door and looked out. The floor was deserted and the hallway dark. She returned to her desk to prepare herself, allowing Pethen to whisper the words she was to say. *This will be easy*, he soothed.

When she was ready, she dialed the number. It rang and rang, until finally– "Sam? Hi, this is Lynette Kulik from CPS. Child Protective Services. I talked with you the other day."

"I remember." He sounded out of breath.

"Have you been running?"

"Yes. I ran down the stairs. But I was coming down anyway to make chicken."

"Oh. Well, as you know, the charges against you are being dropped. I'm sure you're very relieved." Sam was silent. "So am I," Lynette continued. "Is your mother around?"

"No."

"Do you know when she'll be back?"

"No. She said it depends on the weather."

"The reason I'm calling is that there is some paperwork I need you to sign to make sure that the matter is legally ended. I wondered if I could meet with you this evening to do that."

"Meet where?"

"Well, the thing is, the affidavit is in my briefcase which I left at the elementary school earlier today. But I remembered that you worked there and I thought you might know how to get in."

"Why were you at school? It's closed this week."

"Closed," Lynette repeated. "Yes. I was at a special meeting."

"I don't work there anymore."

"But you could get us inside?"

"I know the code."

"Terrific."

"But I don't want to leave right now. It's snowing. And I'm about to start cooking."

"I'm sure that could wait. We really should try to get it done today. There's a deadline, you see."

A long pause. "I don't know," he finally said.

"Well, it's up to you." Lynette kept her voice light. But her frustration was beginning to build. The others were not like this – they never questioned her, not once. Chester Gilbaugh, arrogant and ridiculous; she only had to tell him he was certain to get the part if he came to the theater. And the two-faced church leader was more than happy to meet with her privately for some legal advice; the dumpster was the perfect place for a piece of trash like that. Chris Owen was more difficult, but she had gotten her chance after all.

Chris's probation updates noted that he went to a tutor each Tuesday at 7:30 p.m. The plan was to intercept him on the way, tell him she was having car trouble and ask for a lift. She would bring him somewhere out of the way and then in his car, where he used to do it to Heather – that's where she would *do it* to him. But that night, he didn't go into town, he turned the other way and drove to the park. Turning off her headlights, she followed at a distance. He pulled up to the pool house and got out, carrying something in his hands. She left her own car underneath a stand of trees at the entrance and went after him on foot, staying in the shadows. His failed attempt at suicide unfolded before her; and she watched curiously, without emotion. When it appeared he would not try again, she went back to her car, and cradling the gun in her lap, drove up to meet him. As Pethen would remind her, planning was useful, but the ability to improvise if necessary was equally important.

"Is this the *report*?" Sam was asking.

"Report?"

"My mother told me you were going to issue an 'unfounded' report. Is that what you're going to file?"

Lynette heard eagerness in his voice. "Exactly," she replied.

"So I could get that report tonight?"

"You certainly can, Sam."

Lynette kept her eyes focused on the blank computer screen in front of her while he seemed to be thinking it through. He wouldn't be pushed.

"All right," he finally said. "Should I come to the school?"

"No. Meet me in the parking lot at the Town House, next to the soccer field, so we can go over a few things first."

"Okay, when?"

"The sooner the better. How about in thirty minutes?"

"Okay."

"Can I count on you, Sam?"

"Yes," he said.

"One more thing," Lynette said sweetly. "I feel embarrassed about leaving my briefcase at the school, I'd appreciate it if you wouldn't tell anybody about this."

Silence at the other end.

"Did you hear what I said?"

"I heard you."

Lynette put the receiver down gently and became aware of a new sensation filling her body, unsettling and disturbing. She remained still, trying to examine its source. As a child she would lie immobile in this way after he was finished, waiting for the pain to subside. But this wasn't physical pain. This was different. She was unsure for the first time. He was guilty, wasn't he? Of course he was. Children don't lie about sexual abuse; they are too innocent to lie about something as foreign and terrifying as sex. Yet Sam was rather like a child himself, and hadn't one of the boys confessed to making it up? Lynette heard the familiar mewling child trying to suppress her cries. Was it coming from her own throat? There it was again. She pressed her hands against her temples squeezing the doubt away.

* * *

Sam hung up the phone in the front hall and looked uneasily in the direction of the kitchen where his chicken waited, flanked by the row of spices he had set up. Frankie would call it bad timing. But there was nothing Sam could do about that. He had a deadline. Strange word – how could lines die when they weren't alive to begin with? Of course, what it meant was you have to do something by a certain time whether you want to or not. It made him uncomfortable to have his plans unexpectedly derailed, but this was important. He went straight to the hall closet for his gloves and winter coat. Buttoning up, he peeked out the front door and watched with dismay as big, fat snowflakes drifted through the halos of light at each lamppost. All those little icicles ready to fly in his face.

He almost changed his mind, but remembered that the lady from Child Protective Services would be waiting for him outside the Town Hall. If he didn't show up, he'd miss the deadline. He wasn't sure what the consequences might be, but he wasn't prepared to take the risk, not when he could get the report tonight – now. It was supposed to be over, but the stench of the accusations lingered. Ricky Wilkens' antics yesterday still hurt. More important, Sam wanted his brother back.

At once, Sam brightened with a grand idea – he'd bring Frankie to the meeting where he'd see firsthand that the charges were bogus. Ms. Kulik could hand him that report herself. Sam was so pleased with this scheme that he forgot about writing a note for his mom or checking the answering machine in the kitchen to see if there were any messages. He tugged his winter hat down over his ears, jangled his car keys, and ready to brave the knife-feathers, he headed out.

CHAPTER THIRTY-NINE

T HE CLATTER OF dishes and crackle of logs in the fireplace were comforting. So was the news Roz just heard on the radio: the police and fire department had cleared the overturned oil truck on Route 684; Terry would be home soon. She took the roast out of the oven and poked a fork into one of the potatoes. Letting the pan cool for a moment, Roz wandered into the living room and pressed her head against the picture window. In the yard, a shadow moved against the snow piling up underneath the old swing set and drew her eye to a dog that loped off into the swirling flakes. Its gait was raw and feral, and she realized it wasn't a dog at all, but a coyote. The second one this week. They were getting bolder, coming close to the house, and she made a mental note to tell Kevin and Terry not to let the cat out.

Then Roz spotted the tire tracks in the driveway. Thinking her husband had just pulled in, she went into the mud room and peeked into the garage. It was empty. The tracks looked fresh enough, it must have been someone turning around. Roz poured herself a second glass of Chardonnay and called the boys from the basement. They had to be hungry by now.

Just then, the lights flickered and went out, as they often did in Branford during a storm. Roz crossed her fingers, hoping it would be brief. But the house remained dark and eerily silent. She sighed and made her way back into the mud room for the stash of candles and hurricane lamps; Terry could set up the generator when he got home. One set of footsteps trudged up the basement stairs.

"The power's out," Kevin keenly observed.

"Just in time to give your X-Box eyes a break," his mother commented. He and Frankie had been down in the game room most of the afternoon. "Don't run the water or flush the toilet until Dad sets up the generator. Where's Frankie?"

"He left." Kevin went to the sink and ran his hands under the faucet before wiping them on his jeans.

"What do you mean, he *left*?" his mother asked, then added irritably, "I asked you not to run the water, the pump runs on electricity."

"Sam picked him up."

Roz frowned as she lit another lamp. "How come I didn't see him?"

"He came in downstairs. You were up here."

"Oh." That explained the tire tracks to the basement entrance.

"Sam hates the snow," said Kevin.

"Yes, that's right."

After setting candles on the table, Roz took out a knife and carved a few slices of the roast. "It seems odd that Sam would go out on a night like this," she commented, serving up the meat and vegetables.

Kevin shrugged and tore into his dinner.

Roz sat and sipped her Chardonnay. "Oh well, I guess Ilene is late and asked Sam to pick up Frankie before the roads got too bad."

"No," Kevin said with his mouth full. "Sam said they were meeting someone who was going to prove to Frankie once and for all that he is innocent."

That explanation seemed perfectly satisfactory to Kevin who continued to chew contentedly. But not to his mother.

"I don't understand," she said. "Sam *is* innocent. Jeremy and Dylan made up the whole thing. Doesn't Frankie know that?"

"Yeah, but…"

"But what?"

"I don't know."

She slapped her hand on the table. "Kevin! What has Frankie been saying to you?"

The twelve-year-old huffed and rolled his eyes, but finally relented. "His mother works to protect kids who get, you know, sexually abused, right?"

"Yes. She's a prosecutor."

"Well, she says that kids who say that happened to them don't lie."

"Probably not often, Kev. But obviously some kids do lie, like Jeremy and Dylan.

Kevin countered, "But his mom said, 'Why would a kid make stuff like that up? They don't even know about sex.'"

"I'm sure Ilene was speaking in general terms."

"In what?"

"It's complicated, honey. What I'm concerned about is where they're going, and why tonight? Does Ilene know?"

He shrugged.

"Who were they going to meet?"

"I don't know!" He was getting fed up with his mother's interrogation.

"Kev, I don't think Frankie's mom knows about this. It's important! Who were they going to meet?"

He shoved his chair back and headed for his room. "I don't *know*, Mom! Just some lady who came to their house to talk to Sam. It's not my fault! Sam picks up Frankie all the time. How was I supposed to know?"

Roz was worried. If the woman had come to the house, Ilene surely knew her. But it was unlikely that she would let Sam take the car in this weather, especially with Frankie. Who was this woman? And more troubling, how was she going to explain to her friend that she let Frankie slip out of the house without her knowing? Roz swallowed half the glass of wine to steel herself and reached for the phone.

* * *

Ilene's car slid the last few feet and the right front wheel rode up on the curb. Before the engine was off, she was out and racing toward the darkened house. She flung open the front door and called out Sam's name. The peculiar stillness inside told her he was gone, but she threw down her bag and bolted upstairs, darting into each of the unlit rooms and willing him to be in one of them. *No, no, no,* a voice kept crying inside. *It's impossible, he would not go out in this weather!*

But so much had happened to him in the past few days. And every time she thought she understood her children, every time she thought she had them pegged, they changed and went in a new direction. Sam wanted more responsibility, more independence; he wanted the Hudson State job so much, he was trying to prove himself to earn her blessing. Since he had told her he would cook tonight, he might well have braved the snow if he was missing some ingredients. Surely, in her shock over finding out about Lynette, she was overdramatizing the danger. His abuse case was different from the others. He was innocent, and Lynette knew that. She knew Dylan and Jeremy had lied. She *knew* that.

The harder Ilene tried to convince herself, the more insistently the letters intruded. I was some sort of savior for her, Ilene thought. *What in God's name did she think when she learned Sam was my son? What might she do to him to punish me?* All her instincts told her that Sam hadn't ventured out for something as trivial as bread crumbs or garlic – something important had drawn him from the house.

She felt her way back to the kitchen, where she retrieved a flashlight. Throwing the beam around, she saw a half-defrosted chicken on the counter. She checked the phone which worked. But without power, the answering machine was lifeless; even if Sam had called to leave a message, she wouldn't know.

No note.

Blue and red strobe lights bounced off the walls; a Branford PD squad car was pulling up in front of the house. Ilene darted to the front door in time to see Matt trudging up the walk. He stamped his boots free of snow and stepped into the hall.

"You okay?" he asked Ilene. "Dave said you had a situation at home. What's going on?"

Ilene didn't know where to begin. "Sam's gone," she blurted out, "and it's not D'Ambrosio. It's Lynette."

"What are you talking about?"

"I found something that I thought could tie D'Ambrosio to the other murders, so I went to Secaucus to follow a lead," Ilene said hurriedly.

"New Jersey?" Matt wasn't following, so she tried to slow down.

"Another sex offender was murdered in New Jersey and I thought D'Ambrosio might be involved. But I learned that before she came to Westover, Lynette worked at Social Services there. And we went to see a woman who used to take care of her." Ilene put her head in her hands. "Lynette was viciously abused by her father and her brother, and I think she killed her brother."

"But why would you think–"

"Chief, she wrote the letters!" Ilene cried. "Lynette sent them. Her application for Youth and Family was typed on the same typewriter, there is no doubt. She's psychotic."

Matt's face darkened as he took in her information. "You're telling me D'Ambrosio is innocent?"

Ilene nodded. "She's the link; she worked with each of the kids, in New Jersey and here in Westover. I'll tell you every-thing, but right now, I'm worried about Sam. I don't know where he is."

Just then, the telephone rang.

"Sam?" she picked up breathlessly.

Pause. "It's me, Roz."

"Oh, God, Roz. I'm sorry, something's come up and I totally forgot about Frankie," Ilene rushed. "Do me a favor and hang on to him a while longer. Sam's missing and I have to find him, I just hate that he's out somewhere in this storm–"

"Ilene, Frankie's not here," her friend interrupted. "Sam came to pick him up. I … I assumed you were running late and asked him to."

"No, I didn't," Ilene cried. "When did he pick up Frankie?"

"I guess it was about twenty minutes ago. I didn't see them."

Ilene stood frozen. *What?* Why would Sam get Frankie without telling her?

"...and Sam told Kevin that they were meeting a woman," Roz was saying. "Apparently someone you know, but I was concerned because it had something to do with proving Sam's innocence."

Understanding slammed into her and Ilene's legs gave way as she nearly collapsed to the floor.

Oh my God! She's got them!

Paralyzed with fear, everything around her disappeared. She could only hear a high thin wail in the distance, which she finally recognized was her own voice keening. She clutched the countertop for support.

"What did he say?!" she croaked.

"Ilene?" Roz's voice trembled.

"What did Sam *say* about where he was going?" she screamed.

"Oh, God!" cried Roz.

"Where are they going?"

"I don't know. Sam said some woman–"

"*Where?*" Ilene cut her off sharply.

"I don't know," Roz began to wail. "Sam only told Kevin they were meeting her. What is it? Who is she?"

"I can't talk now. If the boys come back, lock your doors and call the police!"

"Ilene, honey, I'm so sorry–"

Ilene dropped the phone on the counter, sobbing and gasping for air.

The next thing she knew, Matt was gripping her shoulders, steadying her. She felt like she was teetering on a high, narrow ledge and that if she looked down, all she would see were the broken bodies of her two sons and a blackness from which she would never escape. She felt Matt trying to pull her back and she struggled to raise her eyes.

"She's got Sam," she managed to say. "I don't know how she got him out of the house, but he went to Roz's and picked up Frankie. Now she's got them both!"

"When?"

"About twenty minutes ago."

"Could they come back here?" Matt asked.

She shook her head. "Roz said Sam was going to meet her, but he didn't say where. Lynette's tricked him and she's taken them someplace where she…" her voice broke, "…she has to kill Sam."

Ilene burst into tears, but rather than comfort her Matt shook her by the shoulders. "Stop. I need your help. Sam took his car." He pulled out his radio. "It's a Volvo, right? What's the plate number?"

Ilene pressed her hands to her eyes. "NCD … I don't know, there's a nine in there. The car's registered to me."

Matt stepped away to raise headquarters. Speaking into the radio with heightened urgency, he told Cahone to pull everyone off traffic duty and contact the state troopers. Stranded cars would have to wait. "I want an APB on a green Volvo, you'll get the tag from a registration on…" He spelled out Ilene's name and address. "Also, get an address from DMV for a Lynette Kulik. I'll wait." He turned to Ilene. "What do you know about her?" he coaxed. "What kind of car does she drive?"

Wracking her brain, Ilene tried to picture Lynette's car the day she had come to the house, allegedly to pick up Sam's medical records, but perhaps only to find out where they lived. "It's a wagon of some sort, dark blue I think," she said.

A moment later, Cahone had confirmation. Lynette drove a blue Subaru Outback and lived down-county near the government offices. Matt told Cahone to contact the local police to check out the residence and add her vehicle to the APB.

Finally he said, "Cahone, alert everyone that we have an immediate hostage situation." He went on to describe Lynette briefly, adding that she was holding two male victims and should be considered armed and extremely dangerous.

For a moment Ilene felt a glimmer of hope that Matt was taking charge and galvanizing a police presence. But as he related information about Sam and then of Frankie – *twelve-year-old boy, brown hair, blue eyes, five-two* – she came close to losing what was left of her composure as their physical descriptions were replaced by her own treasured images: Sam's look of deep concentration as his fingers moved rapidly over the computer keyboard, Frankie's goofy smile and his pre-teen bravado. She sagged against the counter.

"What else?" Matt asked Ilene.

She shook her head, feeling panic overwhelm her attempt to think. "The *place*," she said. "She's taken them somewhere that has meaning to her." Ilene clenched her fists, trying to squeeze some sanity into her body. "It's part of the punishment."

Matt narrowed his eyes, uncomprehending.

"The killings follow a pattern connected to the abuse committed by the sex offender. A kind of righteous retribution for their sins – and she's playing God. So it's important to her how it's done, and where. This guy in New Jersey, he loved the theater and was murdered at the Crawford Playhouse. And the coach – she went after him in a park where kids play sports."

Even as she tried to make sense of it, something didn't feel right, but she knew that the place was part of the ritual. It sounded like a reasonable theory, and the only one she had.

"Maybe the idea is to get the offender somewhere he's most comfortable or a place he has always loved. And *then*, take it away from him – forever."

Ilene and Matt made eye contact and then said at the same time, "*Basketball.*"

"We'll try Hudson State," said Matt, striding toward the door.

Ilene grabbed her keys and followed. "Anywhere that has a gym! Branford Elementary, the high school, I'll try the courts at the park, and the Boys and Girls Club in Branford. That's where Sam and Frankie go sometimes."

"No. You stay here," insisted Matt. "They might come back."

"She won't bring them here," Ilene said. "And we need as many people looking for them as possible."

Unable to disagree, he relented. "If you think you've spotted them, don't try to do anything on your own, call for backup." With that, Matt wheeled and was out the door.

* * *

The snow had finally stopped falling. But even on the streets where the plows had come through, the wheels of Ilene's car had trouble catching on the slippery pavement. She was suddenly overcome with anger, but not at Lynette – at Sam. *How dumb could you be, Sammy. How could you believe her story? So easily deceived, so clueless! And you think you can be out on your own! If anything happens to Frankie I will never, ever forgive you. If anything happens to you...* Each angry thought was an intolerable dagger to her heart. *Why would you go get Frankie? She doesn't want Frankie. It's you she's after. What did she tell you?* Then she understood. Sam is so worried that Frankie doesn't believe him, and Lynette has told him she has the report. He wants it to show Frankie. Jesus, the very thing that he believes will draw Frankie back into his life might get them both killed.

Ilene passed Branford Elementary where two police cruisers were parked, one of them with the driver's door open. She slowed to see if they had found anything, but seeing no signs of activity, she sped up. There was no sense in duplicating search efforts; no time for emotion. Every minute wasted could mean a minute too late. At the bottom of the next hill, she pulled into the empty lot of the town park and stopped short of the gravel road that snaked around the back of the pool house. She threw open the door and ran towards the basketball courts.

Snow soaked into her heels and the cold bit at her stockinged legs as she tore up the path next to the baseball field. The pristine drifts beneath her feet suggested that no one had come this way, but she had to find out. Ilene reached the chain link fence, winded, with tiny icicles glittering in her hair. She circled the fence, crying out the boys' names. But there was no answer, only the oaks groaning in the wind.

Moments later, she pitched down the hill, stumbling and flailing her arms. She jumped into the car where her frigid fingers could barely turn the ignition key. The tires screamed against the ice.

CHAPTER FORTY

LYNETTE SAT RIGID, feeling Pethen's cold, heavy body draped around her neck and shoulders. Her breath came out in smoky puffs that frosted the windshield. Suddenly the snake contracted, warning her. He was coming.

Sam pulled his car slowly into the parking area behind the Town House, his headlights glancing off the snow-covered cars in the lot. When she saw his tall, mop-haired figure at the wheel, Lynette loosened. He had come at her request, and she was in control. She flashed her lights and he drew in between her and the Meals-on-Wheels van at the back. Lynette swung her legs out the way she thought a movie star might and walked over. Sam rolled down his window a few inches.

"Hi," said Lynette. "Thanks for coming."

He said nothing, busy trying to make sense of the change in her appearance. He recognized her, but was confused about why she looked like a TV game show assistant, her skin painted with make-up and a fake smile frozen on her face.

"Would it be okay if I got in?" Lynette asked. Wearing only a light jacket that she had purposely left open, she coyly wrapped her arms around herself to mime how cold it was.

Sam nodded, and she glided around the front of the car and slipped in next to him. Sensing they weren't alone, she whipped her head around and saw Frankie in the rear seat, pressed against the door.

"What is *he* doing here?" she asked in alarm.

"I wanted him to come so he can see for himself that I'm innocent," Sam explained somberly.

Frankie let out a guttural sigh. "I believe you, Sam. I told you already."

"No, you don't."

"I *do*."

Sam squeezed his eyes closed and rocked slightly. "That's what you *say*, Frankie. But I can tell that you're angry at me."

"Sam. Frankie. It's okay," said Lynette in her most reassuring voice. She turned around to look at the scowling Frankie. "Sam is right. He is absolutely *innocent*." The word left a bitter taste in her mouth.

"Do you believe me now?" asked Sam.

Frankie stared out the window, chewing on his lower lip to try keep the tears at bay. After a moment he looked down and whispered, "I'm sorry. Deep down, I knew you didn't do it, but some of my friends … they're just jerks."

Sam's chin lifted. "It's okay, buddy. That's why we're going to get the unfounded report, so you can show it to them."

Frankie caught Lynette staring at a spot on the seat next to him. "What are you looking at?" he asked her.

"We should probably go, don't you think?" said Lynette.

"Go where?" Frankie demanded.

"She left her briefcase at school," Sam explained dolefully.

"School is *closed*," Frankie exclaimed.

"I can get in, I know the code."

"Let's go, then," said Lynette.

"We're going to get into big trouble, Sam," warned Frankie, but with an edge of excitement in his voice.

"No you won't. Not as long as I'm with you," Lynette said. She gauged Sam's expression. He appeared torn, and she could feel his enthusiasm waning. He didn't seem to be responding to her new look the way she expected, and the brother had complicated things. If he escaped now, Pethen would be angry.

Risking a new tack, she said, "Maybe Frankie's right. We can do this another time. Naturally, I'll have to re-do the affidavit and because there's so much red tape it'll take a few weeks. But, there's no rush."

A few weeks? The idea was unbearable. "Let's go," said Sam. He glanced at Frankie in the rear view mirror. "You can stay in the car if you want."

Frankie shook his head emphatically. "Unh-unh, I'm coming with you." This was actually turning out to be quite an adventure.

Lynette looked at them both. "We'll walk," she announced. "We're so close and there's no point in going all the way around to the front."

She made it sound spur of the moment, but she had chosen this spot carefully. The Town House backed up to the chain link fence bordering Branford Elementary's soccer field, and it was only a short walk across the field to the rear entrance. Their cars would have been spotted right away in the school's open parking lot. Here, behind the Town House they weren't visible from the road, and why would anyone look? Oh, they'd find Sam's car later, but she'd be long gone.

Sam looked anxiously at the white landscape, but Frankie and Lynette were already out of the car. Caught up in the moment, he followed.

An arctic front was pushing the snowstorm out to sea and a lucent moon flitted from behind the clouds. The wind blew mounds of powdery snow into mini-twisters that swirled into his ears and eyes; even with a hat and scarf covering his face, Sam was miserable. These weren't knife-feathers. They were a barrage of a thousand needle pricks. But driven by the need to get Frankie the report, he pushed in front of them and led the way along the fence's path.

As they approached the back entrance, Frankie spotted the red and blue bubble lights of two police cruisers at the front of the building. He grabbed Sam's arm and pulled him against the brick wall, out of sight.

"Shit!" he cried dramatically. "Cops! We are so busted."

Lynette held her breath.

"If we get caught," Frankie added, "I'm gonna say you forced me."

Fighting off the sensory assault of the bitter wind, Sam eased his way along the wall to the corner where he risked a look around.

"They're leaving," he said to Frankie.

The cruiser doors slammed and the sirens gave a short whoop-whoop announcing Branford PD's departure, Joel Levitsky in one car and Phil Gianelli in the other. Their lights sprayed across the soccer field as they made the turn, and then they were gone. Sam was already punching in the code at the door. Lynette was at his back, and Frankie tumbled in behind her. Just inside the door, the battery-operated key pad flashed; Sam tugged off his gloves and tapped out the secondary code to keep the alarm from going off. He flipped the light switch next to the key pad, but nothing happened. He tried again.

"I think the power's out," he said.

They stood in a huddle, the melting snow on their coats and boots dripping onto the slick linoleum floor. Lynette could feel the boys' breath on her face, and for a heart-stopping moment, it smelled sweet to her, almost pure. She remembered standing close to Niles Middleton and nearly recoiling at the foul, putrid odor of his rotting soul. Looking at the boys now she didn't feel sorry about having to kill them; they meant nothing more to her than paper dolls. But the retribution had to be righteous. She wasn't the kind of person who went around killing just *anybody*. She was too close to God to make human mistakes. The boy was guilty, wasn't he?

Pethen brushed against her ankle and began to wind forcefully down the hall, calling out. *The course is set. You have no more choice than a leaf in the wind.* Lynette had felt that was true all her life. Still, she balked. Suddenly, the serpent wheeled, turning into a gigantic hooded cobra that came lunging out of the darkness. *He is guilty!* he spat. *Now!*

Frankie poked his brother at the wide-eyed look on Lynette's face. When she found them both staring at her, she took a deep breath.

"Come along, boys," she said and started down the hall.

* * *

Maneuvering down Haven Street past Branford Elementary, Ilene's haunted eyes flashed from side to side, looking for the Volvo, Lynette's Subaru, or any sign of the boys. In her rear view mirror she saw the two cruisers at the elementary school pull out of the main entrance and split into different directions. She headed for the center of town, toward the high school and middle school campus – where Frankie would go next year. A sob rose in her throat as she pictured him striding confidently into his sixth grade classroom. Was it possible that would never happen? She tried to keep her energy focused on finding them, but doubts threatened to crush her.

As she neared the campus, she saw a cluster of police vehicles haphazardly parked in the circular driveway. She raced to the scene and bolted from the car. Matt spotted her and stepped forward to catch her before she careened into the knot of Branford officers comparing notes with two state troopers.

"They're not in there, Ilene," he said. "We looked everywhere."

"The elementary school?"

"Levitsky and Gianelli just left. They searched the place from top to bottom."

"The university?"

"No. But we've got officers all over Hudson State in case they show up. I promise we'll find them."

Without another word, Ilene whirled around. She threw her car into reverse and backed on to Haven Street before gunning toward Branford. Matt stared after her feeling hopelessly inadequate. They were doing everything they could; he had all his people on the road as well as a half dozen troopers, many of them staying on for a third shift. But it was now almost an hour since Sam had been lured out of the house, and he wasn't sure he could keep his promise.

* * *

They moved slowly as their eyes adjusted to the dark. The air inside was damp and chilly, and their wet shoes squeaked against the floor. Beyond the open doors of the classrooms, little chairs were lined up like soldiers, illuminated by the moon's reflection drifting through the windows. They passed Frankie's third grade homeroom where he had learned about aborigines with Mrs. McClernan. All the kids had to make masks out of papier-mache. This year's class had done the same project, and the masks displayed along the wall leered crazily out of the shadows. The vision of being hailed a hero by his friends for breaking into school over winter vacation had faded, and Frankie was beginning to wish he had stayed at Kevin's house.

"I want to go home," he said to Sam, his voice wobbling in spite of himself.

"As soon as we get it," Sam responded.

But there was hesitancy in his voice, as well. The weather had distracted him from a feeling that he couldn't readily identify. Now, finally away from the knife feathers, he began to recognize what it was. Fear. This was wrong. *She* was wrong, with her painted lips, unnatural smile and mothball scent in her clothes. And her eyes. All his life, people tried to get him to make "eye contact." They kept telling him how important it was, that he could learn about what others were feeling and thinking by looking in their eyes. But it made him uncomfortable, sometimes painfully so. Not because he couldn't read what was there, but because he read too much and it was overwhelming. As early as kindergarten, he saw in his teacher's strained look the effort it took to be patient and pleasant, to cover up her frustration with him – a deluge of information while he was struggling to learn his ABC's. Better to focus on her ear which was silent. It was sometimes a burden to see in his mother's face all the things she wanted for him, all the ways she ached for him. Confusing, too – the conflict between her tender smile and the emotions that poured from her tired eyes. Frankie was the easiest to make "eye contact" with because he only had one thing on his mind at a time. Or he did until the last few days when distrust and embarrassment dulled his features.

Facing him now was this woman who had eyes that screamed out misery, fear, and falsity. He could see it plain as day, but he didn't know what to do. He had never been in this situation before; he had no roadmap, no strategies. His hands began to flap nervously against his damp jeans. A step ahead of him, Lynette turned to see what was making the sound. The atmosphere in the hallway was suddenly charged, the space between them ionized. She couldn't risk that they'd turn and run down the hall. She reached into her handbag for the gun.

"Up to the computer lab," she said, pointing the barrel at Sam's head.

Frankie gasped, and Lynette flicked her wrist to point the gun at him.

"Shut up," she said. Her voice sounded deeper, raspier.

In stunned silence, the boys stood rooted until Lynette stepped behind them and forced them to move. They turned onto an adjoining corridor, past Frankie's fifth grade classroom on one side and the cafeteria on the other, then up the east stairs to the computer lab. Sam's heart beat frantically in his chest, making it even harder to think. He couldn't comprehend what it was this woman wanted or why she had a gun. But he knew they were in a very, very bad situation, and he did as he was told. As he started up the stairs, illuminated by the red glow of the exit sign above the door, he felt Frankie move closer and slip his hand into his own.

* * *

This was futile. The darkened storefronts on Main Street stared back at Ilene as she passed, each window a bleak reminder that she was going nowhere. She reached for her cell phone in the side pocket of her handbag; maybe Matt had news in the past four minutes. No bag, no phone. She had dropped them inside the front door when she ran into the house. As she proceeded on, the helplessness of her situation seemed to slow time to an excruciating crawl.

They couldn't have gone far on a night like tonight, and all the nearby places with basketball courts had been checked, which meant her working theory about where Lynette would take the boys was wrong. Ilene forced herself to throw it away and start over. Who in God's name was Lynette Kulik? What drove her? The person who sent the letters was crying out for help. But was she the whimpering child – imprisoned, injured, afraid? Or was she the abuser herself – powerful, angry, and with an insatiable need for gratification from someone young and helpless? Clearly, she was riddled with conflict, her letters begging to be stopped before she killed again.

Ilene tried to imagine Dr. Paradiz beside her. Even his imaginary presence was reassuring, and remarkably, his voice came through. She's both, he affirmed, a fragmented, twisted soul who has suffered great pain and who needs to inflict it on others to survive. Go back to the source. What happened to cause such pain?

The sexual abuse.

Sometimes it went on for years, as it probably did for Lynette. But it was the first time that cracked the child in two, vanquishing trust, and making a mockery of love.

The first time.

Through the pounding in her head, Ilene tried to recall the young victims avenged by Lynette. Jessica Lane. Remembering the third or fourth taped interview with Jessica: *The first time he kissed you 'down there,' did you have school that day?* He picked me up from school. *And what happened?* We got home and I was in my room, playing with my dolls. *Yes?* He came into my room and got on the bed with me ... on the bed.

For Hayley Martin, the first time was in the little playhouse he had built for her. Gilbaugh was killed at the Crawford *Playhouse!* Lynette's twisted sense of justice?

And Troy ... yes, he was killed at a park, but not outside. In the men's room. Which is where Troy first solicited David Mullen – in the boys' locker room at the school.

The first time!

It seemed so obvious, Ilene didn't know how it had eluded her. The wheels skidded as she made a reckless u-turn in the middle of the street. Levitsky and Gianelli missed them. Perhaps they had been hiding or had gotten there after the police left. But they were at the elementary school. The final destination was the computer lab. The *first time* for Dylan and Jeremy.

CHAPTER FORTY-ONE

O UT OF THE corner of her eye, Lynette saw Frankie reach for Sam's hand. The intimacy and trust in that small gesture triggered memories of Ray, and something erupted inside, a volcano that spewed an intense jealousy and rage at the brothers for having what she never had. She lost her footing and gripped the railing, looking around frantically for Pethen. Where is Pethen? Where is he?

He had first appeared to her when she was twelve, in her father's machine shop. She had to stay there because it was Mrs. Plant's day off. Ray was supposed to work at the shop because Vashni had a doctor's appointment. But Ray was late; he arrived with a couple of friends and asked if he could go out with them first. Vashni got so mad he slapped his son across the face before getting in his car and storming off. Then Ray's buddies slunk away and left just the two of them. His face was red with humiliation, and hoping to comfort her brother, Lynette went over and put her arms around him. As she hugged his wiry, muscular frame, Ray began to feel her and his breathing quickened. He moaned slightly and tried to push her away, but she clung even tighter. She loved Ray and wanted to let him know he wasn't alone. Crying out in frustration, he told her to stop. But she couldn't, she pressed herself against him tighter, burying her face in his chest – they *needed* each other!

Suddenly, Ray growled, a deep, primal sound. He dragged her into the dirty bathroom and threw her on her back. Then

266

he pulled down his jeans and entered her in the rough way Vashni did, his strong hands pinning her shoulders to the floor. Lynette submitted; she always did. But at that moment, she left her body and watched from above. His jaw set, Ray zipped up his pants and went to work, while she looked down and saw that there was a girl crying on the greasy floor – a stupid, ugly, helpless little girl. That was when Pethen appeared out of the corner of the machine shop. Oh, he was a monstrous snake! Magnificent, pulsing with power. He wound his way toward Ray, his triangular head raised off the floor, his tongue flicking in and out. It was Pethen who pushed Ray into the circular saw. Not Lynette! She was an innocent girl who had to close her eyes so she wouldn't have to see.

Now as she pulled herself up the stairs on the heels of Sam and Frankie, she felt heat rising in her face, the gun burning in her hand. The need to destroy the trust they had was overpowering. It never existed in her world. Why should it flourish in theirs? But still she wasn't sure. Where is Pethen? She screamed out his name, her voice exploding in the darkness and ricocheting off the walls. The boys cowered.

And then, duly summoned, she felt him behind her. And he had a brilliant solution.

Put the young man to the test. If he fails, he dies. If he can resist the strength of the viper, he will be saved, they will both be saved. She had to admit, Pethen's plan was perfect. Hadn't she seen it with her own eyes? There she was in the church sanctuary, surrounded by the grown-ups who were swaying, praying, calling out to Jesus. The sinner was propelled forward, pushed into the center of the circle, fear running in rivulets down his face. The preacher dragged over the box and laid his hands on the man's head. *Prove your soul's innocence and Jesus' forgiveness is yours,* he cried. Then he backed away. The man opened the crate revealing a pair of roiling snakes with the feared hourglass markings. He reached in and grabbed one in each hand, and the thick bodies of the copperheads twisted violently around his arms. The bigger one lunged at the man's shoulder and sunk its fangs deep, the other bit him twice, but he never let go. Hallelujah! Within minutes, he vomited and slumped to the floor, letting the snakes go. The congregation made a path for him and he began to crawl through. And at the door of the church, he pulled himself up and stumbled out. Hallelujah! He had fought off the strength of the viper. He was proclaimed *innocent*.

Now she would command Sam to violate his own brother, to touch him the way Jeremy and Dylan had claimed. If he could resist, he would prove his innocence. If he gave in to Satan's call, he would show himself weak and sinful, unworthy of life. It was that simple.

"Keep going," she said.

And the boys complied. When they reached the lab, she shut the door behind them. The boys stood silhouetted against the moonlight streaming through the windows. They were flanked by rows of small desks, a computer on each, with tiny green lights on the power paks glowing like neon eyes. To Lynette they were the eyes of witnesses.

She pointed the gun at Sam and said, "Take off your clothes." She turned to Frankie, "You, too."

Sam tried to swallow, his mouth dry.

"I said take off your clothes." There was no hesitation in her voice, no room for forgiveness.

He didn't understand. "Why?" Sam asked.

"Do it!" commanded Lynette, advancing a step closer. Now he could see the crazed determination in her eyes. But he didn't want to take his clothes off.

"No," he whispered.

The test could not be easy. Lynette swung the gun toward Sam and pulled the trigger. The monitor closest to him exploded and flipped off the desk, crashing to the floor and scattering hard bits of plastic around his feet. Both boys jumped and Frankie began to unzip his jacket with trembling fingers. Sam thought briefly of overpowering her. He was bigger. But she had a gun, and he remembered asking Matt about that one day.

"What do you if someone points a gun at you?"

Matt shook his head. "Try to stay calm and do what they say."

"But they might shoot you anyway."

"Chances are better they'll just take your money and run."

But this woman wasn't asking for money and she had already fired the gun. Maybe that was just to scare them. He wanted to protect Frankie. As long as they did what she said, he might be able to do that. Sam followed his brother's lead and took off his own coat.

In the shadowy room the boys removed their hats and boots. Frankie threw down his gray hoody and the t-shirt underneath. His thin chest rose and fell with every quick, frightened breath. Standing just a few feet away, Sam slowly unbuttoned his dress shirt and pulled it out from the waistband of his khakis. *What is she doing? Why is she making us do this?* When he was bare-chested, he stopped. But Lynette jabbed the gun at them.

"Take *everything* off," she said.

And they did what they were told.

A moment later, Frankie and Sam stood naked in front of Lynette, covered with goose bumps and shivering more from fear than the cold. In their shame, they instinctively clasped their hands in front of them, daring not to look anywhere but the floor.

Lynette took a step forward, keeping the gun trained on Sam, her finger on the trigger. "How much do you want it?" she asked, her voice sultry and low.

Sam kept his gaze locked on the floor. Her voice had the kind of tone he recognized from TV and movies; she was talking about sex. With her? He didn't answer.

"You think about touching him all the time, don't you?" she said.

What? Sam looked up to see Lynette indicating Frankie. He colored a deep red. "I ... I don't know what you mean," he said, but he was afraid that he did.

"Come on. You lie awake at night thinking about putting your hands on your little brother," she taunted. "You thought about it with Dylan and Jeremy, too, didn't you?" Her voice was caressing, but the words sliced like a sharp knife. "If we say we have no sin we deceive ourselves and the truth is not in us."

"No," Sam shook his head.

"Confess your sins, put to death therefore what is earthly in you: impurity, passion, evil desire."

A barely audible sound escaped from Sam's throat.

Lynette came closer to him, her perfume nauseating. "You are a child molester, do not deny it."

Frankie could stand it no longer. "Shut the fuck up!" he cried.

Lynette lashed out with the gun and struck him sharply on the side of his head. He crumpled to the floor. She leapt over and with one arm hauled him to his feet. The dazed twelve-year-old stayed limp in her strong grasp as she put him in a vice-like hold. She pressed the gun to his temple.

"Come closer and touch him," Lynette ordered.

The barrel of the .38 had opened a gash over Frankie's left ear and blood began to drip down his neck and face.

"Just like you did to Jeremy and Dylan," snarled Lynette.

"I didn't do *anything* to them!" moaned Sam. He clamped his hands over his ears to make her go away. He felt as though bolts of lightening were shooting through his head and he began to rock on the balls of his feet. He couldn't look at Frankie or listen to his pitiful ragged breathing anymore. For a moment he thought of heaving himself out of the lab's second floor window – anything to escape the sight of Frankie's terrified, pleading eyes.

But he forced himself to look up and take one step closer.

Anticipating victory, Lynette began to intone, "When lust has conceived, it gives birth to sin; and when sin is manifest, it brings forth death."

Sam inched closer. "Frankie," he whispered.

With a sudden crash, the lab door swung open. Lynette jerked backwards, yanking Frankie with her as she swung the gun in the direction of the sound.

Ilene lurched through the doorway and froze at the sight in front of her.

Catching the glint of light off the gun, it took every ounce of self-control not to scream, not to run at Lynette and claw at her face like a wild animal. *What have you done to my children?!*

But she caught her breath and said as evenly as she could, "Put the gun down, Lynette."

Ilene's plea was lost among the clamor of conflicting voices in Lynette's head. But out of the din, Pethen's emerged and commanded her to run. And take the boy. Gratefully, she obeyed, dragging Frankie across the floor to the exit.

The gun pressed to her son's head kept Ilene frozen. As they staggered past her just a few feet away, her arms ached with the effort to keep them at her side. And in an instant, they were gone, Frankie's pale, naked body an apparition swallowed in the inky blackness of the stairwell.

Ilene turned to Sam who stood trembling, staring at the door. She grabbed his coat from the floor and put it over him, searching for signs of physical injury.

"I'm here, Sammy. You're okay," she said. But the words caught in her throat. He wasn't okay. And Frankie wasn't okay. They were at the mercy of a crazed psychopath with a gun. In her haste to get to the school, she hadn't stopped to call for back-up as Matt had insisted. She just flew, without a thought of what she would do when she found them. They were on their own now. She grabbed Sam by his shoulders and shook him lightly.

"You stay here," she said. "Find a place to hide and don't come out. I'm going after Frankie."

The thought of leaving Sam alone was torture, but Ilene wheeled and raced for the stairs. Halfway down she lost her footing, twisted her ankle and nearly tumbled down the concrete steps. A desperate grab for the railing saved her from a fall. At the bottom of the stairs, with pain shooting up her leg, she hobbled into the hall and held her breath, listening for them. Nothing. She waited. These halls echoed everything. How could she not hear them? She started to call out for Frankie, but stopped herself, fearful that she'd put Frankie in greater danger if Lynette felt pursued.

Unable to stand it any longer, she began to make her way down the hallway using one hand on the wall for support. Past the cafeteria and Frankie's homeroom. At the end, she stood and listened. It was as if the school had devoured them. She looked down the hall toward the back door. Would Lynette try to take him out that way? *Dear God, don't let her hurt him! Please God, keep him safe!* Pushing off the wall, she headed in that direction, trying to ignore the pain in her ankle and the fierce prayers echoing in her head. They could be behind any one of the classroom doors. Ilene paused at each one, straining for a sign.

She had almost reached the end when the muffled sounds of a struggle came from back down the hall. A sharp cry, a grunt, and then running. She knew that sound. She'd heard it a thousand times, the rhythm of Frankie's feet running up and down a basketball court.

And then, the shot rang out.

* * *

"Unit Three to Unit One, do you copy?" the radio crackled.

Matt grabbed for it. "Talk to me, Levitsky."

"I've got the cars, Chief."

"Where?"

"Behind the Town House."

Matt squeezed his eyes closed, afraid to ask the next question. "Anybody in them?"

"Negative."

"Okay. Go ahead and look around, I'm on my way. Call for another unit."

"Roger."

Matt had no sooner made the U-turn when the second call came in from Dave Cahone.

"You won't believe this, Chief," he said in a rush. "Dispatcher just got a dozen 911 calls about a woman with a gun at the elementary school. It must be them. Wait a sec, now he's telling me more are coming in, says the switchboard is lit up like a Christmas tree. What the hell is going on?!"

Matt had no idea. What he did know was that the school backed up to the parking area behind the Town House. He put out a call to all units redirecting them to Branford Elementary, lights and sirens all the way. Then, his voice breaking, he told Cahone to get an ambulance over there, too.

* * *

"Frankie!" Ilene screamed. "Fraaankie!"

She tried to run, stumbling back down the corridor. With each agonizing step, the hall seemed to get longer and longer. The illusion was almost merciful, since she knew that if she turned the corner and found the body of her son, her life would be over as well. Better to just keep running.

When she reached the cafeteria, there was nothing there but the punishing silence. Fear dug its razor claws into her eyes, her ears, her throat. She tried to think. Had Frankie escaped? And if he had, where would he go? His homeroom was down this way. He might feel safe there. She limped down the hall and peered into Mrs. Reynolds' classroom.

"Frankie?" she called softly. "Are you in here?"

No answer. But she heard a noise. Just a sigh, the slightest stirring in the air. He must be afraid to speak, afraid that Lynette was nearby.

"It's me, Frankie," whispered Ilene.

She stepped inside. Unlike the other classrooms, this one had no windows. The only illumination came from the aquarium in the corner, which glowed with an alien hue and cast just enough light to make out the childrens' work tables and chairs. Ilene moved hesitantly along the low bookshelves at the back, her hand sweeping along the top for something she could use as a weapon. Her hand collided with a basket which fell over, pouring out staplers and scissors with an endless clatter. She held her breath and listened for a reaction. It seemed another lifetime that she had last been in this classroom, she and Roz walking down the row of projects dutifully hung on the wall for parents to admire. It was filled with such innocence then, a place for little coats, mismatched mittens, and forgotten paper bag lunches. Now, the innocence had been replaced with menace. Ilene's fingers touched something hard, and they closed around a pair of school scissors. Purposefully dull with rounded ends, they were useless for cutting anything, much less inflicting serious harm, but she tightened her grip.

The possibility that her son was here, hurt or unable to answer, was Ilene's entire universe, blocking out the wail of sirens in the distance. Nor did she hear the rumble of the school generator or feel its vibrations under her feet. It came as a surprise then when ceiling lights began to flicker and hum around her, and suddenly the classroom was awash with light.

Accustomed to the darkness, Ilene put her hand over her eyes to shield them from the cold glare of the fluorescent beams. And she squinted in disbelief.

She was alone.

She hobbled across the room, winding her way around the work tables, looking from side to side. There was no place for a person to hide in here. *But she had heard something!*

"Frankie?" she croaked.

Then, out of the corner of her eye, she saw something move. She spun around.

Lynette was crawling out from under Mrs. Reynolds' old wooden desk. Her shoulders undulated and her head wove side to side, almost like she was ... slithering. She held the gun in her right hand.

Ilene froze, like an animal that recognizes it is cornered prey. For a long moment, the two women stared at one another. Ilene thought she had never seen such lunatic eyes. Then Lynette did an even stranger thing. She made a hissing sound and darted her tongue in and out of her mouth. Ilene stood rooted as Lynette put both hands on the gun and aimed the barrel at Ilene's chest. Lynette's hand tightened and her trigger finger began its inward pressure.

Boom!

Everything went black. But then she heard men's voices and slowly opened her eyes to a blur of movement. Joel Levitsky was lifting her and carrying her into the hall, past more cops storming through the door, others running down the hall. Levitsky was asking if she was all right, and she later remembered thinking, *How can I be hearing and seeing if I'm dead?* Then she was on her feet, and her surroundings came into focus. Matt's solid form was partially blocking the entrance to the classroom. Beyond him was Lynette, who had been knocked backward into the desk, swaying on her knees, her head forward, her hands clutching at the blood spilling from a hole in her chest. Matt stepped close to her to kick away the .38 she had dropped on the floor. Then he backed off, keeping his service revolver trained on her.

With difficulty, Lynette lifted her head and looked past him. Her eyes searched Ilene's and, not finding what they were looking for, darted wildly around the room. Suddenly, she stiffened and stared at a spot on the floor as if everything else had disappeared. Relief washed over her face as she followed an imaginary movement across the floor until it settled next to her. She broke into a childlike smile, then the light went out from her eyes and her heart stopped beating.

"Mom?"

Ilene's heart leapt at the sound of Frankie's voice behind her. She turned and saw her son, very much alive, running down the hall. He was wearing a police officer's parka that went down to his knees, and she thought that the sound of his bare feet slapping against the linoleum was the sweetest sound she had ever heard. She opened her arms and Frankie rushed into them. She held him tight until both their sobs began to subside.

A jacketless officer hovered nearby, talking on his radio. He made no move to intervene until Frankie finally disengaged from his mother's embrace. Then he said gently, "Ma'am, your son Sam is upstairs. He seems to be all right."

"Thank you."

A few yards away, Matt was directing two of his officers to secure the area until the medical examiner could be summoned. Lynette's body was not to be moved; it was a clean police shooting, but there would be a full investigation. Frankie started toward Matt and his mother reached out a hand to stop him. *He mustn't see the body.* But then she realized that Lynette had done her damage and could do nothing more to hurt him. She let him go.

"Is she dead?" Frankie asked Matt, who had placed his weapon in a plastic bag and was handing it to one of the state cops.

Matt looked down at the youngster. "Yes," he said.

"Did you shoot her?"

Matt hesitated, and then said simply, "Yes."

Frankie thought about it, then nodded his head. He went back to his mom and asked to see Sam.

Flanked by police officers, a paramedic gave Ilene a shoulder to lean on as she went up the stairs to the lab. Frankie stayed close to her, frantically pouring out details of his amazing escape. "And then she started acting all weird. I mean, even weirder than she already was, like, whispering to somebody named Puffin, or something. And she kind of let go for a second, so I ran. I ran all the way to the gym. She shot at me, but she missed."

"Oh, Frankie," Ilene breathed. "You took an awful chance."

"Mom, I was naked, I had to do something."

"But she had a *gun.*"

"Well, it was dark and she couldn't see me too well. Plus, I knew I was too fast for her. She never would've got me."

Flush with gratitude that he was there beside her, Ilene didn't try to explain how fast one has to be to outrun a bullet.

* * *

Sam was sitting cross-legged on the floor of the lab with his back against the wall. He had put on his pants and his shirt, which was buttoned haphazardly. Despite the cold, his face glistened with sweat and he stared at a laptop clutched tight in his hands. Standing guard near by was Officer Gianelli; Sergeant Blue was in the back talking quietly to a third man, Terry Wohlman, Roz's husband. The last few minutes had been so harrowing and strange that Ilene didn't even question why he was there.

Terry put a hand out to touch Ilene's elbow.

"We tried to talk to him," he said kindly. "But he won't say anything."

Sergeant Blue nodded. "He's not hurt, Ilene. I think he's okay."

She went over to Sam and knelt down on one side of him. Frankie had already taken up his post on the other. Sam looked up, fear still etched on his face.

"Are you all right, Sammy?" asked Ilene.

He glanced first at his mother, but then lowered his head, his eyes shifting toward Frankie. Ilene could feel the emotional current that ran between them. For the first time, she allowed herself to recall the sight that met her when she ran into the lab. Both boys naked. She suspected that Lynette was forcing them into some kind of sexual contact. But why?

A glimmer of understanding made her wince. Lynette was conflicted about Sam. The rational, functioning part of her may have accepted the evidence that Sam was falsely charged, but the deranged and damaged woman had already decided he had to be punished. Quite possibly, in order to ease the conflict, she had to make *certain* he had sexual contact with a child before killing him. Ilene fought the heartbreak of imagining that she had been successful.

Sam felt the light touch of Frankie's hand on his own.

"She's dead, Sam," said Frankie. "She can't hurt us anymore."

Sam was unable to look his brother in the eye. Frankie probably still blamed him and would always wonder if he would've done what Lynette ordered. Sam wondered the same thing himself. It took an act of courage to finally meet his gaze. The light in Frankie's eyes reflected lingering fear and sadness ... but also something else Sam couldn't read, and it caused a panicky feeling to rise in his chest. His brother had joined the world of adults, like his mom and his teachers and all the people whose eyes were a canvas of too-bright, chaotic patterns. But then Frankie squeezed his hand, and the emotions and colors came together for a moment in a single, recognizable picture – love. It would always be there, and it was enough. Sam squeezed his hand back.

Sergeant Blue and the paramedic approached.

"Excuse me, we should get the boys to a hospital to be checked out," said the paramedic to Ilene. "And he needs some stitches," pointing to her younger son.

"Again?" complained Frankie.

The paramedic came over to take a closer look. "Afraid so, champ."

Ilene bent over Sam. As he got up off the floor, he handed her the laptop. A computer, Ilene thought, feeling tired and sad. He must have reached for it like a security blanket, losing himself in its emotionless, predictable world. But when she saw the screen, she caught her breath. It was flashing a message:

CALL 911 ... EMERGENCY ... BRANFORD ELE-MENTARY ... BOY HURT ... WOMAN WITH GUN ... CALL 911 ... EMERGENCY ...

The message repeated over and over.

"What is this?" Ilene asked.

Matt appeared behind her, and when he saw the screen, he smiled.

"Sam was the one who called for help. With this," he said, taking the computer from her. "Isn't that right, Stats?" he asked Sam.

Sam nodded and began to hunt for his shoes and socks.

"I don't understand," Ilene said.

"Do you know about the Westover School Alert System?" asked Matt.

"Sure. It's how we get emails about school closings and early dismissals."

"And it sends them out instantaneously to *everyone* in the school district," Matt explained. "Sam didn't have a phone, so he grabbed a computer. He had to override the superintendent's password lock, but of course Sam was the one who configured the whole system. He sent out this message to every family in West-over – to their computers, their iPhones, Blackberrys. The dis-patcher started to get calls immediately, and apparently, they're still pouring in. Sam put it on a loop just to make sure."

Suddenly, Ilene realized that she hadn't questioned how the police found them. She turned to Terry Wohlman.

"Is that why you're here?"

He looked slightly sheepish. "I was almost home when I got the message," he said. "I came straight over just as the cops were arriving. Me and about ten other guys."

Matt ran a hand over his head. "Be better if you folks let us handle it."

Terry grinned. "Next time, Chief."

Ilene absorbed the information and then took a long look at the tall, frizzy-haired young man putting on his coat. "I can't imagine what would have happened if... We were completely alone here."

Matt's eyes welled up. "Not for long."

Sam and Frankie finished dressing and hung close to each other, wordlessly trying to make sense of the violence inflicted on them. Ilene knew both her boys had been wounded in a deep, private way that would take time to heal. But she trusted that the bond between them ran deep. One of the paramedics went over to tend to Frankie's head. His partner, who had helped Ilene up the stairs, held his arm out once again.

"Ms. Hart?" he offered.

"Thank you," she said. "But I think my son can help me down."

And there was Sam at her side. She felt his wiry arm close around her waist as she took a final look through the lab windows. Outside she saw the swirling lights of police and ambulance vehicles in the parking lot, and beyond them, a line of cars in both directions. It seemed that the Branford community was still responding to Sam's message. But now with the police in charge, drivers had gotten out and were talking in small groups, silhouetted in their headlights. A couple of state troopers pulled their jackets close and headed out to tell them they could all go home.

Acknowledgements

THANKS TO ERIC Brown and Marley Sims for their thoughtful input on the manuscript in progress. I would also like to acknowledge Dean Oliver for his fascinating work in basketball statistics. Finally, to Kenny – your tireless editing and willingness to read each draft with a fresh eye has kept me going in more ways than you can know.

CPSIA information can be obtained at www.ICGtesting.com
Printed in the USA
LVOW100946150712

290136LV00003B/60/P